BILL KENT
street legal

Thomas Dunne Books / St. Martin's Minotaur New York

THOMAS DUNNE BOOKS.
An imprint of St. Martin's Press.

STREET LEGAL. Copyright © 2006 by Bill Kent. All rights reserved. Printed in the United States of America. No part of this book may be used or reproduced in any manner whatsoever without written permission except in the case of brief quotations embodied in critical articles or reviews. For information, address St. Martin's Press, 175 Fifth Avenue, New York, N.Y. 10010.

www.thomasdunnebooks.com

www.minotaurbooks.com

Library of Congress Cataloging-in-Publication Data

Kent, Bill, 1954–
    Street legal / Bill Kent.—1st ed.
        p. cm.
    ISBN-13: 978-0-312-32885-6
    ISBN-10: 0-312-32885-0
    1. Journalists—Fiction.   2. Women   journalists—Fiction.
3. Philadelphia (Pa.)—Fiction.   4. Organized   crime—Fiction.
I. Title.

PS3561.E516S865 2006
813'.54—dc22

                                                    2006040388

First Edition: June 2006

10 9 8 7 6 5 4 3 2 1

For my wife, Elaine,
my son, Stephen
and the lawyers in my family

acknowledgments

Among the books I read about the history of the law, the courts and legal pathologies, David Marston's *Malice Aforethought* was especially helpful. Professor Michael Goldberg at the Widener University Law School referred me to *The Lion and the Throne*, Catherine Drinker Bowen's excellent biography of Sir Edward Coke.

All characters in this story are imaginary and have no precedents in life. They are not meant to depict existing lawyers, lawyer novelists, law firms, talk radio hosts who happen to be lawyers, chefs, judges, psychiatrists who like to hang out in courtrooms, journalists, consumer electronics repairmen, public relations professionals, law enforcement personnel, plumbers who moonlight as dominatrices, consumer electronics repairmen who collect old television sets, sand sculptors, automobile repair women who were once demolition derby drivers, etc.

Events and locations in this book are fictional. The city of Philadelphia does call a section of Broad Street the "Avenue of the Arts," but it does not have an annual St. Valentine's Day Broad Street Ambulance Chase. The Chadds Ford region has several old mills in incomparably beautiful settings, but none as described here. Atlantic City does not have an aquarium, but does have an Ocean Life Center, a worthy tourist attraction. The Ocean Life Center is not connected with the casino industry, and has no shark habitat.

Jake Elwell provided agenting services. Dr. Mark Gilbert added medical lore. Steve Zatuchni, who is not a lawyer, came up with one of the murder weapons. Architect Michael Prifti provided fascinating facts about concrete pumps and building control systems. I remain grateful to those who continue to share their lives with me.

Because he had become an oracle amongst the people.

—King James I and VI (1566–1625)
explaining why he imprisoned Chief Justice
Sir Edward Coke (1552–1634) in the Tower of London

street legal

1 exit sandman

On the morning after she found the dead lawyer, Andrea "Andy" Cosicki checked the pocked and pitted newsroom bulletin board above the incoming-mail boxes.

Above the announcements about cutbacks in health benefits, the name of a staffer who had just given birth to a baby girl, and the results of last night's Fretzer Awards at the Hot Lead Club, *Philadelphia Press* editor Howard Lange had posted a memo "re: procedures to be used by staff to assist police re: incident re: death of Charles Muckler."

These included Samantha Gross, who edited the puzzle page and wrote the "Daily Twinkle" horoscope under the pseudonym Glinda Starr, and, at the very bottom, "Andrea Cosicki (Mr. Action)."

Neville Shepherd Ladderback, the old, dusty obituary writer who seemed to know everybody, was not on the list.

"Did you know Muckler?" she asked Ladderback as she draped her bomber jacket over the back of her chair, hung her woven shoulder bag on the seat back and confronted the mess of letters, faxes, papers and things that she hadn't yet thrown out.

Behind his thick bifocals, Ladderback's eyes moved like goldfish in a

1

bowl while his stubby, liver-spotted hands danced swiftly over the keyboard. "I knew of him," he said quietly.

Ladderback's immaculate desk was immediately to the left of Andy's. He worked facing a blank wall. The wall extended to a huge series of file cabinets that supposedly contained every obituary Ladderback had written in his who-knows-how-many-years at the *Press,* as well as files of other articles he had clipped and saved.

Before Andy could get to work on the day's Mr. Action, Ladderback took his fingers off his keyboard, turned in his chair to face her and asked, "Would you like an assignment?"

She sat down in her swivel chair and stretched her legs, which looked longer and thinner because she was wearing tight, winter-weight black denim, the bottoms over brown street boots whose edges she'd scuffed from practicing side kicks on fire hydrants, railings, and brick walls. She crossed her arms over a burgundy I'm-not-expecting-to-meet-the-public-today sweater. She took a deep, do-I-really-have-to-take-this-assignment breath. She reminded herself she didn't have to take assignments from him—she was only nominally his assistant.

And his assignments tended to lead her to places she'd rather not go. At the moment, she had enough to do with Mr. Action. On her desk, in her computer and stored in the voice-mail cue on her telephone were questions from readers who wanted to know what to do when the wrong dishwasher is delivered, or when the credit card company raises your rates, or even how many city workers it takes to change a lightbulb in a street lamp. Andy had spent most of yesterday getting the answer: nineteen desk jockeys within the Streets and Sanitation Department's Public Safety Division; ten inspectors who are supposed to spot burned-out lamps, traffic lights and illuminated signs on any of the 36,000 Philadelphia city streets, not including those on state roads and federal highways that are serviced by the Pennsylvania Department of Transportation; seven clerks in the city warehouse where the bulbs are stored; two procurement officers who order new lightbulbs when the supplies are low and attend important yearly conferences in exotic locales so that they can be well versed in the latest illumination technologies; four three-person Service and Maintenance Division teams that actually go out in the truck, ride the cherry picker, take out the old bulbs and put in the new; and, finally, a resource recycling coordinator who contracts for bulb disposal in accordance to current environmental laws and policies, for a total of fifty-three.

The topmost letter on her desk was from a Philadelphia public school student who had asked for advice about something that was "taken from him" that he failed to identify. Today she would have to call the student's home and confirm that he had sent the letter. Before she could decide to include the letter, and its answer, in her column, she would have to find out what, exactly, had been taken.

And then there was that murder she witnessed last night.

As she signed on to her word processor, she saw Ladderback write a telephone number on a reporter's pad. "This is the cell phone number of Schuyler Nordvahl. Twenty years ago he made a great deal of money from litigating asbestos claims. He left his firm and helped found the Delaware Valley Law Watch, which advocates for higher ethical standards in the legal profession. The Law Watch is on the second floor of Jimmy D's. Mr. Nordvahl celebrated his birthday there last night. He also takes his meals there when he is in the city. You could meet him there for lunch today."

Jimmy D's was a dark, wood-paneled surf-and-turf restaurant that Andy's father had used for business luncheons. Ladderback had taken Andy there a few times, and had introduced her to the restaurant's owner, a former Irish mobster named Whitey Goohan. Ladderback wrote what Andy thought was the best obituary she had ever read after Goohan died the past week.

"Mr. Nordvahl is also fluent in Latin," Ladderback continued. "He has lectured on the history of law, and legal ethics at the University of Pennsylvania Law School. He only works pro bono."

Andy wasn't impressed. "So he doesn't charge. There are a lot of lawyers working pro bono. I use a few of them for sources when a reader asks Mr. Action for free legal help."

"Mr. Nordvahl only takes cases that he feels will be *pro summa bono,* for the greatest good," Ladderback continued. "Because many of his cases involve legal malpractice, he tends to be shunned by his colleagues. He lives in a seventeenth century Brandywine River mill in Chadds Ford. Chadds Ford is an exceptionally beautiful place, especially in winter."

She knew Ladderback was agoraphobic, and she sympathized because she was born with a rare neurological disorder called amusa: she couldn't hear music. So much of what others found beautiful and moving was, to her, just noise.

For Ladderback, so much of what human beings inhabited was a terrifying, fearful void.

"How do you know his place is so beautiful?" she asked him.

"I've seen photographs," Ladderback said.

"I don't do articles about people's houses," Andy said. "He's just a lawyer, Shep. He's not news."

Ladderback frowned. He handed her the paper with the phone number.

Andy took it out of his hand and put it on top of the letter from the Philadelphia public school student. "Why don't you tell me the real reason you want me to write him up?"

Ladderback became motionless for about a minute. Then he said, "Last night he celebrated his fiftieth birthday."

Andy said, "He's more than double my age and you want me to use this newspaper to give him all this publicity? Like, we don't have people in this town turning fifty every day?"

Ladderback shifted uncomfortably. "The half-century mark typically inspires a person to look back on his life, take stock of his achievements and his failures and react in a variety of ways, some of them unanticipated."

Andy looked at the ceiling.

"When you interview him," Ladderback added, "be certain to ask him why King James imprisoned Sir Edward Coke in the Tower of London."

Andy let a second go by. Then she picked up a pen and the notepaper with the phone number and asked, "Who was Sir Edward Coke?"

"Schuyler will tell you," Ladderback said. "I'd prefer if you'd call him promptly."

She sighed. "Is this, like, an emergency?"

Ladderback pondered that. "What if I told you it was a matter of life and death?"

"You write obituaries," Andy said. "Everything you do is a matter of life and death."

He shook his head and she stuffed the note in her shoulder bag.

Dear Mr. Action,

I go to the James Lawson Middle School in Rock Hall and Mr. Arasim, my English teacher, wants us to express ourselves by writing to the media to say something that is really important. In the *Press* you answer questions about things. My question is, what do you do when somebody takes something from you and it's real important to you and you can't get it back. Should you go after them? Should you take something of theirs? Should you call the police? Please tell me what to do.

Never been told, Jermaine Haynes, Rock Hall

Andy dialed the phone number at the bottom. A woman who said she was Jermaine Haynes's "half sister" confirmed that the boy lived in the Rock Hall neighborhood. "His fifth-grade English teacher said he was supposed to write some dumb thing to a newspaper or magazine about something important to him."

Had the boy had something stolen from him? Andy asked.

"Why are you asking?" Jermaine's sister replied, immediately suspicious. "Just because Jermaine wrote a letter don't mean you have to ask questions about it."

"I want to make sure I represent his question fairly and accurately before it's printed," Andy said.

"A boy like Jermaine can get himself in all kinds of trouble, talking about what he seen and didn't see, without you trying to represent him any which way. These gangstas, they'll kill you just to have something to do. You're not going to print his name, are you? You print his name and they come after him, it's me that's going to come after you."

Andy explained that identifying details about readers were never printed unless the readers consented. "I only identify sources who provide information in my column," Andy said.

"How come you're calling it your column? You're no Mr. Action. Mr. Action a man. Put him on. I got stuff I got to say."

"Anything you have to say to Mr. Action, you can say to me," Andy said firmly. The woman sputtered words that Andy couldn't quite hear and hung up.

She let the late-morning sounds of tapping keyboards and newsroom phone chatter distract her. She hated it when readers were a pain. Sure, the media gets things wrong every once in a while, but Jermaine's letter sounded as if it were more than just the completion of a school assignment.

She tried a reply:

> Dear Jermaine,
>
> What to do depends on what was taken from you. If you have a problem with someone, common sense should tell you to try to work things out with that person. If you can't settle the problem on your own, you might want to consult an adult or authority figure. If a valuable object was taken, as a citizen, you have a right and obligation to report any criminal activity to the police, as quickly as possible.

Andy paused. Her answer seemed gassy and insubstantial. She needed a good quote from an authority figure. She could call the Philadelphia Police Department's Division of Public Affairs and get a quote from the officially designated spokesperson.

Or she could buttonhole Detective Lieutenant Jeffery Everson of the Homicide Division, who was, at that very moment, inside Howard Lange's office, interviewing newsroom staffers about the demise of Charles Muckler, Esq. Lieutenant Everson had been a friend of her father's, and, though he didn't handle burglaries or stolen cars, he could say a few things that would give the answer some weight.

Just then, her phone rang. A bored, irritated Lange told her, "You're on deck."

She signed off her word processor, took a pad and pen and crossed the newsroom to Lange's office, a glass rectangle against a far wall, shrouded in floor-to-ceiling beige curtains. She approached just as Samantha Gross waddled backward out the door in a huge, clover-patterned crimson dress.

"You sure you don't need anything else from me?" She asked, reluctant to leave.

"If we do," Andy heard the resonant, deeply masculine reply, "I will find you."

Gross paused, turned and sighed at Andy. "He is so . . . ," she sighed again, "*much.*"

She was gone before Andy could ask who was so much, or why. She poked her head into the office and smelled the sour odors of old sandwiches and stale coffee.

"Last one to go!" Lange called out from his desk. He rubbed his face, stuck his fingers in the corners of his eyes, yawned.

Across from the desk, a weary, bleary-eyed Lieutenant Everson was sinking ever deeper into the lumpy brown couch. Andy saw a mustard stain on his pale blue and gray flannel shirt. His badge and I.D. hung on a strap from his neck.

Andy thought Everson might have looked great maybe ten or twenty years ago, when his eyes and mouth lacked the stress marks that came, not just from the sad and terrible crimes he investigated, but also from the bureaucratic complications that, he had once told her, were always a "factor" in "what gets done, who does it and who it gets done to."

Sharing a place on the couch was Everson's assistant, a thick, dark-skinned woman whose lap was piled high with legal pads. She was replacing cassettes in an old portable tape recorder. In a chair near Lange's desk sat a blank-faced Asian man in his twenties, wearing a smartly tailored copper-colored suit, the knot of his gleaming, navy blue tie riding tightly under his neck and a laptop computer, open on his lap, his hands poised.

Andy had never met the *Press*'s lawyer, Michael "Marathon Mike" McSloan. As soon as she saw him, she knew immediately the reason for Samantha Gross's reluctance to leave.

He stood with his face turned away from the window and its view of City Hall. He wore a pale blue silk shirt stretched tightly over long, lanky arms, wide shoulders and a trim, smoothly muscled chest. His blue and gold suspenders were like racing stripes, ending in dark blue trousers that emphasized very long legs.

Lieutenant Everson gave Andy a once-over. "You grow some, or something?"

"I was almost six-one when I last saw you. I'm almost six-two now."

Lange stretched in his chair. "Once a month we put a dust mop on her head and she does the ceiling. You've met Jeff Everson, right, Andy? Good. With him is Sergeant Hess. Here in the chair is Gordon Wu, and the only reason he's here is that our counsel, Marathon Mike, doesn't like to take notes, am I right, Mike?"

The sun was low in the winter sky as the man at the window turned, so the chiseled planes of his face were lit in an amber glow. He was her height, or close to it, with clear, deep set brown eyes, a long nose ending in flaring nostrils, a strong mouth and dimpled chin. He gave her a small smile, as if he really, really liked the fact that, finally, here was a woman with whom he could see eye to eye.

Andy saw the wedding band on his finger. She decided not to sit. She folded her arms and leaned against the curtains so she was directly opposite McSloan.

"Ms. Cosicki," McSloan said with a voice that seemed to echo inside her, "before we begin, let me tell you why I'm here."

To pose in front of the window like some kind of African god, and melt every woman who sees you down to slag, Andy told herself.

"This is to be an informational interview," McSloan went on. "I'm here to make sure you do not answer any questions you do not want to answer, for any reason. Lieutenant Everson has asked to record the proceedings. Your responses do not have to be recorded if you do not desire them to be. What is your *pleasure?*"

Pleasure. The way he said that, you'd think he had just thrown a log on the fire and was about to uncork the champagne.

"You can tape it," she said, her eyes on McSloan. "I don't care."

Sergeant Hess put a cassette in the tape recorder.

"Okay, Andy," Lieutenant Everson began. "Tell us who you are, how old you are, where you live and what you do for a living."

"She's twenty-two," Lange said. "She lives in town and she does our 'Mr. Action' column and the occasional feature. She's famous for her attitude, which she is not going to give us at this time because we've been here all day and we want to wrap this up as quickly as possible. Got me, Andy?"

She got him, but more than what she got from him was a tension between Lange and McSloan that McSloan confirmed when he folded his arms and almost scolded Lange with, "The lady can speak for herself."

Lady? Not once, since Andy was hired in June of last year, had anyone in the newsroom called her a lady. When Ladderback called her it was more like "Yo, Andy" or "Hey, you" but, she had to admit, she liked the way McSloan said it.

Lieutenant Everson covered his mouth as he yawned. "Let's start with why you were at the Hot Lead Club last night. When did you decide to go there?"

"At the last minute," Andy began. "I'd finished up. I saw the announcement on the bulletin board. I'd been to the Hot Lead once before, when I was co-editor of the Penn student newspaper and the Quill Awards were being handed out for the best student newspaper work. I'd heard about the Fretzers. I thought it would be fun."

"Fun," Lange said sourly. "Look, this isn't about you. You were there, you saw the Sandman, and the next thing you know, he's in his car and he's up to his ass in—"

"You want to let me talk?" Andy said to Lange.

"Please," McSloan said. "The lady is speaking."

"Calm down everybody," Everson said. "Now Andy. Could your late father have crossed paths with Muckler? It's likely, in your father's dealings with city hall—"

"He was a sneaky little fixer," Lange said. "She wouldn't have this job if it wasn't for him blowing out my parking tickets."

"You shut *up* about my father," Andy told him.

"I knew Benjamin Cosicki," McSloan said. "I found him very open and forthright."

"Can I ask the questions here?" Everson said. "Did your father ever say anything to you about any dealings with Charlie Muckler?"

"My father never said anything about what he did," Andy said.

"He never told you why they call Muckler the Sandman?"

Andy shook her head. "Not a word. I didn't know about it until I read the paper this morning."

"I love it when my staffers read," Lange said.

"The *Press* article gave a simplified version of what Muckler did," McSloan told Andy. "It's true that he was quite expert at what we call pouring sand into the legal machinery: he caused delays, he failed to file documents in a timely matter, he challenged accepted procedural points and was so difficult to work with that he could force pre-trial settlements, generally in favor of his clients, because no one wanted to meet him in court."

"He was a pain in the ass," Lange said. "Did he bill the same as you? Or less?"

"Less," McSloan said. "Far less."

Everson nodded, as if he had heard this too many times. To Andy, he said, "You didn't expect to see him last night?"

"I never saw or heard of him before last night," Andy said.

"Did you tell anyone that you were going to the Hot Lead Club?"

"Just Ladderback, the guy who sits next to me."

"Our man on the dead beat," Lange said. "I've been trying to get him to retire since I got this job. Shep's out of the loop."

"He is not!" Andy said.

"How did you get to the club?" Everson asked her. "Cab, bus, train, walk?"

Andy had told all of this to the police who had interviewed her last night. "I got my car out of the *Press*'s garage and drove there, so, if it got late, I could drive back."

"Make and model?" Everson cut in.

"Ford Focus. Red. I parked it on Seventeenth Street, right near the Dempsey Lane. The Hot Lead is on Dempsey, so I went down Dempsey."

"That was the first time you saw Charlie Muckler's car?"

"A silver Jaguar parked in this tiny space right next to the club. I didn't know whose car it was when I saw it. But I remember the license plate said SANDMAN."

"Did you wonder why the car was parked there?"

"I figured it was left where it was because whoever the Sandman was, he was either special, or he thought he was special. My father used to leave his car in all kinds of places," Andy said. "He didn't get tickets."

Lange piped up "That's because he was a—"

"That's *enough*, Howard," McSloan scolded. "You may continue, Ms. Cosicki."

Of the numerous professional, regional, semi-professional and prize-in-exchange-for-a-speaker's-fee awards ceremonies that a Philadelphia journalist might attend, the Fretzers were unrivaled in that they were given by the local media, for the local media, and no one else.

They were named for the *Philadelphia Press*'s hard-drinking, chain-smoking gossip columnist Lincoln Fretts, whose L. Fretts Alley column had been widely read up until Fretts died of throat cancer.

They were given out in February at the Hot Lead Club, a private club for media types that Fretzer helped found. After his death, the club lost membership, largely because a city that once had five newspapers suddenly had two, and most radio and TV stations had moved to the suburbs.

And, as it happens to proud, great historic institutions in any city, the end arrives, not with a bang, or a whimper, but with a landlord raising the rent, or, worse, selling the building.

A lawyer named Charles Muckler bought the place because it had a parking space on Dempsey Lane just big enough for one car. The parking space was a short walk to Muckler's offices at Seventeenth and Walnut Streets.

Muckler also put money into the place. He had the upstairs "Malfunction Room" extended over the kitchen so it could accommodate larger crowds. The room had comedians performing on weekends and open-mike nights on Thursdays.

None of this had been explained to Andy Cosicki when she pushed open the club's door and caught the sweet, treacherous scents of cheap liquor and craven ambition. People crowding the tarnished rail of the horseshoe-shaped bar turned to her and scanned her with their eyes. They did not see a young professional who really loved finding things out and writing about them. They did not see a young woman who did not think she was especially good looking and guessed that anyone who looked at her did so because she happened to be taller than all the women and half the men in the room.

In that one respect, Andy was wrong. Andy would have gotten the once-over from the media professionals inside the Hot Lead Club if she had been a potted plant. And, as a potted plant, she would get even more attention if she were the kind of potted plant that had power, access, prestige, the ability to hire and fire, make and unmake a career.

Anything else, and a once-over is all you get.

Which was okay for Andy because Andy just wanted to blend in, fade out, be the proverbial bug on the wall that saw everything but influenced none. She passed a coatrack that was so overloaded that jackets, wraps and swaths of fur that might not be fake had fallen to the floor. She decided to keep her bomber jacket on.

She neared the bar and tried to get close enough to order a drink but none of those huddled around it would provide access. Someone at the far end of the bar was complaining to the bartender about a drink. The bartender looked up and made a peculiar hand sign to a fat-necked, moon-faced man in a snug gray suit sitting at a table against the wall.

The television set over the bar had been hooked up to a camera in the upstairs function room. On the small stage Andy saw Chilton "Chilly" Bains, the *Press*'s current gossip columnist, his stacked red hair even more vivid above his white tuxedo (worn over his trademark Hawaiian shirt), holding a microphone in one hand, announcing the nominees for "the article or broadcast that caused the most distress to a scheming politician, overpaid professional athlete or utterly worthless local celebrity, the winner of which gets to ride in a genuine Speed Care Emergency Services Vehicle during the up-and-coming Ninth Annual St. Valentine's Day Noontime Broad Street Ambulance Chase."

The volume of conversation increased as the articles and personalities were mentioned. Barbara "Bombarella" Ellerbaum was up for a Fretzer for a caustic *Liberty Bell Magazine* article that the reason "Silent Storm" 76ers basketball star Ismail Khan doesn't speak to the media or fans is that he was such an abuser of street drugs in his days as a Rock Hall gangbanger that they crippled his speech center. Varlet & Tinn, the *Philadelphia Standard*'s team of investigative journalists, had done a tedious, humorless but damning five-part "Bang for the Buck" series that ranked numerous local politicians by how well they took care of significant campaign donors. Chilly Bains himself was up for a Fretzer for a column that interviewed an impoverished Rutgers University remedial writing instructor who not only claimed that he had written most of local best-selling novelist Bette Newarr's last novel, as well as all of the forthcoming *Guilty Pleasures,* but also mentioned that Newarr maintained a childhood habit of chewing on the tips of pencils, pens and, most recently, a $500 fountain pen.

"It'll be the Slip." The moon-faced man sitting alone snickered. He waved a ten-dollar bill. "Any bets on the Slip?"

He was referring to Irv "Slip" Kersaw, a wisecracking Northeast Philadelphia personal-injury lawyer, who was now the host of a talk-radio show called "So Sue Me."

The man at the table caught Andy's eye and said, "Whatever you're drinking, it'll be on me, unless you can't hold your liquor. Then it's definitely on me."

Andy wanted to run from this guy.

"That's a joke I got from one of my comics on open-mike night. Hey, you want to know who's going to win? I'll bet you whatever you're drinking."

Andy saw the man had a printed list on the table. "Are those the nominees?" she asked him.

"How much you want to bet?" he demanded. He covered the list with one hand and pulled on her jacket sleeve with the other.

The list was too short to have all the nominees.

"And the winner is," Bains squeaked on the TV set as he opened an envelope, "not me! Slip Kersaw for 'Raiders of the Lost Lingerie'!"

Boos and raspberries drowned out the applause.

"How'd you get the winner's list?" Andy asked the man.

He crumpled the paper under his hand and winked at her. "What list?" he said.

"And that was the last thing Muckler said to you?" Lieutenant Everson asked.

"Absolute last," Andy said.

"Did you see anyone near his table who may have shown interest in him, or who was observing him in some way?"

"Everyone ignored him, me included."

"What did you do after that?"

"I went upstairs, saw a few people I knew."

"Anyone you think we should talk to?" Everson asked.

Andy did not want to mention the name of her former boyfriend, Drew Shaw, *Liberty Bell Magazine*'s editor, who had dumped her last summer and was currently sleeping with Bombarella. "You'll probably get to all of them," Andy said.

"Anyone say anything to you about Muckler?"

"Not a word about him," Andy said.

"How is it you left when you did?"

Andy shrugged. "I waited until the end, until Slip Kersaw got Fretzer of the Year, and I left."

"But your timing . . . ," Everson sighed.

"Ms. Cosicki stated that she left," McSloan said decorously. "Like lawyers and some police, proficient journalists have a talent for being in the right places at the right time."

"Or the wrong places," Lange said. "Sometimes, there's no difference."

Outside the club, Andy drew her bomber jacket around her, hiked up her shoulder bag and tried to walk as quickly as possible back to her car.

As she stepped on to Dempsey Lane, an enormous truck rolled past her. Something inside its engine made an insistent, pinging sound. What was a truck that big doing in a narrow alley like Dempsey at this time of night? Making a delivery?

She was headed up the street to her car when she saw something was very wrong with the silver Jaguar in the small lot right off the alley. The wheels had bent and buckled, as if the car had suddenly become so heavy that the wheels couldn't hold it up.

In the dim light she thought the windows had been painted. Then she noticed the broken glass in the back and the wet sand pouring out of it.

The entire inside of the car had been pumped full of sand. She saw a spot on the windshield. No. Two spots.

She looked closely. They weren't spots. They were fingertips pressed tightly against the glass, and they weren't moving.

"That's when you called 911," Everson said.

"On my cell phone," Andy said. "I was told that somebody had already called."

"A male, possibly an older male, from the sound of the voice, from a pay phone at Seventeenth and Chestnut," Everson said. "He said something screwy was going on Dempsey with a car and truck. Anything else you can tell me about the truck?"

"It was big and smelled of diesel exhaust," Andy said. "The engine made a pinging sound."

"You didn't see the make or license plate?"

"I don't normally look at truck license plates."

"You saw Muckler's license plate," Lange pointed out.

"Because I had time to look at it," Andy said.

"We're checking images on our stop-sign cameras for truck images right now," Everson said. "So far, the only one that's come up that might be a possibility had its license plates obscured. The cameras are designed to get a good view of license plates, but there was either some road grime covering the plate, or, as is the case with illegal haulers, the plate was covered. The truck we're looking for was carrying a rather large pump that is capable of pushing sand suspended in water, or liquid concrete, through a tube into the broken driver's side panel window," Everson said. "We're reasonably sure the sand was taken from this side of the Delaware. The truck could have gone to one of the entrance ramps used by the tourist boats, stuck the intake into the water and pulled it up. Has Mr. Action answered any reader questions about concrete pumps lately?"

"I didn't know they existed until you told me."

"Whoever filled the car had to be pretty sure that he would be in it within an hour, or the liquid in the sand would have frozen. They found him in the car, broke the back window and pumped the sand in so fast Muckler couldn't get out."

"What would have kept him in the car?" Andy asked.

"Muckler may not have known what was happening. Or he could have been threatened in some way." Everson went down his list of questions. "You remained at the scene for . . . how long?"

"About an hour," Andy said. "I wanted to see how you would handle it."

Lange said, "Looking for clues, eh?"

"Don't answer that," McSloan said to Andy. He turned to Lange. "There is no need to impugn the motives of your employees, Howard. It was cold. She could have gone home. She stayed because she was curious. Journalists are supposed to be curious."

"And lawyers are supposed to—"

"What, Howard?" McSloan pressed. "What do you know about lawyers?"

To Everson, Lange said, "That's it. She's the last one."

Everson looked at the newsroom personnel list. "What about Ladderback?"

"He wasn't there. He's out of the loop," Lange said. He nodded at Andy. "You're done."

McSloan asked if there would be an obituary for the Sandman.

"The news story ran on page three today," Lange said. "It's news. An obituary would be redundant and from what I hear about this guy, a lot of people are going to think whoever killed him is doing us all a favor."

McSloan was about to tell Lange what he could do with his favors when Andy asked him if she could speak with him outside the office. McSloan followed her to her desk. She showed him Jermaine's letter. She sat down in her chair, put her hands on the keyboard and asked him for a good, strong quote that would tie everything together.

He leaned over and put his two strong hands on her shoulders. Should she tell him to take them off? She had been taking self-defense classes for four months, and knew that she could trap one hand, spin out and stand up to face him. Then she could grab the arm at the wrist, just above the elbow, take a step back, break his balance, spin him forward and down so he ground his nose into the newsroom's grimy blue industrial carpet.

But she liked his hands on her shoulders, though she wasn't sure exactly why. His grip wasn't threatening as much as it was comforting, and though she didn't need him comforting her, she enjoyed his attention.

So she let him keep his hands there as she typed *Michael McSloan, a Philadelphia lawyer says,* followed by his quote: "If you've been physically injured, if you had an agreement that isn't being honored, if you've been treated badly by anyone for any reason, if you feel your rights have been denied and you're not sure what you're entitled to, see a lawyer first. A lawyer can give you good advice and help you settle your differences, frequently without going to court. A lawyer knows what's right, even if you don't."

He brought his face down until his mouth was near her right ear. "How's that?" he asked her.

She could smell the spicy cologne he wore. "It's okay," she said.

"Okay!?" McSloan said in mock offense. "How about excellent in the extreme? That's the kind of advice that solves all problems."

"It answers the question," Andy said. "But I don't think it's going to solve any problems for this kid. I still have to call him back and find out what was taken from him."

He took his hands off her shoulders. "We should do more. Let's save his soul."

"I answer reader questions," Andy said. "I leave souls alone."

"The saving I do is of a secular variety. You'll be available at four?"

Here it comes, she thought. "For what?"

"I want to address this boy's question personally, and at four P.M. he would be most likely at home, or hanging out on his corner. I would like it if you were there. I have experience with ghetto boys. I once settled a personal injury case involving one. I got him out of the 'hood and into a private school."

"Where he lived happily ever after?" Andy replied. She looked him right in the eye and saw the immediate future: this articulate, smart, *married* man would impress her with his kindness, compassion and willingness to help. He wouldn't try to put the moves on her. He would behave as if being with her were the easiest, most pleasant and fascinating thing he could do with himself. He wouldn't be sleazy. He would ask her to a very good, very expensive dinner, and maybe a visit to a club after that, where he wouldn't try to impress her with all the important people he knew because he would be giving her all his attention. He would find her charming, interesting, clever and then he would make his move. . . .

Why wasn't she offended? Why did she *not* want to run from him, or maybe kick him in his shins?

Because just about every woman in the newsroom was ridiculously jealous.

And Andy felt she was in control. He would call her back and when he suggested dinner she could say no and she would hear that regret in his voice and that would be it.

"Call the boy and make sure he'll be home. I'll come around for you in about an hour."

"I've made plans," Andy said automatically. "But . . . I can change them."

"Do that," he said. Then he turned with just enough reluctance and went back into Howard Lange's office, where he emerged with his jacket and his assistant. Just before he went past the newsroom receptionist, he pointed his finger at Andy and winked.

Andy spun around in her chair and spent a few minutes feeling the heat leave her face. She felt like she was sixteen and a senior on the football team had asked her to the prom.

"The police have finished their inquiries?" Ladderback quietly asked.

"I guess." Andy shrugged.

"So I will not be questioned," Ladderback continued.

"Lange said you weren't there," Andy replied.

Ladderback's eyes moved slowly behind thick bifocals. "Was that all he said?"

"He also said you were out of the loop."

Ladderback returned to an obituary about the former owner of a Kensington produce stand. Soon he heard Andy get up from her chair and go to lunch in the newsroom's cafeteria.

Ladderback picked up his telephone. "What you have done," he said to the man who answered, "is horrible."

"Who said I did anything?" the man replied smugly.

"Was it Muckler against whom you lost the case?"

"Actually, it was Johnny Altmacher, the Papermill. They're similar. Muckler wrecks the legal machinery. Altmacher buries it in paperwork. I hate those shysters. It's a wonder they've both been practicing so long without being cleansed from our midst."

"Cleansing?" Ladderback asked.

"*Ethics* cleansing. I'm surprised it took me so long to come up with the concept: identify the corrupt, lazy, inept, repulsive, disgusting and utterly worthless lawyers, and kill them off in a wonderfully appropriate manner that will draw attention to their sins. Do that often enough, and those who can clean up their acts, will."

"I have another concept for you," Ladderback said. He opened a manila file. *"Enantiodromia."*

"Sounds Greek."

"It is Greek. It is attributed to the philosopher Heraclitus," Ladderback read. "It means 'counter running.' The psychologist Carl Jung found the concept of *enantiodromia* useful in explaining how people with extreme attitudes or beliefs can suddenly behave in a way that runs counter to those beliefs."

"You sound like my wife. Are you seeing her again?"

"I have not seen her since I ended therapy," Ladderback said. "Jung saw *enantiodroma* as a path to redemption. Extremes can cancel themselves out. Or they can be ameliorated by conscience. Have you thought of the grief you have caused among those who loved Mr. Muckler?"

"Nulla remedia tam faciunt dolrem quam quae sunt salutaria."

"No remedies cause as much grief as those that save a life," Ladderback translated to himself.

"The life I'm saving," the man added, "is the life of the law."

Ladderback closed his eyes. "What could make you do this?"

"I've hated lousy lawyers all my life. Last night I turned fifty. Isn't that enough?"

2
slip knot

Ladderback watched Andy leave for her appointment with McSloan. Then he left to keep an appointment of his own. As executor of the estate of Patrick "Whitey" Goohan, owner of Jimmy D's Bar & Grille, Ladderback had scheduled a meeting before the dinner hour to discuss a claim against the estate.

He took the elevator down to the *Press* Building's sub-basement, which opened onto the underground shopping mall and food court beneath Market Street. He took the pedestrian tunnel south toward Chestnut Street and found the set of double doors that opened into the restaurant's basement kitchen, where, he was pleased to note, the staff was busy, prepping the dinner menu. He said hello to those he passed in the kitchen, as he always did, and then made his way up the stairs beside the dumbwaiter that took food up into the dining room.

In his will, Whitey Goohan had directed Ladderback, as executor, to oversee the sale of the restaurant "at a fair price" to the family of Ibrahim Mafouz, a Lebanese immigrant whom Goohan had hired as maitre d' after Goohan's second stroke. Money from the sale, as well as whatever Ladderback could raise from the disposal of Goohan's personal effects, were to be given to a list of current and former employees.

As he mounted the top of the stairs, Ladderback did not see Mafouz in the dining room. But he did recognize Schuyler Nordvahl at the bar.

Their eyes met. A cloud of curly gray hair floated over Nordvahl's ruddy brow. His nose came down in a knife edge. His lips were thin and severe. He wore what Ladderback had come to recognize as his winter uniform: snow boots, dark khaki slacks, a lumpy, knitted sweater and a bright red ski vest, as if he had just tromped through the snow-shrouded Chadds Ford forest.

Ladderback watched him hop off his bar stool, grab a slender black briefcase made of a synthetic fabric and move swiftly across the dining room. He handed Ladderback an envelope. "Herein you will find the check for last night's party."

Ladderback had attended the party. The guests had been limited to members of the Delaware Valley Law Watch, and Nordvahl's odd but rather interesting collection of clients. Ladderback had especially enjoyed speaking to the electronics repairman about collecting old television sets, and the lady plumber who did appearances in community theater groups was quite funny. The only person whose absence Ladderback had noted was Nordvahl's ex-wife.

"You could have given this to Mr. Mafouz," Ladderback said.

"Mr. Mafouz told me about your meeting with Pescecane, so I thought I'd hand it to you personally," Nordvahl said. "Just pretend I'm not here."

"I can handle the meeting by myself," Ladderback replied gruffly. He set off for the only occupied table in the dining room, where three men were finishing what appeared to be an enormous feast.

Ladderback came around to the best-dressed man. "You requested this meeting, Mr. Pescecane?"

Severio Pescecane did not reply immediately. He slowly touched his mouth with a napkin. Then he put down the napkin and turned his head toward the squat, bloated man opposite him and the thinner, younger, twitchy fellow with the white blob of horseradish on his necktie. He rotated his head, like the turret on a tank, showing a face of blotchy skin and a shiny nose and tiny, mincing lips.

"I *insisted* on this meeting, Mr. Ladderback," Pescecane began, "on behalf of my clients, Mr. Fredrick R. Chasen and Mr. Owen Youngblood."

"Your clients are better known, counselor," Nordvahl cut in, "as Slip Disc Chasen, and his boy wonder, Slip Knot, who used to stage fake injuries so that Irving Kersaw could extort settlements in lieu of filing suit."

Chasen grumbled, "Mr. Kersaw would resent your accusations, if he were here to defend himself."

"The man you have defending you, Mr. Chasen, is going to stab you in the back," Nordvahl said. "He is notorious for betraying his clients to the competing interests."

Pescecane eyed Nordvahl as if he would squash him, but didn't think the effort worth his while. "Are you of counsel to the estate?"

"We're supposed to pretend Mr. Nordvahl isn't here," Ladderback said.

Pescecane watched warily as Ladderback and Nordvahl found chairs and pulled them toward the table. Ibrahim Mafouz appeared with Nordvahl's orange juice. Mafouz asked Ladderback if he wanted anything. Ladderback declined. Mafouz then asked Pescecane if his meal had been to his liking.

"I have some thoughts about the service," Slip Disc Chasen piped up. He pointed to the silver cream pitcher. "The cream what's in there was allowed to get warm. That's not right. You can come down with a case of sam-and-ella poisoning from warm cream." He shifted in his chair so his red turtleneck knit pullover bulged out of the chocolate brown sport coat, as if the hypothetical salmonella bacteria were expanding inside him.

Mafouz pulled the cream pitcher away, apologized and said he would not charge for the coffee.

"There are numerous other concerns but . . ." Chasen took out a business card. "I do liability and risk prevention consultations to restaurants the world over. Perhaps we can do business together after our situation here reaches a suitable resolve." He gave a card to Mafouz and slid one across the table to Ladderback, who did not touch it.

Mafouz asked if he could provide anything further. Slip Knot said he wouldn't mind another slice of shoofly pie, but Pescecane said, "We've had enough, thank you."

Mafouz adjusted the check and put it beside Pescecane, who flinched, as if insulted.

"Let me look at that," Ladderback said.

Pescecane seemed pleased that Ladderback appeared to be paying for their food, until Ladderback said, "This appears to be correct," and put it on the table near Pescecane.

Pescecane folded his hands. "You don't appear to have done much estate work previous to this, Mr. Ladderback, am I not correct?"

Nordvahl again cut in. "Mr. Ladderback's experience to this point is immaterial. Show us your claim."

"In due time," Pescecane continued. "Let me create a scenario, if I may. Mr. Ladderback doesn't want to be an executor, but he's doing this in honor of a near and dear friend. Let me assure you, from my professional understanding of situations like this . . ." He stopped when Ladderback scowled. "Excuse me? Did I say something that bothered you?"

"There are no situations *like* this one," Ladderback said. "This situation is unique. Other situations may be *similar* but not *like*. Also, to ask if you are correct, and follow that with, 'am I not,' is redundant."

Pescecane rolled his eyes at Slip Disc. "This is the first time, in all my years of practicing law, in various situations with individuals high and low, that I have had my grammar corrected by a party to a lawsuit."

"You asked if you said something that caused me concern," Ladderback replied. "I answered your question."

"And he is not a party to a lawsuit," Nordvahl said.

"I would not make statements without checking your facts, counselor," Pescecane said to Nordvahl. "I've been in enough of these situations and, let me assure you, what's about to occur is going to be a pain in the ass. I don't know if that's grammatically correct and, personally, I don't give a fuck. How's that?"

"You're being crude and disgusting, counselor," Nordvahl said. *"Vulgus non opus sit."*

24

Vulgarity does not work, Ladderback translated to himself.

"We live in a crude and disgusting world," Pescecane replied. "I wanted to point out that Mr. Ladderback may not have a sufficient understanding of what he's getting into. From the obituaries I have learned that Whitey Goohan never married and he never gave a shit who his parents were or if he had any brothers or sisters."

"He was an orphan," Ladderback said.

"All to my point. We may presume that individuals of all stripes will claim that Goohan promised them a hundred thousand. Maybe two hundred thousand. Whitey used to vacation in Puerto Rico, and what's going to stop a claimant from saying he's his love child, or because he saved Whitey's life, Whitey promised him a hundred thousand? You're going to get suppliers that Whitey stiffed, and now they want what they're owed, plus interest, and it's going to come to a hundred thousand. You're going to get contractors that haven't been paid and they want what's coming to them. Another hundred thousand. Maybe two. Claimants are going to come jumping out of the woodwork, I shit you not. They read obituaries in the paper, they find who died, and they set up their spurious claims. Some of these people are known to me. My office has represented some of them, and the financial hardship on an estate in settling the simplest claim can be, I assure you, sky-high, if not higher. You're going to be up to your eyeteeth in this, drowning in it for at least a year, maybe two, unless you name me of counsel to the estate."

Nordvahl almost knocked over his orange juice. "Have you called this meeting to sell your services counselor?"

Pescecane put his hands flat on the table. "I am being informational, at this point. I'm informing Mr. Ladderback of what he's getting himself into. He's going to need strong, reputable representation that's going to work in his interest. It doesn't have to be me, but, if it *was* me—"

"*Were*," Ladderback said.

"Whatever. What my firm would do, is take it all off your hands, with nothing coming out of your pocket, except, maybe, the liquor license. I can turn that liquor license over faster than the chef can fry an egg, and you could get a cut of that, which is only fair."

"What would be fair," Nordvahl said, "is for you to take your shoddy, ethically compromised business elsewhere."

Pescecane examined his fingernails. "Mr. Nordvahl, I will cease all pretenses. I want to tell you that I am honored to appear on that list you drew up, with Charlie Muckler, Marathon Mike McSloan and all the others, as the top ten lawyers we can do without, though it confuses me to understand who, precisely, 'we' are."

Nordvahl couldn't hide his pleasure. "That list was compiled by the staff of the Delaware Valley Law Watch," Nordvahl said. "They love the law and hate bad lawyers."

"And you had nothing to do with it? Ah, c'mon. You created that list for a reason."

"God created sharks for a reason," Nordvahl said.

Pescecane almost laughed. "He did indeed. As you might be aware, my firm is sponsoring the shark habitat at the new Atlantic City Aquarium. It's opening in a few days. I'd be happy to make sure you get an invite to the dedication ceremony, if you would kindly, kindly, shut your fucking mouth, okay?"

"Before I refuse an invitation that you have no intention of sending," Nordvahl said, "I want to confirm that I heard you offer to represent both your fraudulent claimants as well as Mr. Goohan's estate. Did you state that, counselor? Are you an ambidexter, counselor? In Shakespeare's day, an ambidexter was a lawyer who took money from both sides."

"I don't know from Shakespeare," Pescecane continued. "But I know from sharks. The way it is with sharks, they always have these little fish hanging around with them. When the shark eats, everybody eats. If the shark doesn't eat, he goes after whoever's closest."

Slip Knot, who was closest to Pescecane began to rub his hands nervously.

Ladderback said, "Mr. Goohan's will is to preserve the restaurant and provide for his employees. The liquor license will remain with the restaurant."

"Then we move to the claim," Pescecane said. He opened a slim, chrome-rimmed, black leather attaché and removed several stacks of documents. "This is a judgment for the plaintiff, Owen Youngblood, against defendant Jimmy D's Bar & Grill, for punitive and compensatory damages in an amount not less than $780,650, with interest accruing in event of late or nonpayment, regarding an injury suffered by said plaintiff on or about—"

Nordvahl snatched the documents away. He removed from his briefcase a set of reading glasses and a handheld computer. He put the glasses on the end of his nose, and began reading Pescecane's documents. He said, "You must improve your spelling, counselor. S-t-a-f-f is what you hire and fire. Staphylococcus is commonly abbreviated as s-t-a-p-h."

"I'm sure Mr. Ladderback is not familiar with the situation," Pescecane said to Slip Knot. "Mr. Youngblood, tell Mr. Ladderback your unfortunate story."

Slip Knot stopped rubbing his hands. "It's like, well, I was eating here a while ago, had to go to the bathroom and I washed my hands and I got this cut, see?" He pointed to a faint, crescent-shaped scar on the inside of his left palm.

"Be accurate, kid," Chasen told him. "You can't expect them to listen to what you don't spell out to them."

"What I mean is," Youngblood continued, "I was reaching for the soap thing and I cut myself right here, and it got infected with staph and it got into my body and I had to go to the hospital."

Nordvahl put on a pair of reading glasses. "It says here that the staph infection 'spread throughout plaintiff's body causing pain, discomfort, inability to move freely, temporary damage to kidneys and liver, as well as permanent nerve damage to the plaintiff's left arm.'" He looked over his glasses. "Show me your hand again."

Youngblood became uncomfortable. "I can't do"—he saw Pescecane fluttering his fingers—"what he's doing."

Nordvahl accessed the Internet on his handheld computer while Ladderback studied the hand. Ladderback saw callouses on the inside of the thumb and across the top of the palm. "Do you do much rowing?"

Youngblood brightened. "In the summer, like, on a boat."

Ladderback ignored the ill usage of "like." "Do you row on the Schuylkill, or, perhaps, at the New Jersey shore?" Ladderback continued.

"We gotta—my folks, I mean, have an apartment in Ocean City. It's down from Mr. Pescecane's place. He takes me fishing sometimes."

"Shark fishing," Pescecane grinned at Nordvahl. "Mr. Youngblood rows in the back bays, which, I might add, he cannot do in the manner to which he had been accustomed, due to his injury."

"The Jersey shore meadows can be wonderful for rowing," Ladderback agreed. He raised his hand and Mafouz appeared at his side. Ladderback asked for a Jimmy D'Tini. He also asked for the clam and oyster sampler, unshelled. "I'll open them myself," Ladderback said.

Mafouz wrote it down and rushed away.

Nordvahl thumbed through Pescecane's documents. "It says here that a default judgment has been entered to defendant, Jimmy D's Bar & Grill, who did not appear in court on the date of . . ." He tapped it into his notebook computer. "Ah. Yes. I see."

Severio Pescecane asked for another Bloody Mary. "Forgive me for speaking ill of the dead, but Whitey Goohan had the typical working man's contempt for due process. When Mr. Youngblood sued, neither Goohan or his appointed representative appeared in court. The judge found for the plaintiff and, this was a year and a half ago and we haven't got a dime out of Whitey or his insurer."

Nordvahl sipped his orange juice while his fingers flew over his keyboard. "You have copies of correspondence with the restaurant's insurer?"

"We dealt only with Goohan," Pescecane said. "Goohan was a pain in the ass to deal with about this, and you know what happens to people who don't settle their claims. The interest adds up until . . ." He opened his hands.

Ladderback's Jimmy D'Tini came. Mafouz poured it in a martini glass and left the shaker. Then he positioned the plate of three oysters and three clams nestled on crushed ice, with a side dish of lemon wedges, cocktail sauce and a flat, elliptical shucking knife.

While Nordvahl's fingers tapped his notebook computer, Ladderback put an oyster in the palm of his left hand and tried unsuccessfully to pry the end of the shucking knife into the small gap between the bivalve's shells. "I appear to be having difficulty with this," Ladderback said. "I haven't been to the Jersey shore since I was a child."

"You're out of practice," Youngblood said. "I go clamming and oystering all the time from my boat. The best thing is to just pull 'em up out of the mud and pop 'em open. Let me have one." He reached over for an oyster. Ladderback gave him the shucking knife.

Youngblood put the oyster in his left palm. He gripped the shucking knife in his right and traced the edge of the blade around the outside of the shell. "You gotta tickle it in, like this." The knife slid in and he drove the shells apart.

"Very good," Ladderback said. "You can do the whole plate, if you'd like."

"Only if I get to eat one." Youngblood grinned.

Ladderback watched him until he was on the third oyster. Then, just as Slip Knot was tickling the shell with the knife, Ladderback knocked his martini shaker onto the floor.

It made a clanging crash and Youngblood almost jumped out of his chair. The knife slipped under the shell and almost buried itself in the skin of Slip Knot's left palm.

Ladderback reached over and removed the oyster from Slip Knot's hand. The end of the shucking knife matched precisely the crescent-shaped scar on Slip Knot's palm.

"Your accident may have had another cause," Ladderback said as Mafouz brought napkins to sop up the liquid. "Anyone who has shucked shellfish gets the injury, sooner or later. Though the scar remains, the injury rarely causes any serious difficulties." Ladderback opened his left palm to show a fainter scar.

Youngblood looked helplessly at Pescecane, who said, "Mr. Youngblood's claim still stands. We have a court order here. A judgment that says we're owed and we're here to get what we're owed."

Nordvahl pointed to a page on the documents. "This date when the default judgement was entered—there's no possible mistake about it?"

"Why should there be?" Pescecane said. "They came from the court."

"Would you like me to check?" Nordvahl grinned.

Pescecane removed another document. "What's there to check? The time for stalling is over. I'm a fair individual. I have a payment schedule here."

"Put it away," Nordvahl said. "Your judgment is a forgery and a bad one, done with the expectation that Mr. Ladderback would not have counsel present, or, if he did, counsel would be lazy."

"I resent that!" Chasen said.

"You invented this scam when you heard Whitey died," Nordvahl said. "The judgment is from another case, on a different restaurant, in which Chasen is the plaintiff." He showed Pescecane the small screen on his computer. "You see that judgment here. A search with Chasen's name, and staphylococcus, brings it right up. That judgment was later reversed after the judge was convicted for taking bribes. The Law Watch published an account of this in *Bar Sinister,* so I have a very good memory of this incident, even if it happened ten years ago."

"What we're talking about happened a year and a half ago," Pescecane said. "This is a unique case. Just because it's like, I mean, similar to another, doesn't mean it's the same."

Nordvahl shook his head. "You downloaded the data, inserted different names and numbers and moved the date up. What gives you away is the date. You never checked the date."

Nordvahl pulled up a calendar on his computer. "The date you picked when you say this default judgment was given is a Sunday. That court has never, ever met on a Sunday."

"So the clerk of the court made a mistake," Pescecane said to Ladderback. "This doesn't change the fact that—"

"Must we bother the clerk over this?" Nordvahl said. "Or do you just want to leave?"

"I will ignore that rebuke," Pescecane said. "Mr. Ladderback, we have a situation in which an innocent party has suffered unreasonably because of negligence due to design, placement and cleanliness of sanitary facilities. You understand where we're coming from."

"I do indeed understand from whence you've come," Ladderback said. "I expect you to pay for your food before you leave." He stood and said to Youngblood, "You may finish the shellfish without charge."

"Thanks," Youngblood said, reaching for a clam. "They're really good."

"While consuming this food," Chasen began, "I found ten things wrong with the service and the presentation that could result in liability issues. Any self-respecting establishment would not charge for this meal." He pushed himself violently away from the table so that the chair tipped backward and would have crashed to the floor had not Mafouz swooped in, one hand holding their coats, the other steadying the chair.

They were at the door when Mafouz grabbed the check off the table. Ladderback motioned Mafouz not to chase after them. "We are better off without them," he said.

Nordvahl grinned. "Yes. We are indeed. Lawyers like him should be eaten alive."

Ladderback paused and said, "I have asked my assistant to do a profile about you."

Nordvahl shrugged. "It makes no difference to me if I see my name in a newspaper."

"This time it might," Ladderback said.

3 dysphonia

A young boy peered through one of four diamond-shaped pieces of tinted glass that had been set into the row house's warped door.

Mike McSloan banged his knuckles insistently again and the battered plywood front door came open.

The boy stood meekly in an oversized yellow winter parka, a blue Nautica sweatshirt and baggy indigo Dickies work pants that fell over his shoes, and told them his parents and his sisters were "not around."

Jermaine closed the door and the first thing Andy saw were cockroaches. The row house's shallow parlor had two space heaters glowing so brightly they might have started a fire if the room weren't so cold, and yet the cockroaches frolicked across the frayed, filthy orange remnant stretching from the couch to the TV set as if it were a hot day in July.

They scurried away when McSloan strode in. He spun about so that his long, camel-hair coat swirled outward as if it were a cloak. He inspected the room, nodding at the water damage that had stained the wallpaper, nodding at the torn billowing plastic over the windows.

Then he turned his attention to Jermaine and said, "You have been given gifts."

Andy thought she'd scream if she saw another cockroach but she didn't scream because she couldn't bring herself to interrupt the patronizing performance McSloan was presenting. He circled about Jermaine, who sank glumly on the couch as McSloan said he was "one in a million. Do you have any idea of what that means?"

Andy sensed that McSloan was performing, not for Jermaine, but for her. She stepped between them. "Jermaine, could you tell us what was taken from you?"

"A basketball," he said proudly.

McSloan made a face at Andy, as if to say, these are the kinds of things ghetto kids fight over.

"I do layups," Andy said to Jermaine. "This must have been a special basketball."

"It was!" Jermaine said. "It was autographed by Ismail Khan. I got it at a contest raffle: And these kids come up to me and stole it."

McSloan grinned at Andy. "What would you do," he said to Jermaine, "if I told you Ismail Khan was my client, that I was standing as close to him as I am to you? He's one in a million. So are you."

Jermaine seemed genuinely confused.

"See those boys selling crack on the corner? The folks who buy from them, they're desperate. They can't live without their stuff. Ismail Khan was as desperate for what I could do for him as a crackhead is for his dealer."

Andy came up between them. "Do you know the boys who stole your basketball?"

Jermaine nodded hesitantly.

"Can you ask their parents to make them give it back?"

McSloan laughed. "Girl, this is the *ghet*-to. These boys are *bad*. They don't listen to nobody."

She resented being called a girl. She resented him slipping into dialect. She resented him.

"*Mr.* McSloan," she said to him. "If Ismail Khan was your client, could you ask him if he would sign another basketball? The *Press* will pay to have it delivered to Jermaine." And if Howard Lange wouldn't let her submit that as an expense, she would pay for it herself.

"I am forbidden to discuss the case because of the attorney-client confidentiality," McSloan began. "The nature of the work I did for him was private. Ismail Khan came to me before he was Ismail Khan. He was messed up pretty bad. He couldn't even say his name, you hear me, Jermaine? I got him into a place where he found a new name for himself."

"What kinda place you talking about?" Jermaine asked.

"A place for kids who are one-in-a-million. You know what it means to be one in a million, Jermaine? We talk about how important it is to be an individual in this country, how everybody's unique and got rights. But those rights only apply to the kids that impress us, win the game, make the grade, get the prize. What about the kids with birth defects, rare diseases, or who are messed up in ways we can't figure out? You ever heard of spasmodic dysphonia, Jermaine? That's where you wake up one morning and every word you say comes out like a broken plate. There are all kinds of theories about what causes it, but a theory won't make it any better if you got it."

Jermaine's attention began to wander. McSloan sensed that he was losing his hold on the boy.

Andy said, "Jermaine, I will contact the Philadelphia 76ers myself. I can't say for sure if they'll do it, but if I write it up, they'll probably get Khan to sign a basketball and I'll send it to you myself."

"Why?" Jermaine asked her.

Andy paused.

"Why you want to do this?" he said. "Why you want to help me? I don't want your help. I had a question. You didn't answer my question. You just tell me what you're going to do for me. I didn't ask you to do anything for me. Those boys took my ball. They'll take it again. I don't want nothing nobody's going to take until I'm big enough I can take what I want."

"You want to know what happens to big boys, Jermaine?" McSloan said. "They're only so big until a lawyer takes them down." He began to pace, as if he were lecturing a jury in a courtroom. "I specialize in class-action law. That's where you get a group of people together who have been wronged by a big boy, and you get back at that big boy. Sometimes you don't need a wrong if you can show the possibility of a wrong. I happen to be famous, Jermaine—that's right, *famous*—for what I did to get back at Fulham Health Sports and Manufacturing. They make computer-controlled exercise machines and I showed a jury how easy it is for a remote control—just like the kind you use to operate a TV set—to get screwed up and mess with the treadmill's computer, making it speed up or slow down or do all kinds of dangerous stuff that could throw a person right off the machine, cause serious injury, even death."

Andy previously had done an Internet search about McSloan. She had discovered an article about him and this case in *Bar Sinister*, the monthly newsletter of the Delaware Valley Law Watch—the legal ethics organization that Schuyler Nordvahl had founded. The Law Watch accused McSloan of playing loose with the facts in that case, and then, after winning it, forcing Fulham Health Sports to donate equipment to his health club—a blatant violation of professional ethics. For this reason, the Law Watch had put him on its list of "Lawyers We Could Do Without."

She hadn't planned to bring up what she had read, but she had grown weary of listening to McSloan talk about himself. So she let him have it. "You distorted the facts. The company said it had no problems with remote controls overriding the computers and that these problems were unlikely to occur."

McSloan relished the challenge. "They were trying to confuse fact and probability. If the odds of someone being killed by a piece of machinery are one in a million, then there are upwards of two hundred and fifty people in this country alone who are in mortal danger."

"Hold on," Andy said. "Probability does not determine outcomes. *You* are the one who is confusing fact and probability."

"The jury *believed* me and the case was upheld on appeal," McSloan replied. He came close enough to her for her to see a nervous twitching in his eyes. Then he turned away. "Justice in this country," he told Jermaine, "is about what a judge or a jury is going to believe. It's not about what's right or wrong. It's not about what's fair. It's not about what's cool. It's not even about what's real or true. You get folks to believe you, Jermaine, you can get back just about everything they can take from you."

Andy had had enough. She thanked Jermaine for letting them into his home and mentioned that it was getting late, that they had plans.

When she left the house, she saw that the dreary slum wasn't the kind of place where you could expect a taxi to answer your call. She had no idea how far she was from public transportation, it was already dark out, there was a crowd of kids admiring McSloan's cream and brown leather BMW sedan that were giving her the wrong kind of looks and, from what she'd picked up from self-defense courses, you should never put yourself in a dangerous situation, even if you think you can handle yourself.

Mike McSloan made his coat flare out around himself as he swaggered toward his car. He stared down the kids hanging around and held the door open for Andy.

She got in. He joined her, locked the doors and started the engine.

"Care for some music?" he asked her.

Andy did not care for music and told him so.

He drove quickly toward Kensington Avenue. "I will say anything and do anything to represent the interests of my client."

"And who was your client?"

"You are my client. I was showing him that you care, Andy."

"I didn't ask you to do that. You said you wanted to save his soul!"

He grinned. "Admit it: you were impressed."

She was not impressed. She was so astounded at his arrogance that she was—for a moment—speechless.

"I want you to know I could have sent anyone from my firm to supervise the police interrogation in your newsroom. But I went myself because I was looking for a special individual. Someone like you." He appraised her. "You move like an athlete."

She was too shocked to reply. He seemed to enjoy her outrage as he drove. "I would have been surprised if you had not found out more about me, as I also found out about you."

"Like what?" Andy said, not believing a word of it.

"You're clearly frustrated with your job and the people you work with. You have an inner need, drive, almost a compulsion to take each thing you're given and run with it as far as you can. You know you're destined for great things but you can't see those things happening by answering silly questions."

He was sounding like one of Glinda Starr's horoscopes. "The questions readers ask are not silly," Andy said. "Not all of them."

"But you would not be bothering with them if you were given a chance to become a part of something much greater." He stopped the car at a traffic light and said, "I'm putting together a team of bright, if not brilliant, extremely capable individuals. I'm talking about a chance to leave a mark on this city, to improve the lives of hundreds, if not thousands of people. And to get rid of the corrupt, backstabbing, petty little characters who are holding the city back."

She became aware that his hand was on her thigh. "Re*move* your hand."

"I want you to understand I'm serious."

Andy clamped her hand on top of his and pried the hand away. Before she could tell him where he could let her out, he said, "What I'm serious about is power, and passion."

He put his hand back on the leather-sheathed steering wheel and let the car go forward. "I'm talking about a run for the most important office in this city. I want to knock Senator Hank Tybold off his perch."

Just before she could tell him he was crazy, he added, "I can surround myself with the most professional staff possible, and I will lose the election.

"Or," he continued, putting his hand on the sleeve of her bomber jacket, as if to say, I touched your thigh because I wanted to but now I just want to make a point, "I can reach out and put together a team of really sharp, volatile, energetic, passionate people, people I admire in as many ways as possible . . . ," he caught her eye long enough for her to wonder if he was going to drive into the elevated subway support girder, "people who have never done anything like this before and want to shake the tree and see what falls out."

He took his hand off her arm, made a turn and the gleaming towers of Center City came into view.

Andy told herself McSloan was trying to seduce her, but what he had just revealed to her was a potential news story: nobody, not Parnell O'-Hearn, the *Press's* political columnist, not Chilly Bains, the gossip columnist, or their opposite numbers at the *Philadelphia Standard,* the *Press's* broadsheet competition, had mentioned the city's Republican party's challenge to Henry Tybold, who was up for reelection in November. Even if McSloan was lying to her, with the primaries only three months away, his intentions had to be confirmed.

Andy couldn't help herself. She had to ask: "What makes you think you can win?"

"I don't have to win," he said confidently. "Politics and law is all about power, and power in a democracy comes from getting people, be they a Jermaine Haynes or a judge and a jury, to believe you, to believe *in* you." He grinned again. "I might lay it all out to you. Over dinner."

Andy had to get out of his car. She was looking for a well-lit corner when McSloan's cell phone made a sound that Andy guessed was music.

McSloan's demeanor changed suddenly as he barked into the phone, "I told you not to call me. . . . He's *your* responsibility."

McSloan's arrogant mask had come off—he was so angry he almost drove the car into an SUV. "I can't take him tonight," he yelled. "I can't and I won't!" He took a deep gulp of air, let it out as if his breath were fire and said, "This is the last time I will let you do this to me."

He broke the connection and told Andy that he would drop her off at the newspaper's office because dinner would have to be postponed. He gave her a look that told her she had better not ask why.

So Andy asked why.

He seethed. "My son."

None of what she saw on the Internet mentioned that he had children. Suddenly Andy was interested. "What's the problem?"

He turned the wheel hard and the car zipped obediently up an access ramp onto an elevated portion of Interstate 95, heading south for Center City. "He's not your concern," he snapped at her. "Why do you care?"

"Let me meet him," Andy said, "and I just might lay it out to you."

She could have told him that as the only daughter of two mutually antagonistic, self-absorbed parents who were never the people they were at home when they were in the public eye, she was fascinated by how people in the public eye treated their children.

But he didn't give her the chance. Instead, he floored the car and she heard the eager, happy purr that BMWs make when they're given a chance to break a speed limit. As the digital speedometer soared, the car slid effortlessly across the lanes of densely packed traffic, swooping over at the last minute to take the off-ramp onto the Vine Street Expressway, up the corkscrew spiral onto Fifteenth Street, whipping around and through the tangle of small streets between Ben Franklin Parkway and Spring Garden Street, ducking through the perilously narrow tunnel under Eakins Oval to the the Spring Garden Street bridge over the Schuylkill Expressway and into the tight blocks of indifferently rehabbed row houses and slightly seedy Second Empire mansions-turned-fraternity-houses, racing up and over side streets in a sawtooth pattern that put them past the boxy buildings of Drexel University and the sprawling, architecturally quarrelsome University of Pennsylvania campus to Forty-fifth Street, a few blocks from the Forty-second Street apartment house where Andy lived and the trash-strewn public school basketball courts where she did her layups when the world drove her crazy and she needed a place to work it off.

He zipped past the basketball courts onto Biltmore Avenue and then made a left between two stone pillars into what a small sign on a high stone wall covered with scraggly brown shoots of ivy indicated was the Kendall Home and School.

Inside the gate was what had once been a broad lawn leading to a large, stick-style Victorian house that had been painted a grim, Philadelphia-brownstone brown. The lawn was now an asphalt parking lot lined with stray clumps of filthy gray slush left over from the last snowfall. At the very front of a house where a boxy, modern entrance had been built into what had been a broad porch, a yellow school bus took on wheelchair-bound children with a lift. Standing near the line of wheelchairs was a small figure in baggy winter-weight blue jeans and a crimson ski parka, rocking side to side. A dark stain had spread across the front of the parka from under the boy's tear-streaked face.

When he halted the car inches from the front of the school bus, Mc-Sloan got scowls from the aides helping the wheelchair kids onto the bus. He shoved open his door and rushed out to the boy and began yelling at him, not to cry, not to be mad, not to complain, not to make a fool out of himself, not to embarrass himself in front of people, to just shut up for a change.

Through the open car door, Andy heard a peculiar, choppy shrieking coming from the boy, as if he had been crying so long, his voice had grown so hoarse he could only make short, sharp flute-like screeches. She opened her door, stepped out and heard them more clearly: he seemed to want to say something but the sounds that would have made the words intelligible were emerging in chopped, halting fragments.

"Shut your mouth now!" McSloan yelled.

Couldn't the father see that by yelling at his son he was only increasing the boy's stress and making it harder for him to stop? Andy approached the boy, who looked at her feet first, then looked up higher and higher until his wet eyes found her face.

"I'm Andy," she said, bending at her knees and holding her hand out to him.

"The lady is offering you her hand, Rawle," McSloan said. "Shake the lady's hand."

The boy, who was half his father's height, made one last, halting whoop and then extended a red ski glove. Andy gently shook his hand. "Pleased to meet you."

The bus driver beeped his horn.

"He is named," McSloan said, "after William Rawle, who started the first law firm in America."

Andy saw Rawle's lips flutter. She got down on her knees and moved close to him. She could barely hear him say, *"P-p-plea . . ."*

McSloan began, "What he means to say is—"

"I can hear him," Andy said.

The bus driver beeped his horn again.

"What you're hearing is spasmodic dysphonia," McSloan grumbled.

That was the speech dysfunction McSloan had mentioned in that bogus story he told Jermaine. "Let Rawle speak," Andy said.

McSloan wouldn't. "He's just afraid to open his mouth, think calmly and speak clearly."

"Let your *son* talk," Andy told him.

The bus driver started the bus and beeped his horn insistently.

"It takes him forever," McSloan said, ignoring the driver. "You'll freeze by the time he says a sentence."

"Move the car and wait for us," Andy said firmly.

McSloan threw his hands in the air. Then he stomped off to his car, slammed the door and backed the car away.

Andy sat down on the cold sidewalk beside Rawle. "Let's start over," she said. "I'm Andy. Andy Cosicki. Pleased to meet you, Rawle."

"Pl-l-lease . . . t . . . ooo muh . . . muh . . . eee . . . eet . . . y . . . ooo." He swallowed. "Pleased to meet you." Then he took two deep breaths and slowly, slowly said, "Ah-n-dih-eee."

The sound of his voice touched her in her heart. It made her put her arms around him and hold the tear-soaked front of his jacket close to her. She hoped that he wouldn't see that her eyes had grown wet, too.

"It's okay, Rawle," she said. "I understand you."

She really didn't, but she would. Soon.

4 one in a million

Alone at the bar, Ladderback ate his way through a dinner of grilled lamb chops, cauliflower au gratin and roasted new potatoes. Two months ago, Whitey Goohan would have joined him for a time before he ordered his second Jimmy D'Tini.

Goohan would lean on the side of the bar and he would say something silly, arrogant or outrageous and the conversation, the alcohol and the food would slowly remind Ladderback that there were more important things in a life than what you did for a living.

He chewed on the last remaining lamb chop and looked back on the nearly empty dining room. Mafouz would have to do something to bring more people into this place. He was aware of Mafouz at his side with a plate in his hand. "Mr. Goohan told me I must learn when to speak to customer and when not to."

Ladderback saw the earnestness in his dark face. "The service and the food are up to your usual standards, Mr. Mafouz."

"If you will permit me, Mr. Ladderback, Mr. Goohan said some customers must be approached when they need a tickle."

"A tickle?"

"Mr. Goohan was being metaphorical. Mr. Goohan said most who dine alone would rather not be alone for the duration of their stay. He said they would appreciate something extra from the kitchen, followed by an exchange of words. Would you like an exchange of words at this time, or would you care to taste what I have from the kitchen?"

Ladderback gazed at what resembled a badly mangled croissant dusted with powdered sugar. He touched it carefully—it was warm and slightly yielding.

"Have a taste."

He bit into a sweet, flaky, slightly oily pastry, redolent of cardamom. Ladderback said, "The Italians call this a zeppole."

"Everywhere about the Mediterranean there is a recipe like this. This is from my wife's family," Mafouz said proudly. "*Leshad hashemen* is sweet fried bread. It is shaped like the *lamed,* the Hebrew letter. *Leshad hashemen* is what it says in the Torah that the manna from Heaven tasted like."

"Didn't the passage also say the manna could taste like anything anyone would want?" Ladderback asked.

"It could take the form of any kind of food, but it could also be *ein kol*—nothing at all. It came directly to edge of your tent: very easy to find if you were a righteous man. If you sinned, you had to leave your tent and look for it to find it."

"I must be righteous, then," Ladderback said, taking another bite.

"That is one of the teachings of the manna," Mafouz said proudly, "that, for the righteous, everything that is needed is close at hand."

Ladderback gazed upward for a moment, not at some heavenly source, but in the direction of the psychiatrist's office on the building's second floor. It had seemed so convenient twelve years ago. He could go up to see her without having to go outside.

Then he said, "Since when have you known Hebrew, Mr. Mafouz."

"All my life. I learned it in Lebanon and this was helpful because my wife's family is Israeli. I am, of course, Muslim."

"An implausible combination," Ladderback said.

"Love makes all combinations possible," Mafouz said. "My English isn't as good as I want. My Hebrew is a little better. In Arabic I could tell you perfectly. It is like thinking you need so many things that you don't have, but love makes what you need always close."

Ladderback glanced upstairs again.

"Am I making sense, Mr. Ladderback?"

Ladderback didn't feel close to anything at the moment. "You are, Mr. Mafouz."

"Then why, Mr. Ladderback, if you will permit me to ask, are you troubled?"

"Today," Ladderback grumbled, "I received welcome assistance from a dangerous man."

"Did this person threaten you, Mr. Ladderback?"

"He helped me."

"And this was a bad thing?"

"It was a good thing."

"But you did not want his help."

"The consequences trouble me."

"These consequences will be bad for you?"

Ladderback frowned. "What is the teaching, Mr. Mafouz, when a man decides to punish those he thinks evil in unusually appropriate ways?"

"You mean like in *The Mikado.*" Mafouz recited the emperor's famous proclamation from the Gilbert and Sullivan operetta: " 'My object all sublime I shall achieve in time—to make the punishment fit the crime, the punishment fit the crime.' "

Ladderback took up the lyric. " 'And make each prisoner pent, unwillingly represent, a source of innocent merriment, of innocent merriment.' "

Ladderback put his hand on the stem of his drink. "Whitey Goohan would have said the same thing," he said.

Mafouz brightened. "Then there is no problem."

Ladderback would have contradicted him, but Mafouz excused himself and went back to the dining room. Ladderback thought of calling Andy on her cell phone and canceling the assignment. Why had he been so foolish to think that she could make Nordvahl see the horror of his ways by asking a single question?

Because he had faith that intelligent men who turn fifty can be made to see the error of their ways, and that, having seen their error, they might be inspired to correct it.

Which was exactly why Nordvahl was killing lawyers.

He gulped his drink too quickly and shuddered.

Rawle had problems, Mike McSloan informed Andy, as they took the elevator up from the parking garage in his Center City apartment building to the top floor Skyline Spa. "One of his problems is that he likes his routines and we have to stick to them or Rawle will become even more difficult than he is now."

"He's not being difficult," Andy said. She had almost fallen in love with the boy. "He's being himself."

"He has never been himself from the day he was born." McSloan glared at his son.

Rawle looked at the floor of the elevator.

The doors opened onto a broad, icy white marble foyer enlivened by lush green plants that looked fake even though Andy was sure they were real. A woman Andy's age in a pale blue polo shirt with a white collar sat behind a curving desk and welcomed them.

"She's with Rawle," McSloan said. He told Andy that he was going to get changed and that he would meet her on the balcony. "Rawle never changes his routine. If you're going to stick with him, you'll be outside on the balcony in the sandbox with him while I'm running. I'm in training for the Ambulance Chase. I would have normally run later at night after you and I had a chance to get to know each other better . . ."

Andy glared at him. "The only reason I'm breathing the same air as you right now is your son."

He sneered. "There's a sandbox on the balcony. Rawle likes to sit in it while I run. He does it even when it's freezing outside. There's a hot beverage station right before the balcony so you can grab something to keep warm. If you get disgusted and leave, I'll understand."

"I don't get disgusted with children," Andy said.

"You will when you have one," McSloan said, and went through a round door that resembled the oversized dial of a combination lock.

Andy turned to Rawle, who stood with his arms straight, his head slightly tilted to the right side. She waited for him to move. A minute went by and he didn't move.

She saw his gaze was on her shoulder bag. She took off her shoulder bag and offered it to him. He turned and went through a round, green-tinted glass door that rolled aside as he approached it.

Andy slipped her arm back through the bag's strap and followed him onto a broad catwalk that overlooked a series of coldly bright squash and racquetball courts. The catwalk opened into a great cavern. Dark, geometric sound-absorbing shapes hung from the top and, below them, black, white, red and chrome exercise machines were clustered on risers that held men and women in tight, bright, clinging exercise garb.

None of these furiously exercising people seemed to be sweating. Their ears plugged and their eyes aimed at vast, soundless video screens, they emitted an aura of intense, striving preoccupation as they ran, climbed, pranced, stepped, bicycled, bounced or twisted through the air on a great, rotating gyroscope-like contraptions.

Rawle moved purposefully down a central runway between the machines, leading toward a slice of glass that looked out onto the scarlet-tinted night sky.

He stopped at a glittering self-service coffee and juice bar and took a clear plastic cup and a smaller plastic dessert tray from a stack behind the counter. Then he raced toward two sets of glass doors that obediently swung aside as he ran through onto an open concrete deck that seemed to stretch all the way to the distant red lights on the antenna towers on the Roxborough hillside several miles to the northwest.

Andy could imagine the deck in summer, lined with lounge chairs and small tables holding the latest health drink. On this chilly winter night, with the nearly full moon hiding behind a dense cloud cover, the concrete balcony had the barren, lonely emptiness of a snow-covered field.

At one end of the deck, steam rose from the heated indoor/outdoor swimming pool, at another, islands of light led to a canopied platform where three unused treadmills reminded her of Caspar Friedrich's hauntingly cold painting of empty crosses on a tree-shrouded Golgotha.

About halfway between the pool and the treadmills, Rawle mounted a small circular platform. He lifted the top, revealing a sandbox.

When Andy caught up with him, she found him sitting motionless on his knees, his attention focused on the sandbox before him. She sat on the edge of the sandbox and asked Rawle if he was okay.

He didn't notice her. He didn't move. A gust of chilling wind lifted some of the sand but he did not move. Andy pulled her bomber jacket around her, took out a knitted, woolen cap and put it over her head and ears. She waited, then looked up, past the outdoor lights, at the distant, twinkling beacon of a jet airplane flying high overhead, and the few stars that could shine bright enough to be seen through the red haze. Street noises came up from the lip of the balcony just past the treadmills.

She again asked Rawle if he was okay.

"He's fine," Mike McSloan called from behind her. "He'll start moving as soon as I do."

He strode forward, wearing a skin-tight, hooded, yellow and black all-weather track suit. He aimed a remote controller at the treadmills. The digital readout on the central treadmill's control panel came to life, and a row of white trailing lights countersunk into the concrete flashed on.

Though Rawle's eyes were on the plastic cup, as soon as the lights came on, he extended the index fingers of each hand and made a row of impressions, just like the running lights, leading to the plastic dish.

His father aimed the remote control again and the central treadmill slowly rotated on a turntable. "I insisted on this with the architect," McSloan told her. "I'm on treadmills so much, I get bored with the view. Each treadmill is fully remote-controlled, with built-in cable video, DVD, satellite radio and Internet. Mostly, though, I just look at the view. Check it out."

Andy saw Rawle turning the plastic dessert dish on the sand. Rawle stopped the dish when his father stopped the turntable. The front of the treadmill now pointed southeast. McSloan would be running with his back to the edge of the balcony's waist-high guardrail.

Andy stayed with Rawle, who had begun to fill the plastic cup with sand. He packed the sand hard, inverted the cup on the sand and lifted the cup to create a tower.

Andy heard an electric whirr and saw McSloan taking his first broad steps on the treadmill. He used the remote to adjust the treadmill until he was moving with the wind, which was rolling in over the edge of the balcony, at his back.

Rawle adjusted the dish, then continued making towers.

"Once he makes his sand castle, he just sits there," McSloan called from the treadmill. "I told you, you're going to get disgusted, or cold, or both."

He was right about the cold, but wrong about being disgusted. Rawle wasn't making a sand castle. The placement of each tower corresponded exactly to the positions of other buildings visible from the deck, relative to the dish. He modeled the skyline with unusual accuracy.

And he didn't just sit when he finished the skyline. He turned and looked at her shoulder bag. Andy took the shoulder bag off and put it on the sand beside him. Rawle made a choppy, croaking sound that she eventually heard as "take things out."

She hesitated. She wasn't sure if she wanted to get sand on her small purse, pens, cell phone and dozen other things that had ended up in the bag. Rawle was staring expectantly at the bag, so she decided to remove the largest item, her notebook computer.

He made more choppy sounds that became "Let me."

She took a breath and handed the computer to him. He opened it expertly, turned it on. "You can sign on as a guest," Andy began, but he had already done so. He examined her wireless Internet feature, then pulled up the word processor.

His fingers touched the keyboard. Then he turned it so that the screen faced her. The screen said, *HI ANDE.*

Andy got down on her knees in the sandbox and typed, *Hi Rawle. You can call me Andy. DO YOU KNOW HOW TO USE THIS?*

49

She turned the computer back to him and adjusted it to read, *YES I KNOW HOW TO USE THIS!*

Andy looked at him slyly. She wrote, *Do you know to use CAPS and lowercase?*

I USE BIG and small. I USE BIG SO HE CAN SEE THIS.

Your father?

Rawle wrote, *I have this I don't like.* He closed the notebook computer and put it on the edge of the sandbox. He took a palm-top computer out of his jacket, put it on the dish, opened it, wrote some words with the stylus, switched programs and pressed enter.

A punchy digitized man's voice said, "Too small and not my voice."

"I agree," Andy said. "Your voice is okay with me. And you can use my computer if you want."

He put Andy's laptop on the dish. She saw his eyes turn, very slowly, and come to look in her face. "Th-ah-nk y-oo," he said. He reopened her notebook computer and went directly to her wireless Internet connection. Andy signed him on and then she put on gloves. She felt the breeze freeze the uncovered skin on her face.

"I'm going to get some hot tea," she told him. "Do you want anything? How about hot chocolate?"

He opened a window on the notebook's screen and wrote, *No thank you.*

She debated telling Mike McSloan where she was going, but she saw he had turned the treadmill in another direction away from them, so she got out of the sandbox and took long strides toward the juice and beverage bar.

She went through the glass doors and into the steamy warmth of the spa. She found a tea bag of caffeinated Earl Grey and poured steaming water over it to make herself a cup of tea.

When she returned to the balcony, Rawle was staring at the treadmill, which was whining painfully without anyone on it, its engine at the highest setting.

She heard a woman's scream coming up from Locust Street below. She went to the balcony and looked down twenty-five stories.

In the glare from the streetlights she saw, on the dented roof of a parked car, the smashed body of Mike McSloan, one leg of his bright yellow running suit twisted unnaturally under his torso.

She went to Rawle, whose eyes were open. His lips trembled, his fingers quivered on the keyboard. On her computer, he had written, *ONE IN A MILLION.*

McCale's voice came back to her: when you're in trouble, call a lawyer.

She searched her shoulder bag until she found the note on which Ladderback had written a cell-phone number.

5 manna

Ladderback called Andy and her cell-phone voice mail. She must have turned the cell phone off. He left a message. A recorded voice told him to press the pound key, but the phone he was using didn't have a pound key. It didn't have any keys. It was an old, heavy, black plastic rotary dial phone. Beside that was an adding machine, the kind with buttons you pushed and a crank you pulled that advanced a piece of tape. Whitey Goohan had computerized cash registers, but no computer in his office or anywhere in the restaurant. Jimmy D's didn't even have a Web page.

Through the walls surrounding Whitey Goohan's narrow office came the sounds of the washroom plumbing and the mechanical noises of the dumbwaiter that brought food up from, and dirty dishes down to, the basement kitchen. With the door open Ladderback could also hear, from the dining room's sound system, Tony Bennett singing "Nice Work If You Can Get It."

Because he had researched obituaries about restauranteurs, Ladderback knew that the restaurant business could be nice work, if you had the personality for it, together with a good location, steady clientele, manageable costs and honest, loyal employees. As executor of

Goohan's estate, Ladderback found himself in the peculiar position of temporary boss over a full and part-time staff of forty-eight people, most of whom he had come to know over the years just from coming to the restaurant.

He put his hands on Whitey Goohan's desk. He liked being here. He liked being with these people. It was so different from the newsroom, where he was either ignored or badgered, typically by Howard Lange, to accept the latest early retirement package.

Ladderback reminded himself that Whitey Goohan had specified the restaurant be sold to Mr. Mafouz "at a fair price, a good price." Goohan had dictated the will to Ladderback, who took it down in longhand. "And if Mafouz can't get the money, make sure whoever gets it loves it enough to keep it as it is, and to mind the tenants on the second and third floors. They should be kept happy, too."

Mafouz had asked for a few more days while he arranged financing with his family. That left Ladderback with the problem of what to do with what reposed in a polished metal container at the far right corner of the desk, just in front of the ancient Number 10 Tomato Puree can where Goohan put the bills that had yet to be paid.

Funeral directors told Ladderback of bonded ash-distributing services that would also supply a videotape of the scattering. But Ladderback felt he had to do the job personally. Goohan hadn't said where he wanted to be "dumped." He never spoke about a favorite place. When he was healthy enough to take vacations, he would come back grumbling about rude cab drivers, inferior food and service.

Ladderback couldn't just leave the ashes in the office, and he didn't want to make a shrine by interring Goohan's remains in the wall near the bar or on the maitre d's podium.

He eyed the container. It was a little larger than a thermos bottle. It would fit easily into an airline carry-on bag.

Suddenly, panic replaced Ladderback's moment of happiness. The ashes had to be scattered outside, and whenever Ladderback even thought of being outdoors his agoraphobia kicked in and he shut his eyes and started to cringe.

He reminded himself that he could endure this, that he had endured it for most of his life, that he had learned to live with it. He told himself he might be able to scatter the ashes if he had someone to help him.

And who might that be?

Ladderback found himself staring at the telephone again. He had never traded up to a push-button phone. It sat on the left (Goohan was left-handed) of a blotter stained in rings and blobs from liquids. Stuck into the left edge of the blotter was a printed, year-long calendar on which Goohan had marked birthdays, anniversaries and other significant dates for his customers in a handwriting that had grown increasingly awkward with each stroke.

Ladderback let his eyes wander down the list of anniversaries, birthdays—Nordvahl's among them—and other celebrations. He found a name and a blank beside it.

Danny Bleutner, lead partner in one of the city's most powerful political law firms and a collector of "anything blue," used to table-hop Jimmy D's when it was the city's top power lunch restaurant. He had since taken his daytime business to flashier, trendier places.

The entry on the calendar mentioned a birthday party for Bleutner's father, with a note to call and confirm the date before purchasing a specific brand of Greek kalamata olives for the appetizers.

The birthday was a few days away and Mafouz had not made a note beside the date about whether to confirm if the confirmation had come in. The telephone number was not that of Bleutner's Center City office. On an impulse, Ladderback picked up the phone and dialed.

Bleutner's father answered and, after muting the television set's speaker, told Ladderback that there had been no confirmation because he hadn't heard from his son "in more'n a week, which is unusual for anybody but him, being busy all the time, it's not so unusual. You know, he's got a twenty-four-hour social secretary?"

Ladderback asked if Mr. Bleutner had called his son's office.

"He's supposed to call me once a week, on the dot, on the nose, but, this time, last night, for the first time, not a word. Not a good word, not a bad word, not a discouraging word. What am I supposed to do, call his social secretary to set it up, he's always so busy all the time."

Ladderback asked him if he had the social secretary's telephone number.

"I do indeed, I do, I do."

After thanking him, Ladderback dialed it. He got the phone tree: "If you wish to invite Mr. Bleutner to an arts or culturally related event, press one; if you wish to invite Mr. Bleutner to a political event, press two; it you wish to invite Mr. Bleutner to a religious event in which a gift or donation is expected, press three; if you wish to invite Mr. Bleutner to an evening gathering of under twenty persons, press four; if you are requesting Mr. Bleutner to consider a donation to a political campaign or political action committee, press five; if you are or have been a close personal friend of Mr. Bleutner, press six. . . ."

Ladderback couldn't press any buttons. He let the phone tree play on and on. He did not hear the customary instruction advising callers from a rotary phone to "stay on the line and an operator will assist you."

But, to his surprise, someone did answer after the phone tree had run its course. A woman with an upper-class English accent said, "Danny Bleutner."

Ladderback told her he was calling on behalf of . . . he heard fingers on a computer keyboard.

"Are you the gentleman who writes the obituaries for the *Philadelphia Press*?"

Ladderback said he was, "But my concern at this time is—"

"I'm so delighted that you've rung! Danny has some clients who have relations that have just died and if you want to write them up, he would appreciate it. Let me find that list." Ladderback heard the clattering of a keyboard. "Here it is."

"I am calling for a different reason."

"Everyone calls Mr. Bleutner for different reasons."

Ladderback said he was calling about the elder Bleutner's birthday party at Jimmy D's. The restaurant would appreciate a confirmation, "unless, of course, Mr. Bleutner has decided to have the party elsewhere."

"Elsewhere . . . elsewhere. No. But . . . well, until I hear from Danny, and he's been so unusually hard to reach."

"His father said something similar," Ladderback said. "When was the last time you saw or heard from him?"

"Yesterday evening, before he went home. He hasn't been in the office all day. Nobody knows where he is. This is quite unusual for him. Most times, I can depend on him calling me once an hour, just to see how many parties, weddings and funerals he's been invited to. Right now, I have a list of people who won't go to Charlie Muckler's funeral unless they know he's going to be there. They're a wee sensitive about that list."

"What list?" Ladderback asked.

"The one that Danny was on, with Charlie Muckler. You've seen *Bar Sinister*?"

"I'm aware of the publication," Ladderback said.

"It's the February issue, just this month. I have it right here. Danny is at the top of the 'Lawyers We Could Do Without' list. They call him Danny 'Schmooze and Ooze' Bleutner, followed by Charlie 'Sandman' Muckler, 'Marathon Liar' Mike McSloan. Severio 'Oh the Shark Has Pretty Teeth, Dear' Pescecane—no question about that, don't you agree? But Bette Newarr also made the list—I guess because she hasn't given up her practice even though her novels have taken off. I must admit, I did look through her latest one, the one that's on the best-seller list—*Guilty Pleasures!* The sex scenes are *very* well done. And after Bette is the divorce lawyer Roberta Zetzmeer. They call her the 'Great Divider.' . . ."

"Have you checked Mr. Bleutner's house?" Ladderback asked.

"Which one? There's the Gladwyn address where he keeps his collections, and then the one in the Cayman Islands—for tax purposes, and one in Monte Carlo, also for tax purposes."

"Please go to Mr. Bleutner's Gladwyn house immediately," Ladderback urged. "This is important."

"*Everyone* who says *anything* to me having to do with Danny says it's important."

"Then ask the police to check on the condition of the house," Ladderback said.

"Police don't check up on houses in Gladwyn," she told him. "They've been warned not to pry. Danny has private security because of his art collection and some other things he likes to do."

"Ask the police anyway," Ladderback said forcefully.

"Why *are* you so concerned?"

Ladderback stopped. She was a social secretary and would not believe him if he told her the truth. So he said, "It concerns the olives. This is a special kind of kalamatas. We really must put in the order tonight. Mr. Bleutner will understand."

From her tone, she thought him odd, but she promised she would call him later to confirm. He gave her his home telephone number and hung up.

He went out of the office to the shrouded maitre d' stand, where he took a pack of Jimmy D's matches. Then he found the keys for the small storeroom on the second floor.

The storeroom was at the top of a narrow course of stairs going up behind the dumbwaiter.

How many years ago was it when, twice a week, at around this time, he would get the key from Whitey Goohan, go up those stairs, turn on the lights and pass the boxes of crockery, toilet paper, canned goods, old tablecloths, folding chairs, cases of liquor and boxes of old recipes, letters, files, desk calendars?

If he hadn't suffered from agoraphobia, he could have just walked out of the restaurant to the street and then gone through the door with the steps going up to the second floor.

But he couldn't go outside. So he took the set of keys off the hook beside the desk and went up the stairs into the storeroom.

He had to pause about halfway up to catch his breath. When he had gone up those stairs twelve years ago, he had felt no need to pause. Now the effort left him weary.

He finished the climb, turned on the storeroom light and sat down on a case of tomato-sauce cans. He looked about and found the box that had the old desk calendars. He examined some of those calendars, noted some dates, replaced them in the box, then unlocked the door leading to the hallway.

He closed that door behind him. If he turned left, he would pass the entrance to the offices of the Delaware Valley Law Watch, in what were the former Center City law offices of Schuyler Nordvahl, Attorney-at-Law.

If Ladderback turned right and followed the hallway past the washroom, he would come to the milky blue door with the small sign that said DR. RHEA NORDVAHL, HOURS BY APPOINTMENT.

He told himself he should have called ahead. She might be with a patient and would not be able to see him if he just dropped in.

But if he called, he might get her voice mail, and he could not imagine what he had to say to her about her ex-husband fitting on her voice mail.

Or, if she picked up the phone, she might dismiss him by refusing to discuss anything with him unless he made an appointment to resume therapy.

He put his hand on the doorknob and listened. He didn't hear anyone speaking in the little waiting room.

Mafouz had told him that, for the righteous, what is needed is always close at hand.

He gave the doorknob a turn and went in.

Mrs. Alma McSloan almost fell off her feet as she tried to push past the police at the doors leading out onto the balcony. She would have gone but she stopped when she saw Rawle sitting with his back to the beverage stand and his arms around Andy, her notebook computer open in her lap.

"Get away from that woman!" she yelled, but Rawle only held Andy tighter.

She wobbled to a halt in bone-colored pumps and ankle-length bone-white slacks descending from a malignantly gleaming sable stole that made her look like a sharp, brightly blond helmet of hair riding on a big blob of black fur tottering on two tiny bone-white sticks.

The makeup around her luminous blue eyes had been recently and hastily repaired, perhaps on the elevator ride up, but the pale, pink skin around her bony cheeks was streaked by particles of eyeliner, and her lips were so thin that even though she had thickened them with dark crimson lipstick, they still seemed sharp enough to cut.

"Rawle, let go of that woman!" she shouted.

Rawle gripped Andy even tighter. "N-oh, p . . . pl . . . eess."

"It's okay," Andy whispered to him. She gently moved his other hand away from her. Then she put her notebook computer on the ground in front of Rawle and said to Mrs. McSloan, "This has been terrible for him."

"Oh? Is that what it is?" she snapped, the reek of alcohol on her breath. "Terrible. Michael *knew* I had made plans, that he would have to cancel his cheap little adventures but . . . ," she narrowed her eyes at Andy, ". . . but he had his little adventure anyway."

"I write a column at the *Philadelphia Press*," Andy said. "Your husband was in the newsroom and I asked his help answering a reader's question."

"I'm sure he helped you," she sputtered. "I'm sure he told you what he's told *hundreds* before you, that he was impressed with you, that he admired your individualistic spirit. Did he offer to take you somewhere and *lay it all out for you?*"

Andy took a breath and forced herself to say, "Mrs. McSloan, your son needs you right now."

"*Don't* you tell me what my son needs, unless you think he needs you? Did Mike do it that way? Did Rawle pimp for his father?"

Andy was about to boil over when Schuyler Nordvahl stepped forward, "Mrs. McSloan, the police have requested statements from Ms. Cosicki and your son. I have advised against this, for the time being."

"And *who* are you?"

"A lawyer, Mrs. McSloan. Ms. Cosicki called me and asked for my help. *Res fortuna,* I was nearby."

She sneered at him.

He added, "*Res fortuna* is Latin for a 'fortunate thing.' Lawyers don't use Latin nearly enough as they should."

His pretense enraged her. "And how many hours are you billing?" She snarled. "Not as much as Mike. I'm sure he's billing hours even now."

Nordvahl remained serious, solemn, concerned. "I haven't billed for my services in twenty years, Mrs. McSloan. I may ask of my clients some assistance at a later time, but such assistance is always voluntary. My advice at this moment is for you and your son to make no statements to the police, to the media or any individual between here and your home, which, I believe, is an apartment in this building."

"I do NOT live in this building," Mrs. McSloan insisted. "Mike lives in this building. Mike and I are separated. I live elsewhere."

"Then I suggest you and your son go to wherever you are living and take counsel with someone who can help you—"

"Come, Rawle, we're going to your Uncle Harlan's."

The boy cowered in a corner of the sandbox and began to shriek. While Nordvahl spoke to an increasingly shrill and hysterical Alma McSloan, Rawle's fingers raced across the keys of Andy's computer.

Andy crouched down beside the sandbox and read, *I see it ANDY. I SEE WHO*

He stopped writing when Nordvahl drew near. "You communicate this way with him?" Nordvahl asked, eyeing the screen.

Mrs. McSloan almost stepped on Rawle. "WHAT are you saying to strangers about your Uncle Harlan?"

Rawle typed *NOT PLEAS GO TO HARLN. He YELLS and HATES me*

Andy said, "Is there somewhere else you can take him?"

"My brother's home will serve," Mrs. McSloan insisted. "Rawle, you're coming with me to Harlan's house."

Nordvahl stepped between them. "I don't think so, Mrs. McSloan. This boy's protection is crucial right now. He may be a witness to a complicated liability issue involving his father's death. Or," he paused grandly, "he could be a witness to a murder."

Andy blinked.

"I did *not* have him killed," Alma McSloan yelled, "much as I wanted to."

Rawle reacted as if he had been struck. Then his face went blank.

Andy said, "Mrs. McSloan, Rawle needs a place where he can feel okay. The two of you need to—"

"I can arrange for private security, Mrs. McSloan," Nordvahl said. "I have clients who are in that business. It's important that police not be involved at this point because they will use anything the boy says or does as potential evidence, and the boy's fitness as a witness has not yet been determined. I will also have to appoint a caregiver for him because you are clearly incapable of rendering that service at this time."

"He needs you," Andy said to the boy's mother. "Please help him."

"I have just lost my husband!" Mrs. McSloan said. "I need just as much help, and I don't see anyone offering it." She gave Andy a look of dark contempt. "If you know so much about what he needs, then maybe he can stay with you!" she yelled, wobbling so much that she had to throw her hand at the wall to steady herself. She broke a nail and began to swear.

Rawle put his arms around Andy. He held her back.

"Allowing for your inebriated state," Nordvahl said pitilessly, "I must ask, Mrs. McSloan, if you are aware that you have just made an oral grant of temporary custody of your son to Ms. Cosicki, but that Ms. Cosicki is not bound to accept your grant. Are you aware of what you have said, Mrs. McSloan?"

She appeared genuinely confused. Then she looked at Rawle and tilted her head slightly. "If he won't come with me, then he can do what he wants."

Andy felt Rawle cringe in fright. "Mrs. McSloan," Andy said, "tell your son you didn't mean that. He wants to come with you. I'm sure there's someplace else—"

"Your choices are limited," Nordvahl cut in. "You are about to be put through the sheer hell of notoriety, Mrs. McSloan. Are you capable of handling that *with* your son?"

Andy wasn't sure what she was hearing: was Nordvahl trying to pry the boy away from his mother?

Mrs. McSloan focused her anger on Andy. "The boy likes you. He's holding on to you. Let him *stay* with you!"

For Mrs. McSloan to reject her son at a time when he had just witnessed his father's death was an act of emotional violence so horrifying and obscene that Andy could not summon up the anger to scream back at her. Rawle's embrace had a calming effect on her, and that calm only made Alma McSloan angrier. She yelled more things at her until Andy turned to her and said in a tone so level that it surprised her, "I won't let you speak that way anymore in front of us."

"Oh? *You've* decided what I can say?"

"Yes," Andy said. "I've decided. Your son can stay with me until he wants to be with you. You can find us at—"

Nordvahl put a card in Alma McSloan's hand. "Mrs. McSloan, you will call my office when you feel more composed. Until then, as per your instructions witnessed by me, the boy will stay with Ms. Cosicki. Though I don't anticipate a long stay, you will be expected to reimburse Ms. Cosicki for all monetary expenses pertaining to the boy's shelter, food, clothing, education and entertainment, as well as any therapeutic interventions that this situation may require. Do you hear me, Mrs. McSloan?"

She wagged the finger with the broken nail. "How am I going to get this fixed?" Then she looked at Andy. "Mike always blamed me for him, did he tell you that, too? Mike said I had trash genes. Can you believe what that man said to me?"

Nordvahl withheld his contempt, but barely. "I must also emphasize to you, Mrs. McSloan, not to speak with the police until advised by reputable counsel. Ms. Cosicki and myself will make every effort to adhere to your best wishes regarding your son and we will be consulted before he has any contact with the police."

"The police told me my husband's death was accidental. The machine threw him off."

"And you believed them, Mrs. McSloan?" Nordvahl asked.

She put the hand with the broken nail over her mouth, took a step back, spun around and fled.

When he smelled cigarette smoke and saw the green and orange, zigzaggy lithograph over the slightly larger bonsai tree in the corner, Ladderback knew that the wood-and-earth-toned waiting room hadn't changed.

He noticed, in the dusky, shaded light from the hand-thrown pottery lamp that the blue fabric loveseat had faded and rubbed through in some places. The terra-cotta ashtrays had been replaced with hammered copper dishes.

She had the same magazines on a small coffee table: *Consumer Reports,* the *Atlantic Monthly, Smithsonian* and *Liberty Bell,* the city's glossy lifestyle monthly.

He heard street sounds and felt a chilling draft. He turned quickly from the shaded window that let in winter air. It was bad enough that she smoked cigarettes. Why did she have to keep the window open? When he had told her that the mere knowledge that an open window was nearby could give him moments of panic, she told him to consider it an aspect of his therapy.

That window stayed open in every kind of weather, in every season, even when she ran the air conditioner in her consulting room, even now, with heat flowing from the clicking, banging radiators.

The door to her consulting room was a carefully carved wooden model of a gate from a Burmese Buddhist temple. She had told him, when he asked, that the figures and designs indicated that this was the Door of Compassion.

That door was ajar, indicating she had no patient.

"With you in a moment," she called from within her office, her voice rougher, darker than he remembered, but clear enough to make him recall how fragile it became when she laughed.

Ladderback sat on the loveseat. He heard her turning pages in her office—her appointment book, most likely. She paused, turned more pages, then her chair made that comforting squeak when she got out of it.

He stood as the door opened.

"Mr. Ladderback," she said, almost as a question.

"Dr. Nordvahl," he replied evenly.

She was shorter than he was but she seemed taller. She had sharply carved features that suggested a noble, fiercely predatory bird. He could make out a faint corona of wrinkles around her eyes. Her nose held a pair of spectacles, smaller and lighter than he remembered. The flaw in her nose—it had been broken in a childhood injury—was more obvious now, but just as intriguing. Her hair was a silvery blond mess, especially around the ears, because she played with her hair when she read, smoked and listened, twirling it on the long, flexible, tobacco-stained fingers that, even when she held them, were never quite at rest, giving her an air of whirling distractions, as if she had so many things on her mind that even the sight of him was just not enough to bring her completely back to earth.

A silver and mauve scarf swirled below her head. A woolen, red and purple batik dress hung straight down.

"You didn't make an appointment," she said.

"The last time I saw you, you told me if I wanted to see you again, I would not need one," Ladderback replied.

"Only if you've come to resume therapy," she said. "I knew from the moment the treatment began, that if I gave you what you wanted, you would not come back."

"I want something more, Dr. Nordvahl."

"Treatment?"

"Advice," he said.

She took a long breath and sat down on the loveseat. She reached into an end table and took out a pack of Chesterfield cigarettes.

Ladderback hesitated, then sat beside her. She searched for a match or a lighter. Schuyler would complain to him, not that his wife smoked, but that she was always losing matches and lighters, which was why Ladderback had the Jimmy D's matchbook out, tracing the match head against the striking pad as a flame blossomed from the tip.

She thanked him. She exhaled and the odor of the smoke made the years go away.

"I'm sorry I haven't kept in touch," Ladderback said.

"You were making progress. The therapy was working. How much time did you spend outside before you ended therapy?"

He watched the clouds of her smoke catch the draft from the open window. "I may have opened my eyes once."

"Things were working and they can work again."

"I came to see you for another reason. I want to ask you questions about Schuyler."

"There is only one reason that you would see me," she said. "We start again tomorrow?"

He didn't move. She got up, went into her office to check her appointment schedule. She came out, sat on the couch, blew smoke. "We start now, then."

research and development

"They're coming out!"

Schuyler Nordvahl, his silver hair glowing even brighter in the lights from the TV cameras, stepped forward and asked for consideration, understanding and respect. "This is a terrible situation. I'm sure you understand why none of us can say anything to you right now."

A big, old muddy brown Buick rolled into view. Andy held Rawle tightly as she heard Nordvahl speak of a need to take the survivors "of this incredible homicide" to be in an "undisclosed location" and that further inquiries should be submitted to his office. The parking valet told Andy that the doors were open.

As she put Rawle in the backseat, she heard Nordvahl say he could not speculate as to why anyone would transform a treadmill "into a murder weapon." He folded his arms and announced. *"Ultra posse non est esse."*

The TV reporter blinked. "W-what was that?"

"Anything more is not possible," Nordvahl said as he went toward the car.

Andy closed her door as she moved in beside Rawle. The boy shrank from the floodlight that swept the car as Nordvahl drove past the TV news team to the ramp that took them to the street.

Rawle sat rigidly in the seat and closed his eyes as the car began to move. Andy watched his arms and legs quickly relax. By the time they crossed Broad Street, he was asleep.

Andy asked Nordvahl where they were going.

"Far enough away to catch our breath," Nordvahl said. "At this time of night the drive will be a little less than an hour, south on I-95 with some back roads that look wonderful in moonlight, though I don't see much moonlight tonight. We're supposed to get a little snow later, which, on top of the ice, can make the roads difficult. After we arrive I'll go out and pick up anything you need."

Andy took our her cell phone and wondered if she should tell someone in the newsroom what had happened. She decided to listen to the three messages in her voice mail.

One was from Logan "Logo" Brickle, "quality manager" of the Hampton Bank, telling her that he wasn't sure if they had the kind of relationship in which he was supposed to call her if he was supposed to see her tonight but couldn't see her tonight, because he wasn't sure if he was supposed to see her tonight. "Like, did we arrange anything? I'm up to my nose hairs in meetings that have all been so . . . *lacking* that my brain is totally gone and I am amazed that I can actually call you and tell you that, if anything was supposed to happen, it's not going to happen, which, I guess, is better than nothing. Does that make any sense? I hope not."

A second was from Lucia Cavaletta-Ferko, asking Andy if she could come early and use her key to open the dance studio and maybe start the women's self-defense class going until she arrived?

The third was from Shepherd Ladderback, canceling her assignment. She closed the phone. She pulled her shoulder bag against her side and a wave of weariness overcame her. She leaned her head back against the top of the old cracked leather seat.

"How are you feeling, Ms. Cosicki?"

"I feel drained," Andy said. She sat up. "And grateful that I had your phone number and that you could come as fast as you did."

"We must consider the boy's needs, then. Not having had any offspring, I may not be the best man for this job, but I consider it my professional duty to see this, and the events that will result, to the end. And, if I may say so, I think it is good that you offered to care for the boy."

She looked at Rawle. He appeared so calm, almost angelic, as he slept.

"I'm going to get some professional advice about how to handle him, until we find out what provisions can be made for his care. It's likely that, as soon as Mrs. McSloan gets over her shock, she will be quite firm about getting her boy back."

Andy shuddered. "I can't believe she would dump her own kid."

"One can never anticipate the reactions of victims of sudden loss. I have had many conversations with Shepherd about this."

"How long have you known him?"

"*Ad illo tempore.* To that time. He and I take our meals at the bar at Jimmy D's. When I told him about my interest in legal history, I was surprised that he had read enough not only to know what I was talking about, but argue on interpretations. He told me once that he learned Latin by memorizing quotations when he found them, and then he puzzled out the grammar until he could read Virgil and Cicero. I had to suffer with it in high school and college and, to this day, I'm still not completely sure about the passive subjunctive. You've known Shepherd how long?"

"Less than a year," Andy said, her mind wandering back to the newsroom.

He turned right onto the ramp that led down to the Vine Street Expressway. "Are you the assistant that he assigned to write about me?"

"He canceled the assignment," Andy said.

He examined her in the rearview mirror. "Did he tell you why?"

She shook her head.

"Then you should relax," Nordvahl said. "Would music help?" He turned on the car's radio. When Andy shook her head about the music he said, "Conversation, then?"

He hit a pre-set and Andy heard a familiar voice.

"Slip Kersaw?" Andy said. "I saw him at the Fetzer awards. He was in a neck brace all the time. He reminded me of a picture of Humpty Dumpty."

"That's his trademark. As a personal-injury lawyer, Kersaw originated what is known as the Second Vertebra Claim. He based it on an injury he says he suffered when he was body-surfing at the Jersey shore. He says he cracked the second vertebra, a bone directly below the skull that both supports the skull and encloses the spinal column. He became the local king of slip-and-fall lawsuits by getting ludicrously high compensatory and punitive damages, arguing that trauma to the second vertebra, which can happen from a minor fall, could lead to sudden paralysis and death."

"How come you know so much about him?" Andy asked.

"I'm the reason he is no longer practicing law," Nordvahl said proudly. "A decade ago I sued Kersaw for fraud on behalf of one of his defendants, the owner of a parking lot near the Italian market who was forced to sell his lot when Kersaw won a judgment for negligence in failing to clean organic debris—in the form of a banana peel—that resulted in injury to the plaintiff. I proved that Kersaw had used copies of his own X rays when I insisted that the plaintiff submit to another set. This would have opened up every second vertebra case Kersaw had argued had not Kersaw cut a deal with the judge to compensate my client for damages and cease and desist his personal-injury practice. The proceedings are sealed, of course: if you ask Kersaw, he'll say he fell in love with talk radio. The truth is, some very, very hard work on behalf of myself and the Law Watch made sure that, as the Woody Guthrie song goes, there was one less Philadelphia lawyer in old Philadelphia that night."

Rawle curled over on the seat beside Andy. "So why do you listen to his radio show?"

Nordvahl grinned. "Because he annoys his guests far more than he ever annoyed me. Tell me if this is too loud—I don't want to wake the boy."

Andy heard Kersaw's theme, the chorus from the *Guys & Dolls* song "Sue Me," fade out. Kersaw reminded his "listeners in the Slipstream" of the Ninth Annual St. Valentine's Day Noontime Ambulance Chase, "an all-weather, shameless exercise of positive publicity for the personal-injury law practice established by yours truly nine years ago. More than two hundred criminally out-of-shape legal professionals risk life and limb, not to mention the agony of 'de feet' in a breakneck sprint behind a genuine Speed Care, Inc. emergency services vehicle, in a reckless, willfully negligent sprint up Broad Street. As a special added distraction, Philadelphia 76ers star forward Ismail Khan will be giving a speech before the event. You heard that right, the Silent Storm himself will break his silence, or whatever, probably in answer to that *Liberty Bell Magazine* article that we discussed yesterday with *Liberty Bell*'s very own Ms. Shoanna Ellerbaum."

Andy made a mental note to find out how to get an autographed basketball for Jermaine Haynes.

Kersaw continued, "We expect to have incredible Valentine's Day refreshments from Matthew Plank and his Plank's Constant family of restaurants. I must add that, though this event is not, and never has been, sponsored by the Philadelphia Bar Association, it has raised hundreds of thousands of dollars for local charities and good causes. Hope to see you all there."

Andy yawned and waited for sleep to come.

Kersaw went on, "Taking up where we left off with our guest, best-selling novelist Bette Newarr, author of the new legal thriller *Guilty Pleasures*. Tell me, Bette, you're a tax lawyer, right?"

Andy heard a frail, wispy voice say, "I have a small but active practice in Philadelphia, yes."

"And it's true, is it not, that two of your former clients are suing you for malpractice—alleging that you basically forgot about them while you were off researching your latest legal thriller, *Guilty Pleasures*."

The reply was insistent and menacing. "Doug, I came on this show to talk about my book and only about my book."

"Did you see that you made the Delaware Valley Law Watch 'List of Lawyers We Could Do Without'? How do you feel about that?"

Nordvahl chuckled at the silence that followed.

"Okay, let's talk about the book," Kersaw said. "I'm reading from the book jacket here, that 'as she pursues her shadowy prey from the swank roosts of South Beach to the infamous Berlin sex clubs where everything and anything goes, fiesty Philadelphia tax attorney Daphne Gillespie uncovers a whole new universe of dazzle and slime.' Now, correct me if I'm wrong, but you research these books, right?"

"I certainly do, Irv. If you read in my book about a top-floor five-star hotel suite, a haute couture boutique, a meal in a gourmet restaurant, a table in an exclusive nightclub or the color of the Blue Grotto on the Isle of Capri, you can be sure I have invested time, effort and a small fortune to go to visit those places to make sure I have depicted them accurately."

"So you've been there and done that," Kersaw said. "But what I want to know is, your first book, which I actually read, by the way, had Daphne as this hardworking, struggling single mom who couldn't even afford a car, trying to make partner in the big bad white-shoe law firm while living in her mother's row house in the Northeast, where, I might add, we both come from, right?"

"We didn't come from the same row house, Irv."

Nordvahl said, "Point for Newarr."

"But we went to the same Catholic school. Remember how the nuns would take away your pencil if they found you chewing on it? They'd make you write with a pen, thinking that the taste would get you out of the habit. Chilly Bains, in the *Philadelphia Press,* said you never got out of the habit, even if the only writing you do nowadays is signing checks—"

Bette's nostrils flared. "I write every word of my books with my Mont Noir fountain pen and a vial of my favorite Midnight in Benares India ink which I will be using to sign copies of *Guilty Pleasures* at noon tomorrow at the Center City Bookmarket Superstore & Café."

"And you're expecting all your fans to show up," Kersaw went on. "But what I want to know is, the first book was all about this down and dirty stuff, you know, gritty Philadelphia dives, cheap eats, corner bars and neighborhood hangouts. That was when you got, what, four figures for a book?"

"Irv, the writing is always its own reward. I never dreamed, when I had to write my first novel by candlelight because I couldn't pay the electric bill, that I would be on so many, many bestseller lists."

"And now that you're getting seven figures," Kersaw went on, "you have the very same Daphne driving a Lexus, flying first-class all over the world, staying at five-star hotels, eating at three and four-star Michelin restaurants, going into all these high-priced sex clubs."

"Daphne goes to those places because she's tracking down a notorious international villain who may be leading a double, or even a triple, life. It's all part of the plot."

"What I'm saying, Bette," Kersaw persisted, "is you could have Daphne chase your bad guy any place you want. You could have her in rest-stop burger joints on the New Jersey Turnpike, if you wanted to. How come you have all this stuff happen in overpriced tourist traps halfway around the world?"

Andy could almost feel the woman's contempt. "I have this stuff happen, Irv, because it excites me, personally, and it makes for a great story. My readers have come to expect a great story from my books and, in my latest book, I've written what I think is my greatest, most spectacular—"

"Yeah, yeah. But a great story can happen anywhere, right? What I'm getting at is, all this research you do, all this traveling around, living large, eating large, shopping large in the fancy stores, going to sex clubs and all, you pay for that, right?"

"I most certainly do. And I save every receipt."

"As I'd expect any tax attorney would. All this money you spend is a tax deduction for you, right? Come April fifteenth, you can write all that off."

"The federal tax lawssss," Bette hissed, "treat authors as small businesses. Outlays of cash resulting in an author's research, preparation and production of a book can be considered legitimate business expenses and deducted from earnings from the sale of the manuscript.

"So you're saying to me that it's only because you have this great story about European sex clubs and international villains with triple lives, that you spend all this money and drag yourself halfway around the world?"

More bile: "I don't drag myself anywhere. When I go, I go first-class and, let me tell you, with what they're calling first-class these days, you're almost taking your life in your hands—"

Kersaw cut her off. "It sounds to me like you're using your books as an excuse to live large and, in effect, stick the government with the bill. What I want to get into when we go to the phones, is, with April fifteenth only two months away and all these overpaid authors coming up with wildly improbable plots so that they can write off all these luxuries and indulgences from their taxes, what I want to know is, what would happen if the IRS hired a book critic who would read the book and decide if the rest of America's taxpayers should be subsidizing this? If it's a *To Kill a Mockingbird* or even a *Presumed Innocent,* I can hear that critic say, 'Hey, no problem: the deductions are allowed.' But what if the book makes you sorry for the trees that were killed to print it, the IRS critic disallows the deductions and the government goes after the author to pay his, or *her,* fair share? I'm going to turn this over to our listeners way out in the Slipstream. What's your take on it? You can let Bette have it, after these messages."

Andy had fallen asleep, or she would have heard Nordvahl say, "Yes, we will let her have it, won't we?"

7 undisclosed location

Rhea went to a warm, rosy sand-colored file cabinet that took up the far wall of the waiting area. The cabinet was smaller, but of similar design to the one Ladderback kept in the newsroom beside his desk, in which he put the notes from more than forty years of obituaries, as well as clippings from other newspapers and magazines.

She removed his file. "You stopped therapy because I gave you your medical statement," she said, going through her notes. She pulled out her copy and read, "To Whom It May Concern: I have examined Patient Neville Shepherd Ladderback and have determined that, though he will exhibit anxieties pertaining to the disorder commonly defined as agoraphobia, these symptoms have not interfered with his abilities to perform the job of reporter and writer to date, and do not pose a threat to his abilities in the forseeable future." She put down the copy. "You never told me why you needed it."

"Howard Lange had been promoted to editor of the newspaper," Ladderback said. "He wanted me to take early retirement because obituaries are considered an entry-level job and he could get it done cheaper with new hire. He kept moving my desk to less comfortable parts of the newsroom. When he put me near a window I told him I was agoraphobic and he tried to use that to get me re-listed as disabled. Under the union rules, newsroom staff who become disabled must be transferred to a position appropriate to what abilities they retain. I needed a letter stating that I could accomplish my duties. I mentioned this to your ex-husband during one of our dinners and he advised me to see you and be cured."

"The desire to be cured can interfere with therapy," she said. She found a pair of matches on the bookshelf at whose end there was a framed, black-and-white photograph of sad-eyed William Butler Yeats. She lit a cigarette and emitted a cloud of smoke through her nostrils.

"I had no desire to be cured," Ladderback said. "I wanted a letter from you saying I was not disabled."

She went back to her file. "You also had some anxiety about your fiftieth birthday." She looked up. "Did you discuss any of this with Schuyler?"

"He wanted to believe that, though I was older and had never married, we were similar men with similar interests and similar problems." He was going to tell her that Schuyler had accused Ladderback of having an affair with her, but he kept quiet.

She closed the file.

He asked her why she had not come to Whitey Goohan's wake. She looked away.

Ladderback said, "Whitey kept a calendar on his desk blotter in which he noted birthdays, anniversaries, important dates for his regular customers. My birthday is there, as well as Schuyler's, and your birthday. And the date that you divorced Schuyler."

She inhaled deeply. "You don't have to tell me this."

Ladderback said. "You were married to Schuyler when you and Schuyler rented office space in Whitey's building."

"Should I ask you why you are telling me this?" She stabbed her cigarette into the ashtray.

"Whitey Goohan was a career criminal," Ladderback said. "He gave it all up to acquire this restaurant. He went from an insecure, dangerous life to a very secure, law-abiding situation. This seems to be an example of what you called an *enantiodroma,* I found this fascinating when you suggested it to me."

"Carl Jung is so seductive," she said, "more so than Freud, because Jung's ideas incorporate a sense of spirituality and mystery that Freud abhorred." She found another cigarette. "I mentioned *enantiodroma* so that you might look at your illness in terms of compensation. How is being agoraphobic compensating you for what you want but feel you can't have?"

He wanted to ask her what her ex-husband's compensation might be for killing lawyers. But she had always been so guarded about herself, and her relationship with Goohan. "Whitey also recorded the dates on his calendar when he became your patient."

She did not react.

"Whitey never mentioned to anyone that he was seeing you. I discovered this when I happened to notice some of the older calendars in the storeroom. It made sense, though, in light of the way he became more comfortable in the restaurant at the end of his life."

She turned away.

"I read a great deal about Jung when you mentioned him to me," Ladderback said. "Another one of his ideas concerns vital personalities who enter our lives at unpredictable moments to help us make important transitions that we cannot make alone. We may not appreciate or benefit from everything these personalities do, but, once we make the transition, we will sentimentalize the encounter, and, perhaps, develop affection for this person, not realizing that, for the teacher, ferryman or therapist, the patient's role was just as vital and necessary."

"It is a metaphor for a therapeutic relationship," she said.

"It is more than that," Ladderback said. "Whitey became your patient a year before you divorced Schuyler. Though Schuyler recommended me to you, and he has remained civil to me ever since, he believed that I was responsible for persuading you to divorce him."

She reached for a cigarette but stopped. "I had to leave Schuyler. I had to divorce him." She picked up another cigarette. "Whitey came to see me about nightmares. He was losing sleep and that was making it difficult for him to function. He was a very big man, very physical, and to be defeated by these dreams was deeply troubling to him. We talked about bravery, and strength, what it really means to be weak and . . ." She nodded. "Yes, we went through this transition. What I gave to him is a way of accepting his weakness. What he gave to me was the strength to divorce Schuyler."

"But after you divorced him, you kept your office here," Ladderback noted.

"You mentioned Schuyler being civil to you, even if he feels you were a rival for my affections. As long as he can achieve his ideal, of fighting the good fight, he can maintain standards of behavior that most of us would find difficult. He can also choose to ignore aspects of his personality that might conflict with, or complicate his fight."

"He needs enemies," Ladderback said.

"He burns inside," Rhea said. "He can be quite inspiring if you share his ideals. I found his ideals very attractive and still do. When he had a cause to take on, I could live with him. Even during the divorce, Schuyler and I could always work well together. I still consult on some of his cases."

She leaned back on the love seat and was silent for a while. He sat beside her and the faint warmth from her comforted him. He found himself wishing he had someone to sit beside, someone with whom he could do nothing on cold winter nights.

She let the telephone ring once before she went into her consultation room and answered it. She spoke low enough so that Ladderback didn't have to stop himself from eavesdropping. At one point, he heard her say, "He will be very difficult, especially if he is autistic." And, "Of course, I'll see him."

She hung up and came back into the waiting room. "That was Schuyler. He has a client, a boy with speech difficulties who has witnessed a terrible crime. He wants me to evaluate his client tomorrow in Chadds Ford."

"When are you evaluating this client?" Ladderback asked.

"At breakfast, so I can return and see my patients."

"I want to go with you," Ladderback said.

"These evaluations are confidential," she replied, her mouth tight.

"You can make it part of my therapy."

"Will you resume therapy?"

"We can try," Ladderback said.

After sliding and skidding across the quarter mile of frost-covered serpentine road that spanned the floodplain to the mill, Schuyler Nordvahl turned off the car. Rawle scampered out, and went down on his knees in the snow.

Nordvahl opened the rear door and said gently, "Welcome to Stokes Mill."

Andy opened her eyes and didn't see Rawle. Then she spied him through the open door, forming three small mounds in the snow. It was the place they were in. One mound represented the gabled stone farmhouse behind him. Another was the long, flat stables that had been turned into garages.

The final mound was the narrow, four-story brick tower of the mill, thrusting up from a small rise beside the frozen river like a Gothic castle.

Rawle wouldn't come into the farmhouse until he had finished his snow models. Once inside, he looked at the floor and rocked from side to side on his heels while Nordvahl introduced them to his "butler," Pew. An ancient, grizzled man in a fuzzy fire-engine-red sweater, yellow and gray mucklucks and dun-colored overalls, Pew rose from nursing a fire in the Franklin stove.

Nordvahl said he was going to the mill and that they should put themselves in Pew's hands.

Pew led them up a worn, creaking flight of stairs to three bedrooms. When Andy asked Rawle to decide which bedroom he wanted, he looked down and started to rock from side to side. She asked him if he wanted her to choose and, without stopping, he managed a halting whisper, "Mons-terrrr wa-a-a-tch-ing."

Pew opened a door to the bathroom and said he didn't see any monsters watching, hiding or doing whatever monsters do. Rawle stopped rocking, went in and shut the door.

Pew opened a closet and withdrew a stack of bedding. Rawle emerged in his undershirt and boxers and went straight for the farthest bedroom. Pew gave him bedding and told Andy, "Looks like he wants to say his prayers with you."

Andy found Rawle bent tensely on his knees beside a low, plain Shaker-style twin bed. He had folded his arms stiffly across his chest and had buried his face in the comforter. She knelt beside him. She had not had a religious upbringing. She asked him what he wanted to pray.

His voice was muffled by the bedding: "M-ake m-on-st-er go a-w-ay."

Andy turned around and said, "Listen to me, all you monsters. We need to get some sleep. Go away, okay?"

Rawle didn't move. "Rawle, no monster is getting near you while I'm here. I promise you that."

Some of the tension went out of his body. Without looking at her, he mounted the bed, grabbed the bedding and pulled it to him with his back against the wall. She stayed there until his breathing became regular. She gently closed his door, went into whatever bedroom was closest, threw off most of her clothes and dived under the covers.

Her cell phone chirped. After four chirps, her voice mail took over. She closed her eyes and let her head sink with delicious slowness into the down pillow.

The phone chirped again.

She rolled out of the bed and pulled the phone out of her shoulder bag. "What is it?!"

"Andy, Andy. It's Howard Lange. Was that you I saw tonight on the news, with Marathon Mike's kid, getting into a car?"

"On the news?"

"TV. Was it you with Mike's kid?"

She rubbed her eyes. "Um. Yeah."

"Did the kid really see his father murdered?"

"I don't know. I had gone out to get some tea and . . . why are you calling me?"

"You're with the kid. He say anything to you?"

She became angry. "Why do you want to know?"

"A kid sees his hot-shit lawyer father get thrown off a thirty-story building, he goes into hiding and one of my staffers is with him and you're asking me why I want to know about it? You have your laptop with you?"

She told him she did.

"This is how it's going to play. You are going to get a phone call in fifteen minutes from Chilly Bains, who is going to interview you about the murder and the kid. You're going to tell him that you just happened to be working out at that health club—"

"I wasn't working out!"

"Save it for Chilly. You're going to say that, out of respect for the feelings of the family, you cannot divulge the secret hiding place where the boy is recovering from his ordeal. You're going to tell Chilly that you're with the kid, that he's making no statements to the media because he's very, very upset but he's not going to let the guy who killed his father get away with murder."

Andy said, "No."

"We got this terrific photo of cops looking so very serious in front of the car that McSloan smashed when he landed on it, and you can see just a little bit of his foot in a really, really expensive high-end running shoe sticking out. That's on the cover. Inside, we have the story and a sidebar interview with you, with the picture ripped off the TV of you and the kid getting into the car."

"No," Andy repeated.

"Then, in this box under the picture, we say that *Press* Staff Writer Andrea Cosicki will be filing daily, insider reports of this shocking crime. I'm giving you a byline on this."

"No way."

"Is it snowing down there? Tomorrow, before the TV news trucks arrive, take the kid out and make a snowman or something. Let me know when you're out there and we'll get a shot of that unless you have access to a digital camera. Wait—don't you have a camera on your cell phone? Send us some stills of the kid making a snowman."

"Did you hear what I just told you?" Andy said. "I'm not doing this."

"I heard what I just told you and you're doing it."

"Rawle is in no condition to deal with this kind of attention. To put him through this is—"

"Brilliant, is what it is. He's a kid, right? Kids love attention. We have a wire story waiting to run about Hollywood brats; you know, the sons and daughters of movie stars, and how, contrary to popular notions, being in the white-hot glare of celebrity is kind of cool. I don't care what the kid tells you. I want copy, from you, filed by noon. I want to know what the kid is doing, what he's saying, what he's dreaming, how long he's crying, what he's watching on television, anything and everything, until the cops catch the killer or the readers get bored or we find something sexier to run, whatever comes first."

"Do you hear me when I speak?" Andy asked him. "I'm not doing this."

"You will, because a shitload of people who don't read the paper are going to pick it up and see your byline and say, 'Wow, that Andrea Cosicki, she's really getting the story.' This is exactly the kind of shit that gets you attention, gets you name around, gets you an award or two."

Andy pulled the cell phone away from her ear and glared at it for a second. Yes, she could send and receive video over her cell phone.

She told Lange she absolutely refused.

"You're doing it exactly as I told you or you absolutely won't have a job," Lange said and hung up.

Andy put the phone down. The room was so quiet she could hear her breath rushing in and out. She looked out the window and saw the dark bulk of the mill tower thrusting up against the luminous silver sky. A light shone from a tiny window in the cupola at the top.

She closed her eyes and asked the monsters if they would please, please, please go away.

And the phone chirped.

let's go beach

Andy awoke to find Rawle in his shorts and undershirt at the foot of her bed. His head was down. He rocked slowly from side to side.

She pulled blankets over her. "Rawle? What's wrong?"

He kept rocking. Then Andy saw that he had removed her notebook computer from her shoulder bag and had set it on the bed, its screen facing her.

On the screen he had written *morning?*

She glanced out the window and saw a field of rolling white extending across the floodplain to a ridge of frosted trees. She told him she didn't understand.

He stopped rocking, came around and put his hands on the keyboard. *Use bathroom?*

"Why are you asking?"

First ask then use.

"You don't have to ask me," Andy said.

He continued to rock from side to side.

"Rawle, it's okay. You can use the bathroom."

He took off like a rabbit.

Nordvahl came into the house a few minutes later and told them they were going to have "the best breakfast you've had, anywhere."

When Andy and Rawle had dressed, Pew brought the Buick around. Andy and Rawle got in and Nordvahl slowly guided the car across the unmarked, meandering icy path that spanned the floodplain that isolated the mill and its buildings.

Just before they reached the ramp that went up to the paved road, they passed an abandoned TV news truck that lay pitched forward in the ice. Andy guessed that the news team had tried to drive closer to the mill but the driver had wandered off the path and fallen through a thin patch.

"So they know where we are," Nordvahl said as he drove around it. "But they don't know how to get to us."

"They'll find out," Andy said, thinking of the calls she had taken last night.

"What they'll find out is how difficult it is to pull a vehicle out of a frozen swamp," Nordvahl said.

The car groaned up the slope to a paved road that followed the Brandywine River east to stop at a red light on Route 1. He turned, went about a mile and pulled into a parking lot crowded with trucks, vans and high-end sedans. The lot surrounded a low, flat, vaguely shabby rust-and-dun-colored shed with a few windows and an enclosed porch, with an American flag hanging straight down in still morning and a single red sign over the vestibule door that said BO'S DAY JOB.

"They do an unbelievable mushroom scrapple here," Nordvahl said as he hoisted up his laptop carrying bag and led them into a luncheon-ette with a counter and a small row of booths. "And just about anything you could want for breakfast."

Rawle seemed excited by the odors of frying bacon, sausage and potatoes, and the sweet, vanilla aroma of french toast and waffles, until he saw the people in heavy winter coats huddling at the counter or slurping coffee from oversized mugs in the small row of booths against the wall. He stopped in his tracks, looked down and began to rock on his heels from side to side.

So he drops into this when he's wants something, Andy decided. "Are you waiting for me to say it's okay to come in?" she asked him.

He nodded.

"Rawle, whatever you want to do is okay with me."

In his broken speech, he asked if it was okay to "k-kil-llll m-m-m-m-on-st-errr?"

"I don't see any monsters around here," she told him, giving him a big hug.

Nordvahl led them to a round table for six in the back at which two people were already seated. On the way, Nordvahl said hello to men and women, most of them dressed in rugged winter clothes, as if they had just finished chopping wood. None of them glanced at Andy or Rawle.

"That one's a retired credit card executive," Nordvahl said to Andy as he moved toward the back. "The one over by the counter is an artist. This one here is another artist, a landscape architect. The one he's talking to calls himself a poet but he quit Dupont to run a hedge fund out of his garage."

"No lawyers?" Andy asked.

"Plenty." He said more greetings. Andy thought she recognized some of Nordvahl's birthday party guests. "That woman owns a cable channel and boards horses," he told Andy. "The woman next to her designs water-purification systems. She also does performance art—one-woman shows in West Chester." He halted, then resumed. "And this one," he said when he reached the table, "is somebody you know."

The man in the winter-weight olive drab trenchcoat turned. "Shep!" Andy exclaimed.

"Ms. Cosicki," he said. A chrome-blue chamois opened at his neck to reveal a black knit turtleneck. He added, "You've been in Chadds Ford, I presume."

He turned to the small, bright-eyed woman beside him. "Dr. Rhea Nordvahl, may I present Andrea Cosicki, my assistant, who will probably want you to call her Andy. Ms. Cosicki, Dr. Nordvahl is a psychiatrist."

"Shepherd has told me wonderful things about you, Andy," Rhea said pleasantly.

Andy looked at Ladderback. She wanted to know *why* he was saying wonderful things about her to someone she had never met, but his face revealed nothing. Then she noticed that Rhea and Schuyler had the same last name. They both had gray hair and pale skin. They were *old*.

"You're his sister?" Andy asked her.

Nordvahl cleared his throat. "I am her former husband," he said, pulling off his gloves to show the ringless finger on his right hand.

"And this," Rhea said to the boy, "must be Rawle."

Rawle stopped rocking. Andy urged him to say hello. He looked fearfully at Andy.

"Say hello, Rawle," Andy repeated. "It's okay."

"H-h-h." He squinted, forcing the sounds out. He closed his mouth, took a breath, tried to say hello again, gave up and finished with, "Hi!"

They sat at the table, Andy on Rawle's left, Rhea on his right.

"How come you're not at work?" Andy asked Ladderback.

"I took the morning off," Ladderback said, his face unreadable.

A waitress appeared and they ordered. The food arrived swiftly.

"Scrapple," Nordvahl said, "is what the Pennsylvania Dutch do with cornmeal, onions, anything else they have hanging around and whatever parts of the pig nobody knows what to do with, like the squeal." He sliced into the playing-card-sized slab beside two sunnyside-up eggs and a mound of hash browns. "It has to be cooked thick, like this. Too thin, and it gets crusty, like a cracker, and breaks apart. You want it crisp on the outside, chewy on the inside. The Kennett Square mushrooms are just incredible."

He put a piece in his mouth, chewed and washed it down with orange juice. "Anybody want a taste?" Nordvahl put a square on a fork and aimed it at the boy. "Rawle?"

Rawle was cutting up his banana pancakes dusted with powdered sugar into tiny, precisely proportioned squares. When he heard his name, he froze.

"It's food," Andy said to him. "Schuyler wants you to taste it."

He whispered in her ear. "C-an-t eeee-t s-s-s-s-sqwuh-eel."

"He doesn't want to eat a squeal," Andy told Nordvahl.

Rhea put down a forkful of her egg-white mushroom omelette. "What Rawle just said is significant. A squeal is a wordless sound to us, but to Rawle, it is a physical part of a living thing. This living thing has feelings that Rawle doesn't want to hurt."

Nordvahl frowned at his scrapple.

Rhea continued, "We must assume that Rawle remembers everything we say and do, even when he doesn't respond to us in a way we can easily understand. This is probably the most difficult situation he has ever faced in his life. I have had very little experience with children his age, but I can tell you right now that you have taken a great risk in removing him from his mother's care."

"You wouldn't say that if you saw her," Nordvahl said. "She threw the kid at us. I had to do something to protect the boy."

"Why, Schuyler?" Rhea said. "How can you be sure you're right? You could have waited with the mother. You could have shown sympathy for her situation and waited for her to regain some control of herself. Instead of depriving her of her child, you could have encouraged her to fulfill her role as a parent."

"It was imperative to remove the boy from the scene," Nordvahl said. He finished his orange juice and held up his glass for a refill. "In all the years I've been a member of the Philadelphia Bar, I never heard that Mike and Alma McSloan had a kid. They've kept his existence very quiet."

"To protect him and themselves from the kind of misunderstanding that you have shown," Rhea said.

Nordvahl sawed off a piece of scrapple. "Please deliver your professional opinion as to the boy's capability of offering sworn testimony."

"I can't," Rhea said. "But I feel it would be wrong for him to be questioned or deposed in any way. The boy clearly has some kind of dysphonia—he cannot form words clearly and consistently. This would suggest that spoken communication is problematic. Does he use other methods to express himself?"

"He carries a small voice computer that he doesn't like to use," Andy said. "He likes to type what he wants to say on my computer."

"And you can go back and forth with him?" Rhea asked her. "You can ask and he will answer?"

"So far," Andy said.

"Has he requested information from you or initiated conversations?"

"When his mother wanted him to go to his uncle's house," Andy said, "he wrote on my computer that he didn't want to go there."

Nordvahl sat up. "Did you save that as a file? I want to see everything that he's written on your computer," Nordvahl said.

Andy shook her head. "That's between Rawle and me."

"As it should be," Rhea announced. "Andy, you must continue your conversations with Rawle because conversations build a relationship and it is very important now, for him, to have a relationship with someone he can trust."

Nordvahl swallowed his scrapple. "Sooner or later the cops will want to question him about his father's death. I'm not sure I should let them."

"I cannot be certain if the experience would be good for him," Rhea said. "But it may help him come to terms with what has happened. Rawle might not understand what being under oath is, but, if he is asked a question by someone he trusts, he wouldn't lie."

Nordvahl became quiet.

"Rawle may have highly advanced skills with memory or calculation that he hasn't revealed yet. But he is also a child who is still discovering himself, testing himself and others, in an effort to find out who he is. The most important thing you can do for him is to restore him to his previous environment of comfort and emotional security."

"That may not be possible," Nordvahl said.

"You should make it possible," Rhea told him. She turned to Andy. "How are his motor skills? Can he walk easily? Can he pick up objects and manipulate them to his satisfaction?"

"He likes making models of buildings," Andy said, "I've seen him do it in sand and the snow."

"I want to see how he moves," Rhea said. "Would you like to go for a walk, Rawle?"

Rawle stopped moving. He hunched over. His gaze descended to a point somewhere below his plate. It was a similar to the way he had been when Andy had found him at the foot of her bed.

"I think he needs someone to tell him it's okay," Andy said.

"Would that someone be you?" Rhea asked.

Andy turned to him. "Rawle, Mrs. Nordvahl wants to go for a walk with you."

Rawle sat up and stretched his neck until his lips were near Andy's ear. "Sh-ee w-w-w-an-tsss to se-ee-ee h-owwww I m-oo-ve."

"Show her, Rawle," Andy said. "Show her how you move."

He caught her eye. "I c-c-c-c-annnn m-oo-vuhhhh f-ah-sssssss-t."

"Don't move too fast," Andy replied, aware that she was sounding like a parent.

"I g-g-g-gh-ooh s-sssssss-low f-ah-ssssst."

"What's slow-fast?"

He shot up and zoomed past a waitress toward the restaurant's front door. Rhea put on her jacket and followed him out. Andy was about to follow when Rhea waved her away. "If he needs you, he will come back," she said as she pulled her coat around her.

Nordvahl opened his handheld computer and began to fuss with the machine.

Ladderback said, "Schuyler, are you aware that Andrea's editor has assigned her to file a series of articles about her relationship with Rawle and you? There is a box about it in this morning's *Press*."

Nordvahl wasn't. His fingers fluttered over his handheld computer's keys. Andy saw a tiny version of the *Philadelphia Press*'s Web page on the computer's small screen. "I want to see a copy of everything that's written about the boy before it's printed," he told Andy without looking at her. "What you write may give our adversaries an advantage."

"I can't do that," Andy said. "Everything I write goes straight to my editors."

Nordvahl's face became hard. "Then you are endangering the boy as well as yourself." Nordvahl switched screens. "I've received several e-mails from Roberta Zetzmeer, a reprehensible matrimonial lawyer who says she has been retained by Mrs. McSloan."

"Ms. Zetzmeer is on your list," Ladderback said.

"If you're referring to the Law Watch's list of 'Lawyers We Could Do Without,'" Nordvahl replied, "that is not my list. It was researched and put together by the Law Watch."

"But you had something to do with who was included?" Ladderback pressed.

Nordvahl glanced at the latest e-mail. "Ms. Zetzmeer has demanded that we return Rawle to his mother immediately or face kidnapping charges. That kind of hysterical, antagonizing grandstanding is typical of her. That's why she's known as the 'Great Divider'."

Using one finger, he typed a reply. "I've asked one of my associates at the Law Watch to get some background and, so far, we've been able to determine that Mrs. McSloan's concern isn't so much emotional as it is financial. Mr. and Mrs. McSloan were not living under the same roof and Mike's will puts the majority of his assets into a trust that will . . . ," he called up a document, "pay for a full-time guardian who will house, educate and care for Rawle at a location that will not include his mother or her brother as a full-time resident. Mike named his father as executor. He did not want his wife to get his money."

"He might have had a better reason," Andy said. "Last night, when his mother wanted to take him to his uncle's house, Rawle wrote that his uncle hurt him."

The thin, pale skin around Nordvahl's mouth tightened, as if the knowledge of the boy's suffering had become a physical burden. "Oh, that fits. That fits Harlan Whetson so perfectly." He returned to his laptop.

"I don't understand," Andy said.

"Shepherd, tell Andy who Harlan Whetson is."

"A Philadelphia family court judge," Ladderback said.

"And a huge advocate of so-called family values," Nordvahl said. He gulped more orange juice. "He used to be on the board of a summer camp for dysfunctional and disadvantaged kids. I was real close to re-opening a case that could have held him and that summer camp liable for the injury to a John Doe child. At the last minute, the parents of the kid backed off. They said the kid, who is now an adult, didn't want to revisit the situation."

"Who was the child?" Andy asked.

"John Doe means that I don't even hint about who the kid was," Nordvahl said. He grimaced. "Suffice to say that the kid involved is doing fine now, better than anybody thought possible, despite whatever remedies the law might have provided."

Andy mentioned that she took a call last night on her cell phone from Lieutenant Everson.

"So that's how the TV news found us," Nordvahl said. He pointed a finger at Andy. "You must not say *anything* to the police."

"Lieutenant Everson was a friend of my father's," Andy said. "I didn't tell him where we were and he didn't ask."

"He doesn't have to," Nordvahl added. "The cops have cell-phone locators."

"He wants me to come in for questioning in a few days."

"I will be with you when he questions you," Nordvahl replied. "We must prevent him from making you say what he wants to hear."

"He told me that he had no reason to believe McSloan was murdered. You've been the only person to say he was murdered."

Nordvahl's attention was on his handheld computer. "It doesn't surprise me that the police would come to that conclusion."

"Then Everson said the real reason he was calling me was that he wanted to warn me. From what he's heard, someone seems to have a thing for Philadelphia lawyers."

Nordvahl's bushy brows slid together. "A thing?"

"And you could be next."

Nordvahl paused. Then he let his head fall back and out of his mouth came a single, "Hah!"

Just then, Rawle rushed back into the restaurant, snow still clinging to his fingers. He sat down and stared at Nordvahl's handheld computer.

"You were correct about the modeling," Rhea told her, her face red. "He did some of the trucks and cars. I asked him if he had ever been to the beach and he said he had."

Rawle's eyes stayed on Nordvahl's handheld while he said, "Le-sss go b-b-eee-ch."

Ladderback suggested Atlantic City. "Though most of the historic structures are gone, the boardwalk skyline is impressive."

"How would *you* know?" Nordvahl said.

"I've seen photographs," Ladderback replied quietly.

"The boy needs emotional stability," Rhea said to Nordvahl. "The first thing is to give him back to his mother."

"The first thing is to insure his safety from whoever has this 'thing' for lawyers," Nordvahl fired back at her.

Rhea was about to speak when Nordvahl shouted, "I'm doing what's *right!*"

Then they heard a shriek that silenced the restaurant. Rawle's mouth was open. He had his hands over his ears. He reached for Andy's shoulder bag. Andy brought out her computer. Rawle turned it on and wrote *DONT FIGHT PLEASE IT HURTS WHEN YOU FIGHT.*

Andy turned the screen around so both Nordvahls could see it.

"We're not fighting," Nordvahl said. "We're arguing."

"The boy sees conflict," Rhea said. "For his sake, we must behave differently."

Rawle now rocked from side to side in his chair. Andy offered her computer to him but he seemed not to notice it.

"You must also have him see the social workers who have been treating him," Rhea said. "You've accepted responsibility for him, you must first do what's right for him. He needs to go back to his home."

"His father's apartment has been sealed by the police," Nordvahl said. He signaled for the check. "We should continue this later. You can come with us if you don't have better things to do."

"I have my patients," Rhea said.

"And Shepherd has his restaurant," Nordvahl said finally.

"It is not my restaurant," Ladderback said.

"I have a former client I'd like you to see," Nordvahl said to Ladderback. "He is looking for a job. I told him you might find a place for him. Can I send him over, say, around the lunch hour?"

"Mr. Mafouz will not hire anyone until the restaurant is sold," Ladderback said. "But I will speak with your client."

Rawle stopped rocking. He opened his eyes, cupped his hand over Andy's ear and whispered, "Be-eee-ch!"

Ladderback regarded Nordvahl. He asked Andy if she knew Prosper Mérimée's motto. She didn't.

"I believe it was, 'Remember to be distrustful,' " Nordvahl said as he handed the check back to the waitress with a credit card.

"And you," Rhea encouraged Andy, "be kind with this wonderful boy. Think of the time you are sharing with him as a gift." To Nordvahl she added, "I'll send you a written evauation." She put her arm in Ladderback's and hoisted him up.

Andy had once given Ladderback her arm. They had to take a few steps under the sky from her car. He closed his eyes and clung to her tightly. He was clinging to Rhea now, but it was different. He almost seemed happy.

Had she ever seen him happy? She watched Rhea lead Ladderback away. They reminded her of her parents on one of the rare moments when they had stopped being mad at each other and remembered that they still liked each other.

On the way out, Andy began to think how she could get Rawle to Atlantic City. She almost had a plan when, in the parking lot, she heard a truck engine start. The engine made an odd pinging sound.

She whirled around but saw nothing.

a favor

Nordvahl took a series of back roads that ended at a shopping mall on the Concord Pike in Delaware. When they entered a toy store, Rawle picked out a Lego building set in a plastic case with a handle.

" 'Sometimes it cometh to pass,' " Nordvahl entoned as he paid for it, " 'that men's inclinations are opened more to a toy, than in a serious matter.' Sir Francis Bacon said that."

Andy did not reply. They went to a clothing store and Nordvahl paid for everything she picked out. He wanted her to buy things for herself—new clothing, toiletries, anything. Andy turned him down, hoping to get away long enough when they got to the city so she could go to her apartment and get what she needed there.

They ended up in the food court, where she sat at a table and took out her laptop.

She became aware of him staring at her. Andy said, "You said you had other things to do here."

He looked away. "I have to make some calls. After we're finished I'm going to take you back to the mill and I have to go into the city."

"And do what?" Andy asked as she accessed the Internet.

"That must be confidential," he said.

Something in the way he said that troubled her. Dear Mr. Action, she asked herself, what do you do when a lawyer starts getting creepy?

She closed her laptop. "Just so you know, I'm not writing about you, except as it concerns Rawle. I'm thinking of mentioning what your ex-wife—"

Nordvahl pressed his lips so tightly together that his face turned red.

"What she said about getting Rawle to someone who knows how to care for him as soon as possible. If you can't set that up to happen today, then I'm going to set it up to happen tomorrow."

"Will you?" he asked sarcastically. "How can you presume to find these people?"

"I make phone calls. I do Web searches. I find out," Andy replied.

"But how can you find the *good* people, the right people? Corruption is endemic to human activities. You cannot hope to distinguish competency with a few telephone calls."

"I have one source," Andy said. She asked Rawle what school he went to. He typed *KENDALL.* "Do you like the people there?" He nodded that he did and asked if he could go back to his building set.

"I will have one of my assistants call them and set up an appointment," Nordvahl said, making a note on his handheld computer.

"I can do it," Andy said, holding her cell phone in the air.

"You may encounter difficulty getting the boy's records," Nordvahl said. "The rights of the handicapped tend to be circumscribed."

"I can handle it," Andy said. "And after I handle it, I'm going back to my job. I don't want to spend any more of my time making Rawle's private life public. This is not why I wanted to be a journalist and I am doing my absolute 100 percent best to make sure that nothing appears in the *Press* that's going to hurt Rawle."

She watched Rawle played with his building set, seemingly oblivious to what she and Nordvahl were saying.

"I insist you give me a copy of what you write before you send it in. You can send it to my computer here. I will give you the address."

Andy took her hands off the keyboard. "What I'm going to write today will be about sleeping in a nice old house, having a nice breakfast and a trip to the mall. That's it? Okay? Then I'm going to see about getting an autographed basketball for a reader and continue working on my column."

"We are each industrious people," Nordvahl said. He checked his handheld's message queue. "During legal proceedings that will follow regarding Mrs. McSloan, you will have to assist in verifying Mrs. McSloan's statements. You will be asked to describe Rawle's health and well-being while he was in your care. At the very least you'll be asked to answer to depositions."

"If it'll help Rawle," she said, "I'll do it."

"I must insist you say absolutely nothing to the police."

"There's nothing to talk about," Andy said. "I didn't see anything."

"You don't know what you saw, or didn't see. You haven't been deposed yet, and, in that respect, the police are no different than a defense lawyer, or members of your own profession: they can get you to say just about anything they want, under oath. Or they can make it appear as if you are not telling the truth as *they* see it. Don't you think the killer knows that?"

Where was this going?

He leaned close. "In this mall, we are safe. We blend in: we're just people spending money. But as soon as you go to your newspaper, you become Andrea Cosicki, a person with regular habits, a person with an address, a person who could be in danger."

For a second, she became terrified. Then she remembered the last time she had been in danger. What had happened? She had not fallen apart. She had not run away. She had fought back and she had survived.

"Don't patronize me," she said.

He pushed back his chair. "Everything I have been doing, and continue to do, is for the absolute good. You may come in contact with those who would say otherwise. You may discover information that runs contrary to what I have said and done. As Rawle's lawyer, and yours, I must ask you to trust me. You will do that."

Andy sighed. "Sure."

He got up and walked off.

She went to the *Press*'s Web page to see how the Mr. Action column had appeared. Its cut line had been changed to MCSLOAN'S LAST WORDS! with a note that implied that answering Jermaine Haynes's question was a "final interview" with the "slain lawyer."

Andy wanted to pick up her cell phone, call Howard Lange and scream at him. Why did her newspaper have to be so sleazy? It was true: her father had gotten her the job at the *Press* after the stuffier, provincial, only occasionally sleazy *Philadelphia Standard* had turned her down. Should she apply at the *Standard?* And would they hire a consumer reporter, who had only had a handful of bylines that had gone unnoticed by most everyone in the newsroom except Shep Ladderback?

She looked at Rawle playing with his Lego bricks and she melted. Who was this person that he could just turn so much righteous anger into love?

She went back to the Web page and glanced at her account of the last night's activities in Chilly Bains's column. Chilly had quoted her fairly, but when she saw him refer to her as "courageous and hard-hitting" she grinned.

She spent a few minutes searching for information about events in Atlantic City. She noted three and then sent descriptions of them to Chilly Bains in an e-mail, adding an explanation that Rawle wanted to go to Atlantic City and Andy wanted to make it more than just a day at the beach. Which of the events listed could Bains get them into?

She concluded with a question: who do I talk to at the Philadelphia 76'ers to get a basketball autographed by Ismail Khan?

She glanced at her personal e-mails and then accessed the queue of e-mails addressed to Mr. Action. Though Howard Lange had suspended her duties on the column, she saw that, with her cell phone and laptop, she was capable of answering some questions and sending them in.

She read a few questions and copied them to her active file. Even though she couldn't stand being in the newsroom with a stack of stupid questions to answer, she wanted to be in the newsroom with a stack of stupid questions to answer.

She listened to her cell-phone messages again, called Lucia Cavaletta-Ferko and told her that, though she had "a few variables" in her life right now, she just might be able to open up the dance studio for tomorrow night's "Valentine's Day Special" self-defense class.

"I wouldn't call what you're into a variable," Lucia said. "I saw the paper this morning. If you want to blow the class off, let me know. I'll work something out."

What Andy wanted to do was work Rawle in, and Lucia agreed that, though the class was limited to women, Lucia had no objections against a youngster watching, or even participating.

Then Andy said that Mr. Action had been given a question: what's the best way to help someone who has watched a loved one die?

"You wouldn't be asking me if it was a peaceful death," Lucia said.

"You got that right."

"Seeing someone you love turned into a victim has an incredible destructive power. You have to find the source of your strength, of your confidence. You have to learn to trust yourself again."

She watched Rawle pick up a small figure, a stylized human being included in the parts in the building set. The figure was about an inch tall. He placed that figure in a small square. He turned suddenly to face her and, without making eye contact, pushed the figure in front of her face. "Ahhnnnnn-deee!"

Was this what a mother felt like when a kid interrupted her? Should she tell Rawle that she was on the phone and that if he wanted to talk to her he should wait and say excuse me?

Again, before she could say anything, Rawle turned and put the second figure in the square. "R-r-r-r-ol-eeee."

Andy told Lucia to hold on. She leaned forward and saw he had positioned a third figure on a small, raised platform near a low railing. Beyond that were numerous towers that, Andy realized, corresponded to the buildings visible from the health club's balcony.

The third figure was "Dahhhh-d-d-d-deeeee."

She saw a fourth figure behind a wall near the patch of blue bricks that represented the indoor/outdoor pool.

Without turning around, Rawle pointed to that figure and said, "Mahhhn-sssst-er."

Monster.

Rhea Nordvahl's Honda Accord had a computer direction system that would not stop announcing where they were going. Though Rhea had the volume of the computerized voice turned down, Ladderback heard every word and could not stop from visualizing the world outside the car. He gripped the inside door handle so tightly his hand began to cramp.

"We'll be stopping soon," Rhea told him.

Ladderback heard her put the car in reverse. "You're parking," Ladderback said gratefully, his eyes shut tight.

"I am."

He felt the car slip into the space.

She asked, "Was it you who told me that you had memorized the Philadelphia street map so that when you have to take a taxi you can make sure the driver takes you to the right place?"

"C'est moi."

"You work so very hard to accommodate your difficulties. Why not make things less difficult. Open your eyes, just once. See that you are safe."

"Opening my eyes outside is very, very difficult."

"So was not smoking for me. Didn't we agree that we'd each do one thing to make things better? How many cigarettes have I had since we left Chadds Ford?"

"None," Ladderback said.

"Do you know how difficult it is not to have a cigarette after food?"

"I don't have addictions," Ladderback said, uneasy with the fact that he would soon have to leave the car. "You'll have to walk me to the restaurant."

"I will do that, but I want you to imagine for a moment that it isn't me that you are with, but Whitey Goohan. Whitey would not want you clinging to his arm like a blind man. He would want you to stand up straight and proud. He would want you to try, just for a few seconds, to open your eyes in the light of day."

"He would first get me a drink," Ladderback said.

"Not if he was in this car, sitting beside you."

"He got rid of his car after he had his first stroke."

"Shepherd, I want you to open the door by yourself."

He groped for the handle, heard it click as he pulled it. Then he smelled the city air, so foul and acrid compared to the chilly crispness of Chadds Ford. The grumbling vibrations of a truck shook the car. He waited for the truck to pass before gently opening the door.

An automobile horn shrieked at him and he slammed the door shut.

Rhea sighed. "Perhaps it's too soon to open the door in traffic. Let me get it for you."

"Schuyler," Ladderback said suddenly. "Schuyler has changed, Rhea."

"So have we all. And you can change, too."

"You have to see him without me," Ladderback told her when he heard her open her door. "You have to tell him that he has a capacity for doing harm."

She closed the door. "We are divorced. He does not need me telling him what he is capable of."

"He must be stopped," Ladderback said.

"By bringing him up at this moment, Shepherd, you are attempting to divert attention from yourself. I will not let you do that. You and Schuyler share the trait of the crusader. You must be doing good for others so that you can relieve yourself of the frustration you have with your own character. You have made a long accommodation with your difficulties. You are resisting me now because you are afraid of what you would lose."

"I am afraid of the outside, Rhea. It is my only fear."

"It is not! You are afraid to tell me something, right now. I can hear it in your voice. Open up. Tell me. Get it over with."

"Schuyler may have killed the boy's father."

"Shepherd, I was married to that man for twenty-two years. He believes too much in the law for him to even think of physical violence."

"He is doing more than thinking."

"And on what do you base this?"

"He made statements."

"When he is involved in his work, Schuyler will say all kinds of things about other lawyers. Surely you heard him say these things over the years when you ate with him. Why believe him now?"

"Because I believe anyone who makes claims as to the goodness of his character and his cause also has the capacity to commit evil."

"So tell me, Shepherd, what is this evil that you are so afraid of doing?"

"The evil of doing nothing when the heart demands otherwise," he said. And yet, he did not move. She waited for about a minute. Then she came around and opened his door.

The wind raced around him, the noises of the city intruded. She felt him put his hand in her gloved palm.

He used a light grip. He felt her lead him around the car. He touched the curb with the side of his foot and stepped up.

"There is nothing you could tell me about Schuyler that I don't already know," she said. "He resents you for being with me, as much as he would resent any man. When I was younger, I would have been flattered that he would want my attention. Now I see it as so much foolishness. I am aware that he has turned fifty. He is confronting his mortality. Anyone who confronts the certainty of death must, in the end, learn to be satisfied with what he has achieved and to accept the present for what it is, not what it should be. Again, I must insist you not use him to deflect attention from your immediate situation."

Ladderback tensed. He felt her movements slow. From the tug on his hand, he guessed she was turning toward him. "When was the last time you were outside Jimmy D's, Shepherd?"

He squeezed his lids tighter over his eyes. "I can't remember."

He felt her take his other hand. "But there must have been times when you walked unassisted on the street and came in through the front door, before your illness made it difficult."

"Not difficult," Ladderback said. "Impossible."

"Not impossible," she corrected him. "I will prescribe anti-anxiety medication that would reduce the difficulty. Then I will have you gradually increase your exposure to the phobic trigger over a period of several months. We will explore what brings forth your anxiety. You will learn to recognize and counter these things. Finally, I will reduce the medication dosage. Let's begin right now."

Ladderback tensed.

"I will ask you to open your eyes just once, and if you won't do it, or if it hurts you too much, I will not ask you again."

He felt her holding his arm. The warmth of her breath touched his face. "Look at me, Shepherd. Think of it as . . . nothing. You are so afraid to do nothing. Just open your eyes and . . . do it."

He told himself that if he saw her eyes he would just look at her eyes and that would be enough. Then he heard the door of the restaurant groan open, and he remembered how different that groan sounded now that he was standing outside next to it, rather than when he heard it inside, at the bar.

And that made him remember Whitey Goohan, who always looked toward the door when it made that sound, to see if the person coming in required special attention. And now Whitey was dead and Mafouz had told Ladderback that they would have to get a new, automatic sliding door because the handicapped access laws had changed and, even if they hadn't, nobody who goes into a decent restaurant wants to open a door that sounds like it needs fixing.

Hearing that sound now, with the sounds of people passing around him, the traffic on the street, the distant growl of a helicopter, he could only agree with Mafouz. No matter how we grow accustomed to them . . . some things should be fixed.

He saw windblown blush on her skin, the bright red of her lipstick. He saw her lower lip tremble slightly. His eyes went lower, and below her chin he saw a slice of bright, searing morning light on her coat.

He shut his eyes before his knees gave out. He felt her try to hold him. She tried to stop him from falling but he went down anyway. He hit his knees on the cold concrete and then fell sideways into a fetal ball as the awful terror cut through him and took his breath away.

He heard her say, "Shepherd, Shepherd," but he could not move, could not react, could not do anything until . . . he started breathing again. With his eyelids clamped shut, he put one hand on the sidewalk, then another, then pushed himself up on his knees like a baby about to crawl. He pulled a knee up, put one foot down and another foot and slowly stood up.

"Shepherd, I'm so sorry," she said as she moved him toward the door. "I should not have been so impatient with you."

He found the handle, yanked it open and heard the reassuring groan. He went through the inner door and inhaled the restaurant's warm, reassuring, pre-lunchtime odors of baking bread, roasting garlic, gruyere cheese browning atop the French onion soup, the dash of thyme and Worchestershire in the New England clam chowder, sweet sherry simmering in the snapper soup and, so subtle that only a man who had spent far too much time in the restaurant would notice, the faint, metallic tang of the busboy's clothes iron as he rubbed away the wrinkles on the spotless white tablecloths.

He opened his eyes and saw the worry on her face. "No harm done," he said.

Her face cleared. "Good," she said. "I'm going now. I must see my patients." She stepped behind him. He heard the outside door groan open, and then the fainter squeak of the door leading up the stairs to the second floor.

Helen Sylvian, the new, blithely beautiful lunchtime maitre d' that Whitey had hired away from an Olde City martini bar, appeared at Ladderback's side.

"How are we for lunch, Ms. Sylvian?" Shepherd asked her.

"We are kicking for lunch, Mr. Ladderback," she replied brightly. "We have seventeen reservations. Also, Daniel Bleutner's social secretary wanted to speak with you regarding Mr. Bleutner."

"*Fils* or *pere*?"

Helen knew five languages. "*Fils*. Mr. Bleutner may decide to visit us, though the visit is contingent on you being here. Will you be here?"

"I may stay for lunch," Ladderback said. "Few things would make me happier."

Ms. Sylvian said she would call Bleutner's secretary back and confirm the reservation. "One more thing, Mr. Ladderback. A Mr. Popov has asked for you." She came close. "He's a sashimi chef and he wants a job."

"Popov? A Russian sashimi chef?"

"American-born Russian, from what he told me. He told me he studied for eleven years in Japan."

"The only thing that is remotely Japanese on the menu is chicken teriyaki," Ladderback said.

"He said he will be arriving sometime shortly. He said he first has to do someone a favor."

Later witnesses would remember Bette Newarr emerging from a taxi minutes before noon in the front of the Center City Book Superstore & Café in a sensational red-lavender-and-gold-printed knit scarf over a mauve quilted winter walking coat. Her fans were mostly female, mostly Bette's age, some with their husbands, a few with boyfriends and co-workers. Bette let them throng around her and they became a triumphal procession, with one fan rushing forward to wave at the motion detector above the bookshop's automatic doors so they slid away just as they crowded in, then mounted the escalator to the second floor where copies of *Guilty Pleasures* were stacked into two pyramids on either side of the signing table, with another table laden with paperback and hardcover copies of her previous novels.

At the center of the table was an unopened bottle of water and a Midnight in Benares inkwell, open and waiting.

Ladderback found a reedy, youthful man with flamboyantly curled blond hair waiting near the bar in a smartly pressed, shiny sky-blue suit. In one hand he carried a case of chef's knives, in another, a folder and a book.

"Mr. Popov," Ladderback said. "Let's talk about this in my office."

He caught himself as he moved past the bar. My office? What made this office his? Why was he becoming possessive over what had been for him just a dining room and a place to meet friends?

He unlocked the office door and turned on the light. As he took off his coat, he pointed toward a battered dining room chair shoved against the wall.

"My card," Popov said. Ladderback accepted it and Popov let himself down carefully into the chair.

Ladderback plopped down on Goohan's office chair. He examined the card. He noted Popov's name and address, and a series of Japanese characters, and a shape that resembled a cucumber. "My name is Yuri but I was called Kyuri in Japan. Kyuri means cucumber," he explained. "That I am very experienced in sashami, sushi, tempura and"—he made a face—"tepanaki. And that I am very loyal," he said. Ladderback's eyes went to the book he was carrying. Popov noticed Ladderback's glance and put the book behind his case of knives.

Because Ladderback read books constantly he couldn't stop himself from glancing at what another person was reading, even if the book was in a bookstore bag. It must have been recently purchased. "Tell me about your relationship with Mr. Nordvahl," Ladderback said. "Have you cooked for him in the past?"

"I have not had the honor," Popov said, averting his eyes. "I would do it in an instant. I would do anything he would ask of me."

"You've encountered him socially?"

"Not . . . socially."

"Professionally, then? Mr. Nordvahl represented you in some legal matter?"

Popov's fist was clenched so tightly his knuckles were turning white. "A legal matter, yes."

Ladderback waited.

"I hope this will not prejudice you against hiring me," Popov began.

"It will not," Ladderback assured him.

Popov set his jaw. "I was taken to court in the matter of food prepared when I was employed with a caterer."

"Mr. Nordvahl defended you?"

"He agreed to take my case, yes. He was a guest at the dinner where my food was served."

"Mr. Nordvahl only takes cases in which he feels he can right a wrong or accomplish the highest good," Ladderback said.

Popov cringed. "I was accused of negligence in the handling and preparation of takifugu resulting in a near fatal case of food poisoning."

Ladderback sat back on the bar stool. "Takifugu is the blowfish, or pufferfish found in tropical waters. I believe there are many species . . ."

"One hundred and twenty species," Popov said. "It was part of my training. I supplemented my training with outside study. I told you, Mr. Ladderback. I wished to be the best."

"The toxin the fish produces is named for the teeth of the fish, am I correct?"

"Tetrodotoxin," Popov said carefully.

"Four tooth poison," Ladderback said. "My father was a medical examiner. He once did a rather challenging autopsy involving it. The victim was from a small Haitian community in North Philadelphia and some had claimed that he had died from being cursed. My father knew that tetrodotoxin was one of a handful of substances used in some tribal rites intended to turn a living human being into a zombie. He found traces of those other substances in the decedent and identified the cause of death as tetrodotoxin poisoning. The toxin was extracted from the fish in liquid form and added, with the other ingredients, to a mango drink, whose residues my father also identified. The fish itself was never found. I believe the poisonous varieties have been banned in the U.S."

"It is not imported in quantity to the U.S. as a food source," Popov agreed. "But there are ways to get a single fish, if you might want to try it, Mr. Ladderback."

"I would rather not, thank you," Ladderback said, "at least, not the wild variety. One curious thing my father told me about the tetrodotoxin is that blowfish raised in captivity do not produce the poison."

"This was what I told Mr. Nordvahl and that was the point he made when he defended me. The poison is made by bacteria that the fish acquires while in the wild. I obtained documents attesting that the fish I served was farm-raised. Still, several guests claimed to get the tingling sensation in the lips and the throat that is caused by minute amounts of the poison in the fish. Mr. Nordvahl showed that the heart attack suffered by the guest who sued me was due to pre-existing conditions."

"I'm glad he was able to exonerate you," Ladderback said. "You must have been relieved."

"I was very, very grateful," Popov said. "To have a legal problem is a complicated, confusing, terrifying thing. I do not make much money, even at my level of skill, because most restaurants that serve sashimi only hire Japanese chefs. Mr. Nordvahl believes that the law should serve the people who are victimized by lawyers. He did not ask for any payment, not even for costs."

"Your gratitude must inspire feelings of loyalty," Ladderback said.

Popov became solemn. "There is nothing I would not do for Mr. Nordvahl if he asked me."

"He doesn't ask for much, I assume."

"He asked me to see you while I was in the city."

"You mentioned to my maitre d' that you were doing someone a favor today. Would that be Mr. Nordvahl?"

Popov looked him in the eye and nodded.

Ladderback didn't move for a few seconds. Then he said, "I enjoyed speaking with you, Mr. Popov."

Popov didn't nod as much as he looked down and tilted his upper body two inches forward from the waist. His face became tense. "I thank you very much for speaking with me, Mr. Ladderback."

"There will be no hiring, unfortunately, until the restaurant passes to its new owner. Until then, I'll make sure the new owner gets your card and anything else you may leave."

Ladderback moved his chair forward so he could see the bookstore bag. Through the thin, translucent plastic, he saw the title. "You didn't mention to me, Mr. Popov, that you read popular fiction," Ladderback said.

"I don't. It's for Mr. Nordvahl." He opened it to show Ladderback the autograph:

> To all at the Delaware Valley Law Watch. They say all publicity is good publicity though yours is the kind I would much rather be without. Love and guilty pleasures, Bette Newarr

After Nordvahl dropped them off at the mill house, Pew took their purchases inside the miller's house. He promised he would make something warm for lunch.

Rawle then asked Andy if he could make things in the snow and Andy said he could, if he would stay where she could see him. He ran about ten yards away, to a point where the earth rose in a gentle mound.

Andy found a pale green painted rocking chair under the porch roof and brushed some of the windblown snow off the seat. She pulled her bomber jacket around her and opened her computer on her knees. Then she closed her computer and took out her cell phone. It had a camera above the screen. She stood and wandered through the snow, taking pictures of Rawle modeling what eventually became the mill tower and the miller's house, as well as the small, frozen rises and valleys in the floodplain.

He didn't seem to get cold as he shaped the snow in his new gloves. Andy glanced up at the gray, frozen sky. There was no wind and for a moment, the gentle sound of Rawle's gloves crushing the snow was the loudest thing she heard.

Andy had to stop and admit how quietly beautiful the landscape was. The news truck had been towed away and windblown snow covered the crevice where it had been imprisoned. Andy saw only snow, scraggly trees and a few dark patches of grass that the snow had not claimed.

She felt safe. She felt secure. She had a sudden childish urge to build a snowman, or to run up and dive into the soft curving dunes of snow.

Then she remembered she was an employee of a major metropolitan daily newspaper. She went back to the porch, opened up her computer and wrote about Rawle in the snow so it might suffice for her next day's entry, ending with a description of Rawle making ice castles in the snow.

She sent the photos she had taken, as well as her article, to the copydesk. She saw that Chilly Bains had responded to one of her e-mails about Ismail Khan:

Forgeddaboud him! The Silent Storm has NEVER granted an interview to the media in his EN-TIRE LIFE! He is impossible to contact. The word is, he contacts YOU, you can't contact him. I am INSANELY JEALOUS that Kersaw got him for the Ambulance Chase—and I just found out— an hour ago!!!—that Khan is actually going to give a SPEECH there. I think the connection had to do with the Kendall School. Khan went there and some of the proceeds from this Chase are supposed to go there. What's the BIG DEAL about a basketball anyway? HUGE buzz about your adventures with the kid. Love and hisses! Chill

Pew came out with two steaming mugs of hot chocolate. Before she could take the second mug to Rawle, her phone went off.

It was Night City Editor Bardo Nackels, who, though he was the night city editor and was supposed to work nights, tended to remain in the newsroom for most of the morning, sometimes until the afternoon. He was editing her column for tomorrow.

"So, like, you mean to say here," Nackels said as he read her work, "that it's all been, like, a nice day? I mean, this crap about scrapple is okay. A *lot* of people around here talk about scrapple but they never really eat it and you never say if the kid ate any."

"Look in the next paragraph," Andy said, a copy of her writing on the laptop's screen.

"Oh. He didn't want to eat a squeal. That's cute. I like that. You sure you didn't make that up?"

"You want to trust me?"

"It's not about trust. It's about . . . wait. Hold on." She heard him talking to someone. "She *what*? Just now?" Then, "Hey, Andy, you read books, right? Ever heard of a Betty . . . Newhard or Newark or something? Writes lawyer novels. She's supposed to be local, or was."

Andy said she didn't read lawyer novels.

"It's . . . it's coming in right now over the police scanner. She just dropped dead while doing a signing at Bookmarket."

"That's awful," Andy said.

"Actually, it's great. For us, I mean. I'm going to write a headline on this that you won't believe. Guess what she died of?"

Before Andy could tell him she was in no mood to guess, he said, "Chewing on the nib of a poisoned pen!"

10 make them happy

First, Danny Bleutner talked about the weather. Then he talked about sports—how "there must be some kind of curse on Philadelphia because, you'd think, with the kind of teams we got in this town, and the money being spent, there should be some championships being won. I'm being serious, now. Really."

While Danny Bleutner talked, Ladderback sipped his turtle soup and studied the man's small palms, stubby fingers and perfectly manicured fingernails. The flesh of Bleutner's hands had been scrubbed so much that it glowed an angry red. Narrow grooves of pinched skin between the knuckles on the fingers indicated where numerous rings had been. Gone from those fingers were the rings that signified his attendance at high school, college and law school, and the additional rings that had precious and semiprecious stones of various shades of blue.

The rawness of his hands extended to his wrists. A patch of shorter hairs on his left wrist might have been the site of his watch's wristband. If so, the watch was not visible.

Everything Ladderback could see on Bleutner's body was new. Tiny holes in the fabric on the sleeve of his navy pinstripe blazer indicated that a label had been plucked off recently. The azure shirt, worn buttoned to the neck but without a tie, retained creases and small pinholes. Bleutner's neck and face also glowed red and the sharpness of the dark, tightly curled mat of hair that hugged his head suggested it had been cut that morning.

After exhausting sports, Bleutner held forth on the city's commercial real-estate market, the mayor's eating habits, a planned cruise ship terminal, gossip about how the city's slot parlors were being managed.

And then his eyes suddenly unfocused and his mouth hung open with nothing coming out.

"You'll excuse me," he said after a few seconds. "I'm still . . . I get these moments when my mind wanders and I'm . . . back there, in my basement, up to my neck in . . . you don't want to know."

Ladderback had an idea of what had happened. He saw in this morning's *Press,* in Chilly Bains's column, that "the Bleutner Bird of Happiness has failed to bill some hours because of a plumbing accident in his Gladwyne aerie."

Bleutner rubbed his forehead. "Sorry about these blackouts."

"You have nothing for which to be sorry," Ladderback said. "You're alive, Mr. Bleutner. We don't need to discuss your father's birthday dinner at this time."

"You think I came here to be my father's social secretary?" Bleutner said archly. "I got twenty people in my office who could set it up for my old man, no problem."

"Can you give me the name of the person who tried to kill you?" Ladderback asked quickly.

Bleutner held up both hands. "No names. We both know who is behind this, but you will hear no name come out of my mouth. The things I do, every phone line, every time I turn around, I just assume I'm being watched and listened to, and it doesn't bother me, because nobody would want to be listening in, if they didn't think I had something to say. And I do have something to say, to you."

He took a bite of his sliced pork sandwich and washed it down with a gulp of low carbohydrate beer. "Before I say it, I have to ask, personally, why is it that you, of all people, called my secretary and had her send the cops to break down my door, just at the time things were getting serious?"

"In what way were they serious, Mr. Bleutner?"

"By the time they found me in the basement, I was restrained."

Ladderback paused, creating a hole of silence that Bleutner eagerly filled. He whispered, "By the time the cops found me the shit was up to here." He made a slicing motion with his hand under his chin.

Ladderback remembered the description of Bleutner, and the fate he should suffer, from the article in Delaware Valley Law Watch about the "Lawyers We Could Do Without." "You couldn't escape?"

Bleutner drummed his fingers on the heavily shellacked wood table. "When I'm alone in my house and the wife is out of town, I occasionally have a lady over." Instead of drawing closer, as most men might when confiding about their sex lives, Bleutner leaned back in his chair. "We do things involving restraints. My basement is set up for this kind of thing. So, when I have a lady over, whatever we feel like, rope, leather strips, chains, garbage bag twist-ties, we can do. This lady was—I thought—from a reputable source. First thing she says when she comes in is, where are the chains? Then, when things were getting interesting and I was, you know . . ."

For just a second, Bleutner had to think about the right words. "Bound, gagged and chained to the wall with chrome steel links. That's when she opened this other bag she was carrying and it was full of plumbing equipment. She went to the toilet and did something so it started to come back up. Slowly. I think she had some kind of pump. The septic tank starts to back up and then she just leaves."

"Did she say anything to indicate to you who may have sent her?"

He put his hands flat on the table. "The only thing anybody's going to hear about it, is that it was a plumbing incident, or accident, or whatever . . ."

Ladderback inhaled the steamy scents of garlic, parsley and lemon juice rising from his osso bucco. He scooped a bit of the marrow from the veal shank, placed it on a chunk of Italian bread that was still warm from the oven, put it in his mouth and had one of those moments when he wanted to tell the Roman statesman Cicero that he got it backwards: it is far, far better to live to eat. "When I spoke to your social secretary," Ladderback said, "I had no prior knowledge of your situation."

Bleutner chomped on his sandwich. "So I'm a lucky so-and-so that you happened to call?"

Ladderback sampled the risotto. "I was fortunate to obtain sufficient information to presume you were in danger. You were fortunate that your secretary was willing to do as I advised."

"I would've fired that British babe a long time ago but . . . with what she knows about me, I haven't quite figured out how to make her so happy she'll want to quit. What she did is, she called the cops on me because she figured, if I was there and I was still with that lady, it would piss me off to have a bunch of cops busting in on me. If I wasn't up to my neck in shit, it just might have. When the cops got me out of there, it required a lot of 'good will' so those cops would be happy enough to keep their mouths shut. But they are happy, and I am happy that they are happy."

He leaned back. "So . . . what can I do to keep Mr. Shepherd happy?"

Ladderback quietly finished his veal.

Bleutner found Ladderback's silence unnerving. "Maybe I should pay double, no, triple, for my father's party? Say you have to get some rare kind of thing, and you don't serve it, but you bill me for it, okay?"

Ladderback dabbed his mouth with a napkin.

"C'mon, Mr. Shepherd," Bleutner pressed. Then, "What the hell kind of name is that, Shepherd?"

Ladderback's expression became cold. "It is less awkward than my first name."

"Neville." Bleutner grinned. "Hey, I had my people do some background on you before I came down here. I know all about Whitey putting you in charge of this place. But what do you know about the food business? I'm going to get Matt Plank to look at this place. The kid is a pure genius with food. You see what he did with Loup Garou? You been to Rivincita, his Corsican place? You can't get a reservation for four months. Come in with me, there's a table waiting." He stuffed the rest of the sandwich in his mouth. "My firm does Plank's legal work, his taxes, his deals with the city." He swallowed. "I'm thinking now, but, what if I just buy into this place and bring in Matt? I can get the city to declare this land blighted, which will qualify you for a seriously huge state grant to tear the place down and start over. Not that you need to start over, but I know you're not exactly making money hand-over-fist here. That would make you happy, right?"

"We must stop him from killing, Mr. Bleutner," Ladderback said.

It took Bleutner a second to figure out Ladderback was speaking about Nordvahl. Then Bleutner said, "Why?"

Ladderback blinked.

"You want to know the real reason I'm here?" Bleutner said, his voice low. "You want to get to the top of the heap in this town, and stay at the top, you want to be the Number One lawyer on that stupid Law Watch list, you don't do that by going for blood, like Severio Pescecane, or kicking sand in their faces, like Charlie Muckler. You do it by making people happy."

"Mr. Bleutner, I was speaking about—"

"No names!" Bleutner finished his beer and snapped his fingers for another. "Back when Jimmy D's was the lunchroom of the Philadelphia Bar Association, I'd see our Pro Bono Boy eating at the bar, and I'd see you eating at the bar. I know you talked with him. I know you were at that birthday party of his. So, what I'm telling you to do is: you're going to call him up. Get him on the phone. Talk to him. Tell him you think he's doing a first-class job killing off all these lawyers and, could he just tell you who's next? Then, whatever you get from him, you give it to me."

"What will you do to help me stop him?" Ladderback asked.

Bleutner's beer came and he took a gulp. "Why should we?"

Ladderback sat up straight. He almost wished that Bleutner had drowned in the contents of his septic tank. Almost.

"I can see from the way you're reacting, or not reacting," Bleutner said, "that you're not happy. No problem. The *Press* is making a big deal out of that reporter hanging out with McSloan's kid. Andrea Cosicki. I ran into her at Loup Garou when Matt was there and Matt and I were very impressed. Matt especially."

"Mr. Plank sent her orchids on a wooden plank for her birthday," Ladderback said. "She is my assistant."

Bleutner covered his mouth to mask a beery belch. "You tell her to call me when she finds out who his next victim is."

"The list has been printed," Ladderback said. "It has been posted on the Internet."

"But we don't know who's next. You find out who's next, and you tell me. I could warn the next victim or I could not."

"We must stop the killing," Ladderback repeated.

"Hey, what's your rush? Let's be realistic. We have too many lawyers already in this town. It's time somebody thinned the herd."

"Mr. Bleutner, you should let the police know the full extent of what happened," Ladderback said. "And then you should get some rest."

Bleutner's face became rigid. "I'm serious here. I want to know who his next victim is and how he's going to do it, though, if it were me doing it, I must admit, there are some people whose elimination could inspire me. Who knows? Maybe he'll take requests."

"You haven't tried to call him?" Ladderback said.

"Too risky, with all the people watching me. Nah. I have to get to him through a third party. What do you call them—unidentified sources. You be that for me, or your assistant, and you'll both end up happy, whether you want to or not."

Ladderback sat back. "Perhaps I should go to the police."

"You stay away from them," Bleutner warned him. When Ladderback didn't react, Bleutner added, "Or all this you see around you, I'll take away." Bleutner tossed down his napkin. "By 10 A.M. tomorrow morning, if I don't hear from you about Pro Bono Boy's next victim, then this will all be gone. Unless you want to be happy. You want to be happy, you know what to do." He shoved his chair back and headed for the door.

Ladderback took the tunnels connecting Jimmy D's to the pedestrian mall beneath the *Philadelphia Press* Building. Entering through the sub-basement, he rode the elevator to the eleventh floor. No one noticed him when he entered the newsroom, shrugged off his coat and put it on a hanger on the rack near the men's lavatory.

He glanced at the U-shaped copydesk and saw Bardo Nackels editing a story for the front page about lawyer novelist Bette Newarr dying from a poisoned pen. Then he went toward his desk, averting his eyes as he passed in front of windows. He looked past the cluttered pile of mail on Andy's desk and saw, on his, a copy of today's newspaper and a printout of tomorrow's death notices, with a note clipped to it telling him that as of tomorrow, in an effort to improve productivity, printouts of death notices would no longer be delivered to his desk. If he wished to see the death notices, he could access them at Press/advert/deathnot/(insert date as first three letters of the month followed by two digit date, starting with 01 for the first of the month).

He frowned. This had nothing to do with productivity. Howard Lange was trying to save a few more pennies from his operating budget by slowly eliminating the copy aides who were paid minimum wage to deliver mail, newspapers and interdepartmental communications.

A second note clipped to the first said that mail and daily copies of the *Press* would no longer be delivered to his desk. Mail would be placed in departmental boxes in the newsroom reception area, with copies of the day's newspaper. Packages, overnight mail envelopes requiring signatures and hand-delivered items would also be stored there.

Ladderback sat down slowly. Having his mail, a copy of the newspaper and the death notices printed out and delivered a day before they were published had been such a small privilege. He would study the printout, observe the awkward prose typically composed by a funeral director and observe which notices included photographs of the deceased.

Sometimes he would take his glasses off and stare closely at the photographs, searching the blur of benday dots for insights into the decedent's personality. He couldn't do that on his word-processor screen. The images weren't reproduced sharply enough and, the closer one drew to a machine, the more one noticed that everything—pictures, type, lines—was all a bunch of pixels, light and dark spots of color like a Seurat painting.

Hold a piece of paper up to your eyes, and the type is still type. It doesn't move. It doesn't flicker during a power outage. It doesn't strain your eyes with reflective glare. You can hold the paper in your hands, underline important words and passages. Yes, he could have the page printed out, but it would not be the same as having it waiting for him when he arrived in the mornings.

He sat down and held the death notices page in his hand and, was it coincidental that, on the day that Lange was eliminating the copy aides, here was a death notice mentioning the passing of one of the *Press*'s retired sports reporters, who had started his career in journalism as a copy aide?

Ladderback was tempted to forget the sense of urgency that made him come to the newspaper and compose an obituary about that man. Though obituary writing was the most despised job at the newspaper, Ladderback loved it so much that when he was hungover, angry, depressed, confused, exhausted, when his girth around his middle weighed down upon him, when he thought his heart would stop, when he was so infuriated with the sleazy content of the publication that employed him that he was about to quit, he would pick up the phone, get a list of relatives from a funeral director, call the pastor of the church the deceased belonged to, talk to people who knew the deceased, who loved the deceased or hated the deceased and had anecdotes about why the deceased was the most important, the most unusual, the most valuable, the most loving individual and why did God take him? Why did he have to die the way he did? Ladderback would ask a few questions and lose himself in the emotional intensity of the replies until he could understand, again, the sense of wonder that animates every human life. And then he would condense it all into three to five paragraphs—sometimes more if space permitted—and feel absolutely certain, when he was finished, that he had accomplished something wonderful.

He did not fight the temptation to do his job as much as he withheld it, for a while. He had come to the newsroom to access the Internet.

He signed on to his word processor, accessed the Internet and pulled up a Web page of legal search engines. He tried several engines until he saw one whose Web page matched the one that Nordvahl had used to discredit Severio Pescecane's bogus estate claim. He did a search including the words "takifugu," "Popov" and "Nordvahl," that brought up the name, date and filing documents about the sashimi chef's legal difficulties.

Danny Bleutner had told him that the woman he had hired had made his septic tank back up through the basement toilet. A search with the words "Nordvahl," "plumbing," "ms., mrs., or miss" produced no results. He tried substituting "septic tank" and, again, got no results.

A septic tank is part of a sewer or wastewater system. He tried those terms and found a malpractice case in which Nordvahl had sued the divorce attorney who had represented the former wife of a West Chester water-purification system designer. The lawsuit alleged that the woman's attorney had failed to identify accurately and list all of her assets and holdings within the design firm that she owned jointly with her husband, many of which were given to her husband when the couple's assets were divided. The suit was settled before litigation and details of the settlement were sealed.

Ladderback did a search for news articles with the name of the husband and former wife, and the design firm's name and, even though the town of West Chester was outside the *Philadelphia Press*'s circulation area, he found a mention in Chilly Bains's column about the original divorce. In an item called "Kitchen Kink," Bains reported that the husband had accused his wife of assault, citing abrasions to his buttocks and inner thighs that were later proved to have been self-inflicted with—of all things—scouring pads. The divorce was initiated by the man's wife after he was arrested at a North Philadelphia sex club called The Stockyard.

He also saw a review in the *Philadelphia Standard*'s weekend section in which the same woman was mentioned as starring in "Married to the Beast," a show playing at the West Chester Little Theater about the wives and mistresses of the notorious British cult leader Aleister Crowley.

Ladderback made printouts of Bains's column, as well as a more detailed series of articles about the divorce, and the subsequent malpractice suit, in the West Chester *Clarion.*

He went back to a legal search engine. A search including "Nordvahl" and "Charles Muckler" yielded no results. He pushed himself away from his word processor, folded his arms and closed his eyes for a few minutes. When he opened them, he saw a copy of today's *Press* on his desk, with a copy of the *Philadelphia Standard,* the *Press*'s staid broadsheet competition.

The *Standard* had a front-page refer—CONSTRUCTION TOOL OR MURDER WEAPON?—to a business section story about a Lansdowne company that leases varieties of concrete pumps that Philadelphia police "theorize could have inadvertently or intentionally discharged a mixture of salt water and Delaware River sand" into the vehicle of lawyer Charles Muckler.

Ladderback opened the newspaper to the business section and saw a color photograph of a young balding man with a moustache and goatee, his body filling an awkwardly fitting brown suit worn with a red and yellow striped tie. He had his right hand affectionately placed atop a squat tangle of tubes, coils and machinery.

The article quoted the company's president: "These babies have been used for a lot of different construction, hydrodynamic compression and earth-moving applications, but this is the first I ever heard of turning them on a human being."

The article stressed that police had no evidence suggesting that any of this man's machines had been involved. Lieutenant Everson was quoted: "We're looking at any and every explanation."

This company, Ladderback read, leases, sells and services several models of a German-made, diesel or gasoline-powered hydraulic pump. Among its most common use is pumping concrete and other liquefied building materials from a ground floor mixing or delivery site up as many as fifty stories. Similar pumps are used as dredges that open small boat channels. "We get our biggest rental demand," the company owner said, "in the late winter, early spring and the fall, right after storms bring those big floods. You hook one of these babies up and you can move a lot of muddy water and liquid debris out of basements, parking lots, low-lying areas."

Ladderback went back on the Internet and visited Web pages about the Chadds Ford region. He learned that the water of the Brandywine River, which flows through Chadds Ford, was so free of impurities that Eleuthère Irénée Du Pont de Nemours chose the banks of the Brandywine, on the outskirts of Wilmington, Delaware, to build his gunpowder manufacturing plant. Ladderback also learned that gunpowder operations had to be suspended when the Brandywine flooded, which tended to happen at least twice each year, in the spring and fall.

Ladderback went to an Internet Yellow Pages directory, typed in the Chadds Ford zip code, and did a search for emergency water removal services. He found several plumbing and sewerage system contractors.

He went back to his legal search engine and tried every plumber and sewerage contractor, with "Nordvahl," and had no results. He tried other combinations and came up dry.

He turned to the enormous file cabinet that took up most of the wall beside his desk. It contained copies of nearly every obituary and news article he had written and his notes and supplemental files of clippings from the *Press,* the *Standard* and other newspapers and magazines that he found interesting.

He extracted a rather large SAND file from the S drawer. He glanced at articles he had included about beach erosion, an obituary of a muncipal golf course groundskeeper who was proudest, not of his greens, but of the spotless condition of his sand traps; an obituary of a retired SEPTA passenger rail systems manager who had been fired and then rehired when he became a "whistle-blower" stating that the company that manufactured some of its passenger cars had used defective sandboxes and thus the trains could not be relied upon to start and stop efficiently on wet, icy or leaf-strewn rails; an article on the mineral-rich marl, or "green sand" found in southern New Jersey in which remains of the first dinosaur ever found on the North American continent, unearthed in 1858 and named Hadrosaurus for the town of Haddonfield, where bones of the duck-billed creature were discovered. . . .

He lost himself in the file until he saw an item from the *Press*'s Jersey shore stringer. "The third time would be the charm" for Carlin Charteris, a Pennsbury Township landscape architect and "professional sand sculptor" whose first and second attempts at modeling a life-sized, three-dimensional replica in sand of General George Washington Crossing the Delaware in the parking lot of a Wildwood, New Jersey, pizzeria had been destroyed before they could be completed by July Fourth weekend rain.

Ladderback learned that "Charteris uses local sand but mixes in " 'a cohesive agent, also known as glue' and then employs a gas-operated hydraulic compression pump to 'pack' the sand so it will be soft and pliable but will retain its shape for several days after it dries." The glue is made of "environmentally safe, naturally occurring substances" that, according to Charteris, "cost a pretty penny."

The article suggested that the third attempt had been stalled for two weeks because the pizzeria's owner refused to pay the Charteris's expenses.

The article quoted Schuyler Nordvahl, a board member of the Delaware Valley Law Watch, who said he had agreed to underwrite Chateris's expenses "as long as he makes sure that there are no lawyers on Washington's boat."

Nordvahl was further quoted, describing Chateris as a "fabulous landscape architect and a great neighbor. I can't tell you how many times he's showed up with his truck and helped clear the access road to my property when the river floods. When he told me about this, I couldn't see him disappoint the children who were looking forward to this."

Ladderback picked up his phone, dialed the Philadelphia Police Department and asked for Lieutenant Jeffery Everson, Homicide Division.

Another police detective answered. Ladderback identified himself.

"You're with the media?" the detective asked. "You have to go through the media office."

"I am not asking for a statement," Ladderback said. "I want to give Lieutenant Everson information that may explain a series of murders."

"A series of murders? You mean more than one?"

"They involve lawyers, one of whom was Daniel Bleutner, though that attempt did not succeed."

"That would depend on what you call success," the detective replied. "I can personally vouch for a lot of people who are very happy at the thought of the Blue Boy stewing in his own prunes." He guffawed. "Now let's back up a little. You said you're with the *Press* and you want to explain to Jeff why anybody would want to kill all these disgusting, incompetent, overpaid, full-of-themselves lawyers."

"That is correct," Ladderback said.

"It just so happens that Jeff is not here to take your call because he's gone up around Penns Oak, the old Birks Container factory. You wouldn't be familiar with a lawyer, name of Johnny Altmacher, would you?"

Ladderback went to the Delaware Valley Law Watch Web page and called up the list of "Lawyers We Could Do Without." John Altmacher was number eight for "relentlessly clogging the process of due process with excessive, redundant and all-too-typically incomprehensible paperwork."

"So what happens next, we get a call from an exterminating service that has a contract on the Birks Container building, which has been converted as a document storage facility for the city. Seems they got an anonymous call shortly after the lunch hour about a rodent infestation around the Birks Container building. They wouldn't normally go out on an anonymous call, but they don't have much on their plate and so out they go. They go to the building, which is used to house municipal records and documents, and the clerks take them to a second building on the site that is part of the facility where municipal court records are kept. There's this huge pile of documents and debris and sticking out of that is a leg and a shoe."

"That would be Mr. Altmacher's?"

"The way Jeff sees it, Altmacher came in through another door, which was open. He didn't sign in to the main part of the building, which is the usual procedure. Two of the three clerks that work there said they didn't hear anything but there's this other one that called in sick that we are attempting to locate."

"Ask the clerks if they have had a professional relationship with a lawyer named—"

"Hold on there," the detective said, "do people that don't do your job tell you how to do your job?"

"Occasionally," Ladderback said.

"Jeff says there was well over a ton of documents on top of the victim. Altmacher was just about completely buried. No rats, unless you want to count the victim." He paused and added, "I hope I didn't just gross you out," in a tone that implied he hoped he had.

"I am most concerned about loss," Ladderback said, "and the effect that loss can have on those who cared deeply about the deceased."

"We've asked around. I don't know if anybody gave a rat's ass about this guy." He guffawed again.

"Someone always cares," Ladderback said, "no matter how the deceased is judged by his family, by his society, by his enemies or his peers. It is our nature to love. It is inescapable."

"That a fact?" the detective continued. "You ever speak to Jeff before?"

"He knows of me," Ladderback replied. "I write obituaries."

"He knows *of* you," the detective repeated, giggling. "And you want to tell him *of* whom is killing all these lawyers. Pray tell, you sound like you're in a Shakespeare play. You know, Shakespeare said we should kill all the lawyers."

Ladderback frowned. "Shakespeare included jokes about lawyers in some of the plays, but they were not intended to be taken seriously. The statement about killing is made in Part Two of *Henry the Sixth* by a member of a mob, and his comment, with others, is Shakespeare's way of satirizing the opinions of the ignorant."

"I think you've got it backwards," the detective said. "If you're in the mob, it's going to be the lawyer that'll pull your ass out of the fire. If you're a victim, if you're the mother of the victim, if you're the cop that busted his nuts trying to take some scumbag off the street, you come away with different opinions."

"Shakespeare was referring to the rabble, not organized crime," Ladderback replied.

"We've had that quote hanging up on the wall here as long as any of us can remember. It always gets a laugh."

Ladderback closed his eyes. "Please tell Lieutenant Everson I have important information regarding these crimes."

"What is it you're calling a crime? You ask anyone around here, they're more likely to call it a public service."

Ladderback put down his telephone in disgust. He saw the stack of files on his desk and rapidly returned them to the file cabinet. He cleared his desk of paper.

It took a few minutes before he could began working on the obituary about the sports-writer who had started as a *Philadelphia Press* copy aide.

11 i know what to do

After they finished Pew's lunch of grilled Vermont cheddar sandwiches on whole wheat sourdough bread, with bowls of steaming, meatless minestrone, Rawle meticulously placed his bowl on top of his plate and handed it to Pew. Andy did the same and saw that Rawle had turned on the small television set mounted over the modern kitchen's sink. Then he sat on the floor and began staring intensely at a soap opera.

Pew stepped around the boy. Andy asked Rawle to move but he did not move. Andy suggested they go outside and make a snowman.

Rawle didn't move.

Andy turned off the set and Rawle screamed so loud that Pew dropped a plate. Rawle ran out of the kitchen and up the stairs. Andy followed him and as soon as he saw her he made the same scream and ran into the room he had slept in and slammed the door in her face.

She called to him through the closed door and he screamed even louder. She said she didn't mean to upset him but she didn't think he should just waste his time in front of a television set. She didn't add that this was precisely what her parents had told her when she was Rawle's age and what she had found on television had been more fun than just about anything.

She asked him if she could come in. She heard no reply. She gently opened the door and something flew past her face. She heard it bounce off the wall and saw he had thrown one of his building bricks at her.

She threw the door open and told him he would *not* throw anything at her or anyone and that he would have to apologize right then or . . .

She found him cowering, folded into a fetal ball at the edge of the bed. The anger left her and she tried to touch him but he screamed. She tried to say something but he answered her with another scream. She said nothing and he screamed a third time, loud enough to hurt her ears.

For the next few minutes, he screamed no matter what she did. He even screamed when Pew appeared in the doorway and asked if there was anything he could do to help. She shook her head. As far as she could tell, shaking her head didn't make a sound, but he screamed and she found him looking at her, his face red and wet with tears, his eyes showing an insolent anger that Andy hadn't seen previously.

She took a breath to say something and he screamed.

She covered her ears and he screamed again. She wanted to tell him that she would leave him alone if he kept this up, but she remembered her mother yelling at her, making ridiculous threats to her that she never believed. Andy couldn't leave Rawle alone because he was her responsibility.

Then she asked herself, why couldn't she leave him alone? So many things could happen to him but they'd been together for so much of the day. What if he just wanted to be alone?

She took her hands away from her ears. She stood and went to the door and she watched him unfold himself and sit on the floor with his back against the wall. She heard him speak, slowly but firmly, the words chopped and stretched until she could barely understand them, but his meaning was clear.

He told her he wanted his father. He wanted her to find his father and tell him that he wanted him to come back.

Dear Mr. Action: How do you *do* this?

Andy looked him straight in his beautiful brown eyes and said, "Your father can't come back."

He didn't scream. He didn't rock from side to side. He looked away. After a while he said, "Oh k-k-k-ay."

She waited. Then she said, "Do you want me to leave you alone?"

He turned toward her, wiped his nose and shook his head.

"Do you want to come outside with me and build a snowman?"

Rawle rocked from side to side for a while and then was still for a long time. Finally, he told Andy that she couldn't make a man out of snow.

She smiled and said, "Let's try."

He followed her outside reluctantly. He stood unmoving as she packed some snow into a ball and began to roll it on the ground until it became the size of a basketball. His eyes followed her as she hoisted up the ball and pretended to try to make a basketball foul shot.

He rushed toward her and yanked the snowball out of her arms. It fell apart in his hands and he reacted with a shocked surprise, as if a balloon had burst and the noise had startled him.

Andy told him it was okay and tried to approach him but he stepped back, then ran away. She called out to him and told him not to go too far. She went to the top of a rise and tried to see him but saw only undulating curves of white broken by outcrops of snow-swept trees and marsh grasses. She called for him again. She thought she heard the faint crunching sound of boots on snow but she could not be sure.

She had wanted to play with him, to enjoy him like a big sister with a younger brother. If he could make his models, why couldn't she? She checked her wristwatch, saw the time was nearly 3 P.M. and began to make another ball. She kept pushing it until she had a good-sized boulder. When she put a second, smaller boulder on top of that, he emerged from behind a dune.

He wouldn't help her. She asked him to find some twigs for the arms, or some stones for the face. He didn't move.

When she was finished he studied the snowman for such a long time that Andy began to shiver. She noticed that the sun—a faintly luminous portion of the sky—was nearing the horizon. She told Rawle she wanted to go in.

He approached the snowman and glared at it. He said, *Can't come back*. Then he went back to the house.

Andy tried not to cry. A few tears escaped, icy cold on her face. She wiped them away with the back of her snow-encrusted glove which only felt worse.

Andy let Rawle watch television for the rest of the afternoon in the kitchen, where the rustic, thickly painted cabinets and open (though unused) brick fireplace contrasted with the gray and steel refrigerator, six-burner gas range and other modern appliances.

Andy insisted that Rawle sit in a chair, instead of on the floor. He complied silently as Pew, in an apron, started on the dinner. He said that Mr. Nordvahl would not be joining them so, if they did not mind, could he make a meatless meal? He had in mind slow-roasted winter squash with a cracked barley pilaf of mushrooms, sweet yellow peppers and toasted hazelnuts.

Rawle, lost in the images on the screen, did not reply.

"If he'll eat it," Andy said, who would have preferred a hamburger and fried potatoes, or one of Matthew Plank's magnificent cheese steaks, only because greasy, salty food tended to take her out of low moods when exercise would not. She was in an especially low mood now, even it she was getting a definite caffeine lift as she sipped a cup of domestic orange pekoe tea that Pew had enhanced by adding a few orange peels to the pot. He served it with a plate of flat bread, a mild goat cheese and a sweet lingonberry relish.

"This isn't what Nordvahl eats?" Andy asked.

"Mr. Nordvahl is interested in his orange juice, but tends to have more conventional tastes about his meals." The wrinkles around Pew's face turned upward. "Before Mr. Nordvahl asked me to help out, I was with a local family, rather well-known. They experienced financial reversals and became quite stingy. They let their property deteriorate and looked for reasons to eliminate staff. I was fired, and my pension removed, over a case of truffles from a local grower. The missus felt I should have used less expensive imported truffles. Mr. Nordvahl helped me negotiate a more favorable settlement and invited me to come here. My only instruction is to do what's best for the property, and those who visit."

"Do you get many visitors?"

He took out a small sack of barley from the crowded pantry and busied himself with the preparations. "I mostly see Mr. Nordvahl's clients. They're from all walks of life, mostly people like myself, who needed help and had no one to turn to until he offered to help. Beyond us, he doesn't have much of a social circle. Not as many as my previous family. Those folks went back three generations and hadn't done a thing for their property but sell off pieces of it whenever the tax codes changed. Mr. Nordvahl bought this place after it was almost completely ruined by a flood. He spent a fortune to bring it back, re-landscaped it and put in new drainage systems and an emergency power supply so, when the river overruns its banks, it doesn't come into the buildings. It's quite a sight, actually, when we get a flood. We become an island unto ourselves. I come out on the porch, make myself a little glass of brandy and watch the water and the things in it slowly go by."

Andy saw Rawle's attention fixed on Nickelodeon with the same motionless stare that he had given her when she had told him that his father wasn't coming back.

A small window beside the kitchen table showed her that the sky had grown dark. She left the kitchen, went to her room and looked out on the floodplain. She tried to imagine how it would be in a flood and turned away.

She checked her phone messages: Ladderback cautioning her about accepting telephone calls from Daniel Bleutner or anyone employed by his firm. He suggested that she not return any telephone calls made by, or for, Bleutner.

Bleutner was Matt Plank's lawyer. She didn't see anything from him on her message queue.

She thought of Ladderback. Would he be able to tell her how to help a child like Rawle understand what had happened to him? She almost dialed him, but stopped when she noticed that Chilly Bains had called back. She listened to him say that he'd picked the third Atlantic City event of those she'd recommended, and, yes, she could attend it with Rawle and maybe even send him a line or two about what happened because "the spy I rely on for Atlantic City material is going to a Gamblers Anonymous meeting that night and I really didn't want to cover this but it's got a local angle, so, send me a line or two about the color of his tuxedo or if any celebs show up, especially if they do something stupid." He gave her an e-mail address and the phone number of the development director of the Atlantic City Aquarium and told her to mention his name.

"But if you really want to help me out, I need a spy at that stupid Valentine's Day race because Ismail Khan is going to be there and he's actually going to speak, or so they say, and I am just *not* awake and functioning before noon. If you get past his bodyguards, he might give you an autograph but I doubt it. If you're tied up with the boy, let me know and we'll assign somebody."

The last message was from Logo Brickle. What, he wanted to know, was she doing on Valentine's Day?

She couldn't think about Valentine's Day. She tried to busy herself in her work, in writing, in surfing the Internet for answers to questions that readers had e-mailed to Mr. Action, but she found herself drawn to the darkening view of the floodplain. She did not know how long she had been staring at it when Pew called her down to dinner.

Rawle said nothing during the meal. He divided the food into different areas of his plate, then ate one section after the other. Then he went up to his room. She glanced in once to see how he was doing and saw that the room was empty. She went to her room and saw him typing on her computer. She stayed in the hall. When he emerged, he did not act as if he had seen her.

She saw he had written: *Im okay I know what to do.*

He closed the door to the bathroom. She heard him turn on the sink faucet and brush his teeth. He came out and was about to close the door to his room when she said, "Rawle?"

He gave her the same look he had given the television and closed the door.

She went back to her room and, after a while, saw a car's headlights sweep across the floodplain. The big car bounced and swayed and then came to a rest in front of the mill. She heard the door of the miller's house open. The porch light came on and Pew went out to greet Nordvahl. They talked for a while, then Nordvahl opened the trunk of his car. He and Pew carried out two large boxes of documents from the trunk and left them beside the door to the mill. Pew went back to the house as Nordvahl opened the door, carried the boxes in and shut the door.

Two minutes later, Andy's cell phone rang. It was Nordvahl. "I've scheduled a meeting for you and the boy at the Kendall School. You'll get some documents there and they'll answer questions about how you can take care of him for the next few days until I resolve the situation regarding his mother and his father's will."

"Rawle asked for his father," Andy said.

Nordvahl became guarded. "How did you handle it?"

"I told him his father wasn't coming back. Since then, he's been very quiet. There was one point when he was screaming for a while, when I wouldn't let him watch television. Then he got quiet. We went out and built a snowman; I mean, I built a snowman. Then, later, he wrote that he was okay and that he knew what he had to do."

"He didn't elaborate?"

"Not another word. He just went to bed."

"And you're telling me this because you want my advice about what to tell your readers?"

"This isn't about my *job,*" Andy said. "I just don't know what to do for him. As soon as I think I understand him, he just goes off. It was really hard for me when I lost my father, and I see him going through that now, and I want to help him but I just don't know how."

"Sleep on it. *Nebecula est, cito transbit.* It is darkness that will soon pass. 'Things will be different in the morning.' They always are."

"And what if I can't sleep?"

"You will, eventually. *Tempus edax rerum, tempus omnia relevat.* Time consumes all things, time reveals all things."

She hated it when he quoted Latin at her. She saw a light on in the cupola atop the mill tower. "You sure about that?" she asked him.

"Absolutely," he replied, and said good night.

She turned off the phone and waited for the light in the cupola to go off. It stayed on.

She opened her computer and checked her Mr. Action e-mails. In the subject line of another e-mail with a screen name and address that looked like it had been created by a spammer were two words: Ismail Khan.

Andy opened it.

```
Make sure you listen to him. He may not have a
voice but he can speak. IK
```

It was a hoax. It had to be. Andy remembered the *Liberty Bell Magazine* article that Barbara "Bombarella" Ellerbaum had written about Khan, the one that almost won a Fretzer. Bombarella had interviewed dozens of sources who said that the reason Khan had never been interviewed and refused to speak to the press was that he had suffered brain damage due to a drug overdose and could barely put a sentence together. She described him as a robot who could play brilliant basketball but who was controlled entirely by his agent, his manager and his parents.

Andy got a lot of spam and bogus e-mails and was about to delete this one when she thought of Nordvahl's quote about time revealing all things. Why would anyone *pretend* to be Ismail Khan? She wasn't obligated to reply to reader e-mails, but she didn't like being told to do what she was already doing.

```
I am listening to him and what he says is beau-
tiful. AC
```

She closed her computer and tried to go to sleep. She turned over and saw the light was still on in the mill.

She put on her shoes, ran across the snow and moved a heavy latch over a door so big and old she was amazed she could move it. She found herself in a small glass-enclosed windbreak.

She passed through the windbreak and saw all four stories inside the mill had been gutted, replaced with a series of open wooden landings around a spiral staircase of rough-hewn timbers. From where she stood she could see places for sleeping, clothes closets, a library of legal references, an electronics workshop, a server and computer space and a lavatory with a shower and a sink.

She saw no art, no decoration, no color beyond that of the dark wood and ruddy exposed brick walls. She saw nothing that would signify luxury, self-indulgence or even comfort.

She heard a book slam shut. Nordvahl appeared at the top of the staircase in a frayed, full-length, belted maroon smoking jacket and demanded to know why she was there.

His tone of voice made Andy just a little bit angry. What was his problem? Should she have knocked? She didn't remember seeing a bell or a knocker or one of those metal things that you pull that sets off chimes, like the one at the side entrance to the Brickle estate that Logo used to pull all the time to annoy his mother.

"I saw a light on," Andy said.

"I specifically instructed you not to come here."

She looked him in the eye and said, "I couldn't sleep, okay?"

He didn't move. "Ask Pew to make you a hot toddy."

She shook her head. "I don't want to eat or drink anything.' "

His voice became strained. "And this gives you the right to violate my privacy?"

She looked away. "You didn't have kids, did you?"

"None," Nordvahl said. "I was too busy with the law, and my wife had doubts."

"About your marriage?"

"About herself!" Nordvahl said.

"Not you?"

"Why are you bothering me?" he asked her.

"Rawle creeped me out," Andy said.

"I take it he disturbed you in some way?"

"Just like you did when we were in the mall, telling me about some murderer who would find me out as soon as I went back to work. I could almost believe that you weren't just some super lawyer who came to our rescue and had a plan for everything. It was more like you were that killer and you weren't being a super lawyer to help Rawle, you were putting Rawle and me in this very nice cage until you could find out exactly what we saw. That creeped me out."

He took a long breath, then frowned. "I don't believe that 'creep out,' as you've used it, is a verb."

She pointed a finger at him. "See what you just did? You were just like Ladderback when he gets on my nerves: treating me like I'm a child because I said something that makes perfect sense to both of us, but, because you're older, you think you should correct me."

He narrowed his eyes. "*Quisnam igitur—*"

"Or you sling Latin at me. I didn't learn Latin, okay? I'm not a member of the club."

He curled his lip. "Obviously."

"So what happened today is, you creeped me out at noon and Rawle creeped me out after dinner and I can't sleep, okay?" She sat on one of the stair rungs and hugged herself. "I guess I want company."

He took a step down the stairs.

Andy held herself tightly.

"I hope it doesn't . . . creep you out," Nordvahl began, "if I tell you that my reason for telling you not to come here is that this is where I go when I don't want company. This is my Bat Cave, my Fortress of Solitude. I was a great fan of comic books when I was a child."

She saw his worn moccasin slippers move down the stairs. He sat down a rung above her. "Every superhero needed a place he could go to be alone."

"So what do you do here, when you're alone?"

"The law," he said. "I study it constantly."

"You do this by yourself? You don't have an assistant?"

"In Philadelphia, some of the staff of the Delaware Valley Law Watch work part-time for me. They're very competent, eager and self-directed." He removed his handheld computer from his robe. "With this, I am connected to them. I am connected to law libraries, databases and the Internet, as well as all kinds of machines. Without this, I'd only be dreaming of what I could accomplish. This makes my life possible."

"But you don't have to do this, right? You've made enough money so you can just kick back and enjoy yourself?"

He put the computer back in his robe. "This is how I enjoy myself. I fight the good fight, as do you."

"I don't see it as a fight," Andy said. "I like finding things out, even if what I'm supposed to know is obvious, right in front of my face. I want to dig for it because it's like I'm hungry and I have to keep finding out things until I'm full."

"I'm the same way," he agreed. "If I am involved with an individual, I gather as much information as possible. I don't feel full until I know her birthplace, education, addresses, tastes, employment history—"

"You're doing it again," Andy said. "You're acting like a different person. You're saying you investigated me."

"I did. In the law, as well as your profession, information is crucial. Didn't you investigate me?"

"No," Andy said. "I could have but . . . at this point, I want to trust you, I want to rely on you, I want to believe what you tell me, because, with Rawle needing me as much as he does, that's all I can handle."

"What you're saying is that you don't want to trust me, as much as you want to trust your opinion of me," Nordvahl said. "You don't want additional facts to threaten your initial impression."

"You're doing it *again!*" Andy said. "If I were interviewing you, I'd think, just from the way you said that, that there are some things about you that you definitely don't want me to find out."

Nordvahl narrowed his eyes. "Such as?"

"You want me to guess? Okay: you got there *really* fast when I called you after McSloan died. So you were in the neighborhood. Rawle didn't have to be taken away from his mother. You could have smoothed things over between me and her, or you could have at least tried. It's weird the way you're so obsessed about Rawle answering police questions under oath. What's he going to say that's so important? And who says it's ever going to get that far? You said the police could put words in his mouth or mine, but you're the one who put words in *their* mouth by saying that McSloan was murdered when they hadn't even figured out how it happened. It's like you wanted them to know how he was killed."

"Just an assumption," Nordvahl said carefully.

"That's Mr. Creep Out talking to me. If I were being a reporter right now, I'd say you know something about who killed Mike McSloan, or why, and you might know something about what happened to those other lawyers. You're just like Rawle telling me about this monster on the balcony—"

"A monster?" Nordvahl asked slowly.

"There you go again. That tone of voice. When you and Rawle creep me out, it's like you're the same person," Andy said. "You have this secret that you know you're not supposed to tell, so you're going around telling me, in effect, I have this secret, but you're going to have to guess. But the reason you want me to guess the secret is not because you want me to know the truth. What you really want is to play a game and keep me guessing. You want to stretch that game out as long as you can, because once I guess the truth, whatever relationship we have is over."

Though the mill was warm, Andy shivered. "There," she said. "I guessed."

She heard Nordvahl breathe slowly. "Do you want me to tell you if you've guessed correctly?"

"Not if I'm being Rawle's substitute mother," Andy said. "That boy has found the maternal part of me and that's all that matters now. I want to help him, comfort him, keep him happy because it feels *right*. When it's easy—when all he needs is a hug or some attention—I feel better than I've ever felt. But sometimes, it can be scary."

142

"Could it be that we're all just worrying a little too much?" Nordvahl asked her. "You've come to me for reassurance, which is one of the major reasons individuals consult lawyers. You could probably wipe out a third of all the billable hours if clients didn't want their lawyers to tell them not to worry. So, I'll tell you, pro bono, don't worry."

So why was it, every time Andy ever met a person who told her not to worry, it made her worry even more?

Nordvahl rose. "I'm very happy that we've had our conversation. I must return to my work—"

As worried as Andy was, she had one more thing she had to ask him.

"When Shep wanted me to interview you, he said I should ask you about why some king sent William Coke to the tower of London."

"That would be James the First, also known as James the First and Sixth, because he was the sixth James to rule Scotland. He was the son of Mary, Queen of Scots and assumed the English throne when Queen Elizabeth died. And the man to whom you are referring is one of the most brilliant legal minds ever: Sir *Edward* Coke. Why did Shepherd tell you to ask me that?"

"He never tells me why."

Nordvahl became thoughtful. "When I studied law, I became fascinated with the relationship between Edward Coke and Francis Bacon—the same Bacon who invented the English essay and codified the scientific method. They were bitter rivals, better known in their day for their accomplishments as lawyers, judges and members of Parliament under Queen Elizabeth and King James."

"So why was Coke sent to the Tower?" Andy asked.

"Bacon and Coke fought over a woman, a widow, the Lady Elizabeth Hatton. Bacon wanted to marry her for her money. Coke wanted to marry her for her charm because Coke was a bit of a bumpkin and she was good at giving parties. She became Coke's second wife and later sued Coke, with Bacon representing her, when Coke tried to marry off her daughter by her first marriage. The suit failed because—"

"The Tower," Andy said.

Nordvahl became flustered. "Are you always this impertinent?"

"All I did was ask you a question," Andy said.

Nordvahl paused to collect his thoughts. "Toward the end of his life, Sir Edward Coke was a member of Parliament. He began to challenge the royal prerogative, the ability of the king to make and unmake laws by royal decree. The king was offended. He said Coke had become an 'oracle of the people,' in that he was speaking for people instead of the Crown. Francis Bacon may have had something to do with uncovering the debt that Lady Hatton's first husband never repaid to Queen Elizabeth. Coke had either forgotten about this debt after he married her, or was never told about it. So Coke stayed in the Tower for seven months until the King decreed he could be let go. Thereafter, Coke kept his mouth shut about the prerogative. But he recorded his thoughts about the law in his *Reports,* a series of volumes that survived the English Civil War and were used as a legal precedent for the American Revolution."

Nordvahl frowned briefly. "I can't imagine why Shepherd would have you ask me this. Unless . . ."

Andy sat up.

"When Coke became the Queen's attorney general, he was quite zealous for the Crown. He believed that the law descended from the Crown and he persecuted many people in service to the Crown. But he changed his ways; he went from one extreme to the other. In expressing the will of the people against their king, it was almost as if Coke developed a sense of conscience. He began to see the law as a kind of civic conscience, something greater than all men—including those who wear a crown; something that, when practiced virtuously, impeccably and compassionately, could save men from themselves in ways that nothing else could."

He became quiet. Then he put his hands over his face.

Andy asked him. "Is something wrong?"

"I must ask you," he began. "How would you respond if you discovered that Rawle's father was murdered by an individual who thought what he was doing was right and fair?"

She became afraid again. "If I was being a journalist," she said slowly, "I'd suppress my personal feelings and report the story and hope that the people who decide what to do with murderers have all the facts.

"But if I was what I am now—a mother for a boy who has suffered in ways no one should have to . . ." Andy's eyes filled with tears. "When I see that boy suffering, I think of how I suffered when my father died, and how Rawle doesn't even know how difficult his life is going to be. . . ."

"Would you want to help bring this killer to justice?" Nordvahl said after a while.

"I don't care about justice," Andy said. "I want him dead."

Ladderback stood in the center of his studio apartment, with book-shelves covering every wall and every window, the two-day-old remains of a bagel on the tray beside the recliner that he slept in when he was too lazy to unfold the bed from his sleep sofa.

He set down his satchel. He took off his hat and coat. He put the breakfast tray in the small, galley-sized kitchen, where the sink was already crowded with dishes. He stood in front of the sink. As king of his sink, he could exercise his royal prerogative and let them stay.

He remembered Mafouz, the way they traded off lines from Gilbert & Sullivan's *The Mikado*. He went to the shelves that held his collection of recorded music. He had a two-disc set of performances of Gilbert & Sullivan's *HMS Pinafore* and, tacked on to the last disc, their short, very funny first collaborative effort, *Trial by Jury.*

He rewarmed the two-day-old coffee sitting in the coffeemaker, found some chocolate-covered tea biscuits in the pantry, inserted the disc into the player, slipped on his headphones and settled into his recliner.

Trial by Jury is a loony farce based, in part, on Offenbach's Paris operettas, Gilbert's early efforts as a barrister and a general cyni-cism about the machinery of justice, which comes to an appropriately grinding halt in a breach-of-promise suit involving a man who wants to "marry one woman today, the other tomorrow." Events reach a crescendo when the Learned Judge exclaims, "a nice dilemma we have here," followed by the wonderfully silly choral repeat.

A nice dilemma indeed. Ladderback picked up the remote control and stopped the music. He put down the tea biscuit that was in his other hand. He took off the headphones. He picked up the computer keyboard from the table next to the recliner, accessed the Internet and did a search for the Honorable Harlan Whetson, Philadelphia family court judge.

12 not alone

Andy awoke on the morning of Valentine's Day to see Rawle again at her bedside. He was dressed in his new clothes and smiling. He said, "He's g-g-g-one."

Andy sat up and pulled the covers around her. "Schuyler?"

He nodded happily.

"He was supposed to take us into the city today. We were supposed to visit your school, see some people."

He told her that he did not want to make a snowman. He wanted to go home.

She looked out the window at the undulating plain of snow. "I'll get you home," she told him, without knowing how.

He didn't move. She asked him to leave her alone while she dressed. He asked her why.

"Because I like to be alone when I dress. You're alone when you dress, right? So let me alone."

He began to rock from side to side. Andy called his name and he stopped. Then he told her that he didn't want to be alone.

"I'm not going anywhere without you. I just want some privacy."

Privacy. He repeated the word in his broken, tortured speech. He asked her how you get that.

"You don't get it," Andy said. "People give it to you. You have privacy when other people agree to let you do what you want, when they don't watch you all the time, when they leave you alone, when they don't bother you."

He asked her if he was bothering her and, of course, she said no. "I just want to get dressed by myself. Go down and see what Pew has made for breakfast."

He went to her computer, opened it up, typed on the keyboard and then showed her the screen.

Not want you to be alone.

"How can I be alone when you're with me?" Andy said.

He smiled and sat down on the rug near her bed.

"So just let me be by myself for a while."

He shot up and was out of the door. What had she said this time? "Let me be by myself." To her it meant the same as being alone. Was one idiom so much different to him than the other?

She was about to get out of bed when she saw his eyes peering at her through the crack in the door. She asked him to close the door. She had to tell him to close it *all the way*. She waited until she heard the stairs creaking as he descended.

She dressed and went to the kitchen. Pew had a breakfast of eggs, no-meat mushroom-and-sage sausages, winterberry oat muffins, and the most delicious maple syrup.

"Not all the maple trees are in Vermont," Pew said. "We have a few here."

She asked Pew if he had a car. "I do not," he said proudly. "Most of our supplies here are delivered. I live in a house across the road, just past that break of trees, on the high ground. I am proud to say I walk to work."

"How do you get into Philadelphia?"

"I don't," he said as he went to the kitchen sink. He began to clean the dishes. "If it's a city you need, we're closer to Wilmington. Mr. Nordvahl said for me to tell you to just relax and enjoy yourselves. There's no bus to catch that stops anywhere near here. There isn't a taxi driver crazy enough to come out here this time of the year, though you could always call. You're in one of the most beautiful places you're ever going to find. I have games and things to keep the both of you busy. I have sketch paper and paints, if you feel artistic. The piano in the parlor is all tuned up, if you have a song in your heart." He finished arranging the dishes in the drying rack. "It's unseemly to be in a hurry in wintertime, when nothing feels better than slowing down."

Andy wanted to speed up. "What's the name of this place?"

"It's always been Stokes Mill," Pew replied. "When Mr. Nordvahl restored it, he had it put on the National Register of Historic Places." He led her out of the kitchen to a closet under the stairs that was piled high with board games.

"Mr. Nordvahl wanted me to tell you he might be back in the late afternoon. He had to go off to a meeting."

"Without us," Andy said, ignoring the board games.

"I wouldn't let it concern you, Ms. Cosicki. Mr. Nordvahl always knows what he's doing."

"We were supposed to meet with Rawle's teacher today." She also had that ambulance chase to cover, and she had told Rawle she would take him home.

Rawle took out a chess and checkers set and began making towers with the checkers. Andy went upstairs, opened up her computer, accessed the Internet and did a search including "Stokes Mill," "Chadds Ford," and "historic places."

She found it listed as a private residence, not open to tours. And she found a street address. She used that to get directions from Center City, Philadelphia. On a hunch, she checked if Nordvahl's name was listed in the telephone directory. It was!

Now that she knew where she was, she did a search of SEPTA bus schedules. She found there was no scheduled service between Chadds Ford and Philadelphia. The closest stop was at the intersection of Route 202 and Route 1, much too far to walk.

Maybe the newspaper might send someone out from the *Press*'s Wilmington bureau. She called the *Press* newsroom and told Bardo Nackels, the night city editor, that Chilly Bains had wanted her to attend the Valentine's Day Ambulance Chase but she didn't have access to a car.

"So?" he said.

"The chase is at noon. I might be able to get into the city in time if you can send somebody out from the Wilmington bureau."

"And I just might send another reporter to cover it," Nackels grumbled. "When're you sending in your next column?"

"Soon," Andy said.

"How about now?"

"I have to write it first."

"What are you waiting for?" Nackels said and hung up on her.

Her brain was empty. She had absolutely no idea how to begin. So she checked e-mail. The queue was longer now, with even more readers responding directly to the series about Andy. There was another e-mail purporting to be from Ismail Khan.

> Listen to his body. As long as the heart beats, the body is never silent. I.K.

What did that mean? Andy wrote back:

> I don't know who you are, but if you're the basketball player, then there's a kid named Jermaine Hayes who had a basketball you autographed taken from him and could you please autograph another and have it sent to the Philadelphia Press so I can give it to him?

She sent the e-mail and almost immediately got a response.

```
He will speak for me. IK
```

Okay, she could see a nice mystical connection but, as far as she could tell, the only thing Rawle accomplished with his body was to make little models. That, and he moved fast.

Andy wanted to reply but she had that column to write before she could figure out how to get back to the city. Maybe she could talk Chilly Bains into getting the *Press* to send out a taxi or something.

She stared at the snow. She was grappling with columnist's freeze-up, a form of writer's block she had never experienced because she saw herself more as a reporter—an individual who pursued information and brought it to readers—rather than a writer, who makes art with words. When she began doing journalism in high school, later rising to the position of co-editor of the University of Pennsylvania's student news-paper, she avoided writing editorials, culture overviews, humor, what-it-all-means analyses and other permutations of "think" pieces, because they always read like an exercise in sounding like you knew what you were talking about. She would rather fill the space she was given with information that readers needed to know.

And yet, she had read so many superb columns as a young journalist. She devoured the collected columns of Mike Royko and Jimmy Breslin. Breslin had once said that if it doesn't take six hours to write, it isn't a column, and that the hardest thing to write was the ending.

She didn't have six hours. She had to find some way to get into the city and bring Rawle home.

Then she remembered what Rawle had told her yesterday: *I know what to do.*

She thought back on other times she was with the boy, when she was afraid for his safety, enraged at his suffering or infuriated that others did not understand his vulnerability.

What if, despite his youth, disabilities, the abuse he had endured and the loss he had not even begun to understand, he really did know how to live his life, to help himself, to make the necessary decisions that are the weight and measure of a free life?

She thought of the things they did yesterday, the very normal things they did. Yes, there had been a few strange moments. She had been a typical mom and tried to stop him from watching too much television. And her heart had almost stopped when he had asked her about his father.

But there had been other times that were remarkably pleasant. It was winter and they'd played in the snow. She remembered how fast he moved, how he always kept two steps ahead of her. She imagined him in a race—no—in sports. She could see him on a football field, running with a ball. No one would catch him.

She wrote about chasing him across the floodplain. And the pleasant times they had. She ended with Rawle's assertion: I know what to do.

Maybe he does know what to do, for himself and those he loves, she wrote. *Maybe all we have to do is stand back and let him find his way.*

She looked at what she wrote and it seemed precious and naive.

This might seem a little naive, she added. *What if the way Rawle finds takes him into a ditch? What should we do then?*

She had her ending.

You reach out, give him a hand, and pull him out.

As she sent that to the newspaper, she heard the sound of an automobile's tires slipping on the snow.

A dark blue Honda Accord floundered at the base of the ramp that led down what she now knew was Pennsylvania State Road 100 and buried its front end in a snowdrift. Andy watched the car squirm back and foward until it broke free.

Pew had said nothing about any visitors. Andy watched the car head straight across the floodplain. It wobbled and skidded and then the front end fell deep into the snow at just about the same place where the TV news truck got stuck.

Andy raced downstairs, grabbed her jacket and ran outside.

The snow was thicker, heavier. It almost grabbed at her shoes. She squinted in the reflected glare and caught the aroma of a wood-burning fireplace. She saw exposed patches of dark, tangled marsh grass.

The car was pitched forward at an angle so steep that it would not be able to back its way out under its own power. Andy saw Rhea Nordvahl inside.

Rhea saw Andy and turned off the engine. Andy pulled the door open and helped her out.

"Are you okay?" Andy asked.

Rhea looked at the mill. "He's not here. He puts a light in the third window when he's here." She stepped back and fell down in the snow. Andy helped her up. "I have to take you and the boy away from him."

"Not with your car that way," Andy said. "He went into Philadelphia."

"The car is not the problem," she said. "You and the boy are safe?"

Andy nodded.

Rhea set off for the mill house. "I used to live in that house. He would live in the mill. It was an impossible marriage."

Pew stepped out onto the porch, followed by Rawle, who slipped past Pew and was in front of Rhea almost before she could see him. Rawle glanced at Andy. He seemed to want her approval so she nodded and then Rawle jumped on Rhea and knocked her down on a snowdrift.

"Rawle," Andy said, "that's not nice!" As she pulled Rhea up, Rawle began to rock back and forth.

"It's okay," Rhea said. "We have to get him someplace safe."

"What's wrong with where we are?"

Rhea shivered. "I got a telephone call today from that woman who is representing Mrs. McSloan: Roberta Zetzmeer. She knows I was married to Schuyler and she said the most awful things to me, awful things. She made threats about what she would do to Schuyler. She says she knows where Schuyler's mill is and that the things that were happening to the other lawyers were nothing compared to what she would do to him."

"And you believed her?" Andy asked.

"I did not have to be married to my husband for twenty-two years to learn that the legal profession provides a safe haven for those who would be easily classified as sociopathic. This woman has serious personality disorders. I have never heard such hateful language in my life, and, believe me, I have heard plenty. She has threatened to kill Schuyler. Can you believe that? She made death threats to me! She said she had clients who would kill for her!"

"People say that all the time."

"You do not understand the nature of the attorney-client relationship!" Rhea said. She went on to the mill house, stamping her feet to shake off the snow. "Some clients will do anything for their lawyers to get out of paying the fee."

"Schuyler doesn't charge a fee."

"Neither does Roberta Zetzmeer!" Rhea said and entered the house.

Ladderback awoke, sat up in his recliner and discovered from the clock on his DVD player that he had overslept.

He glanced around his single room and saw the printouts he had made while searching through the Internet for information about Judge Whetson.

He pulled the computer keyboard toward him, accessed the Internet, signed on to the *Press*'s Web page and then pulled up his list of obituaries and saw that he had written far enough ahead so that he really didn't have to go into the newsroom.

But he always went into the newspaper. It was his place to do things, talk on the telephone, cut up newspapers and magazines and file them away.

It was his place to be with people even if most of those people, with the exception of Andy Cosicki, didn't talk to him, ignored him, left him alone.

He remembered that it was Valentine's Day, and that he had a valentine.

He went to his closet and saw his so-dark-blue-it-might-as-well-be-black double-breasted worsted wool suit. He had bought it so long ago that it probably didn't fit.

On a lark, he tried it on. It fit and he looked great in it.

He needed a place to wear it, and he needed a person to wear it with. He knew where to find both.

Inside the house, Rhea called one of Schuyler Nordvahl's clients. "He says we're lucky. The truck's been in the shop all morning and he's just getting it out now."

Pew made hot chocolate for Rawle, a bracing cup of English Breakfast tea for Andy. Rhea began to chain-smoke cigarettes.

Then Pew set down a plate of tea sandwiches on whole grain bread, a creamed goat cheese and thinly sliced cucumbers.

Rawle gobbled everything in front of him. Andy almost told him that he shouldn't eat too much or he would get fat, but she stopped because her mother had said the *exact* same thing to her when she was Rawle's age and, at six feet, two-and-half inches, Andy was not only an inch and a half taller than her mother, she was so thin she couldn't imagine what it was like to be fat.

After lunch, Andy opened her laptop, accessed the Internet and went to the Delaware Valley Law Watch's Web page. Andy noticed that Roberta Zetzmeer was on that list.

She called the Law Watch and asked for whoever kept track of Nordvahl's appointments. She got a young, bright, eager male voice who said he was Kenneth and he had been reading her columns. Andy told him that Nordvahl was supposed to be meeting with Roberta Zetzmeer about Rawle—was that meeting, perhaps, scheduled for today?

"It was supposed to be yesterday but Mr. Nordvahl asked to have it moved to this morning," Kenneth said. "Changing the time of a meeting, especially at the informal stages, can put the opposing counsel off balance. It's a pretty common tactic and the only sensible way to deal with Roberta Zetzmeer."

Andy told him about Rhea. "Completely understandable," Kenneth said. "Did you see the Law Watch list? We called her the 'Great Divider,' because she's so antagonistic. She made a pile when she divorced her husband and she only takes a case if it's going to let her sound off. The woman screams. She throws things. She slams doors. She has been known to stand on the threshold of an elevator and not get in or out—effectively trapping anyone in the elevator there—just so she can have the last word. Many matrimonial lawyers in town won't take her phone calls. A lot of judges don't want her in their chambers."

"She must get results."

"That depends on what you mean by results. Matrimonial lawyers get clients who are hurting in some way. Zetzmeer gets clients who want her to make those who hurt them, hurt even more."

"I don't want to keep Rawle from his mother anymore," Andy said. "Could you set something up?"

"If you want Rawle to see his mother, I'm sure Mr. Nordvahl will make that happen. But he's saving both of you a lot of grief by keeping you away from Roberta Zetzmeer. She makes bad situations worse."

"Tell him, when he checks in, that we'll be in the city and that we'll meet him somewhere. Is he going to the Ambulance Chase?"

"Mr. Nordvahl avoids that, especially since we discovered that it's a fraud."

"There's no chase?"

"There's a chase, all right. Slip Kersaw gets a big turnout among the personal-injury lawyers, and others who are athletically inclined. He'll probably get the biggest he's ever had with Ismail Khan giving a speech. The chase is real. It's the charitable aspect that's the fraud."

"He says it's supposed to go to worthy causes."

"What he says is that it goes to local charities and good causes. The lawyers, through their firms, pay to enter the race, and the sponsors pay a lot more. Kersaw trademarked the phrase 'local charities and good causes' and registered it as a non-profit corporation. All the money goes into that corporation. Guess who owns, controls and, as far as we know, *is* the corporation?"

"Irv Kersaw," Andy said.

"We've done a pretty significant investigation and we haven't found a single charity, local or otherwise, that's gotten a dime out of Local Charities and Good Causes in the last five years. It's going to be our lead feature in the *Law Watch Journal* for March."

"I was supposed to cover it," Andy said. "I'm thinking of taking Rawle there. Then we'll go to his school. Did you set up that meeting at Rawle's school?"

"I did. Ask for a Mr. Deheulos. Just call before you show up."

"Great. There's something else. I'm taking Rawle back home."

"Where he lived with his father? The police probably have that sealed."

"I want it unsealed. I want Rawle to get his own clothes and spend time in his own room."

"You're asking a lot. But I'll tell Mr. Nordvahl about it. If anybody can get you in there, he can."

"One more thing," Andy said. "That list of bad lawyers you put together—"

"It was a group effort. We all had input."

"How is it that so many people on that list have died?"

"The police asked us the same thing yesterday. Mr. Nordvahl told us not to comment to anyone, for any reason."

"But you must have some theory."

"Only that if an individual or group is accused, that individual or group has a right to competent, professional representation, just like everybody else."

"Whoever is doing this is going after your own. You wouldn't rather have the judge appoint an *incompetent* to defend them?"

"If these people keep it up, we won't have any incompetents left."

Carlin Charteris said he wasn't going to pull Rhea Nordvahl's car out of the ditch as much as he was going to restore harmony.

He clambered around the car, the snow catching on his ripped denim jacket. He adjusted the dented, French Foreign Legion kepi on his shoulder-length tangle of coppery blond hair. He pulled on his long, Fu Manchu moustache. Then, taking big steps for a man with short legs, he bounded down and crouched behind the car. He took off a huge, Day-Glo orange glove, put his pink fingers into the snow, picked up a blob and tasted it.

"Warm front coming," he said. "I wouldn't be surprised if all this turns to mud in a couple of days."

Rhea offered to pay him anything he wanted. Charteris said accepting money was "out of the question."

Andy asked Charteris what he did for a living. "I am a *noted* landscape architect and environmental artist," he said, putting on his glove. He hopped into the cab of his big, grimy white Kenwood flatbed diesel and started the truck.

The sound of the engine made Andy turn her head. She had gone back to be with Rawle, who was sitting in the snow, oblivious to the cold, with his building set open. He was making a precise model of the truck and the car.

She studied the truck. Her eyes began at the curving snout of the truck's cab and went back to the bright blue tarp tied down to the flatbed. The tarp covered some kind of machinery.

She'd heard that deep, throaty rumbling before, but it had been different. It had made a pinging sound.

She watched Charteris position the front bumper of the cab until it was less than six feet from the car's rear bumper. Then, with the engine running, he scrambled back on the flatbed, pulled back the tarp, opened a metal box and withdrew two links of heavy chains. He attached the chains to the underside of the car, then slid under the cab and fixed the chains to the truck.

He said something to Rhea that, because of the truck's engine, Andy couldn't hear completely. It was something about "apologizing to the earth." He bowed in the directions of the compass points. Then he got back into his truck, put the gears into reverse, and slowly backed away.

The car slid out. Rhea stepped in and started it. She lowered the driver's side window and cheered.

Andy told Rawle it was time to go. The boy obediently closed his building set and followed her to the car. On the way, Andy said to

Charteris, "Were you at that restaurant yesterday morning, for break-fast?"

"That was you and him with that old guy who was at Mr. Nordvahl's birthday party," he said as he disconnected the chains. She watched him put the chains away and secure the tarp.

Andy asked him if that birthday party had been in Philadelphia. Charteris said it was.

"To go to the party, you drove this truck into the city, right?" she said, glancing at the machinery under the tarp.

"Why shouldn't I?" he asked her. "It's my truck."

She got into the backseat of the car beside Rawle. Rhea, in the dri-ver's seat, thanked Charteris, gave him her business card and told him to consider, seriously, a small but focused publicity campaign that would "get the word out" about his art, or whatever he wanted to call it.

He put his gloved hands on the car. "The time to do this would be in the spring. I'm going to be doing a sand sculpture for the Atlantic City Aquarium this summer."

"You make sand castles?" Andy said, sitting up.

"The idea," he told her, "is to illustrate the reaffirming nature of envi-ronmental processes as opposed to the temporal nature of human en-deavor. I'm going to pump sand from the Absecon Inlet and position it in the Aquarium's parking area, right behind the new shark habitat. Then I'll make a larger-than-life portrait of Gunnar Champ, you know, the guy who has his name on the top of all those casinos. Then I'll wait for rain."

"But won't that destroy your sculpture?" Andy asked.

"It won't destroy anything. It'll just become sand again, and *dis-appear*."

Rhea looked back at Andy. "You really should write this fellow up. The *world* should know about him."

Andy asked him for his business card.

"I don't have them," Charteris said. "Not for my art. I'm in the phone book under landscape architects."

Rhea said good-bye and aimed the car for the road. Rawle waved.

Andy looked back and copied down the truck's license plate number.

13 interesting men

Ladderback went right to the striking woman in the wooden chair sitting against the back wall of Philadelphia family court, room G.

They can appear just about anywhere they want and fit in perfectly, just because the world has such a shortage of beautiful things and accommodates them easily, eagerly.

He saw that she was sitting on a vinyl cushion, the kind that sports fans bring when they sit in the least expensive stadium seats. She had slipped a flat pillow behind her back. A white knitted cap snugly held tangled gray hair that hung out of the cap in curled strands. A full-length magenta down coat enclosed her small shoulders. She had opened the coat, showing a white sweater. Her hands were in a mismatched pair of gloves—both leather, though the brown glove was much older than the black.

Ladderback guessed that she'd probably take off the gloves and her coat as the building's ancient steam heater slowly warmed the place. He tried not to look too long at her face, whose features, no matter how they had aged, still proclaimed that this woman had not been beautiful when she was younger. She had been astonishing.

He noticed the chairs beside her. He had not anticipated that she might surround herself with so many things.

On the chair to her right was a portable coffee cup and a plastic water bottle. On the chair to her left she had neatly arranged a notebook, three ballpoint pens, three pencils, a small box of stationery and a portable radio with a headset. A blue canvas shopping bag, with which she had brought these items, lay in the aisle in front of her.

Ladderback moved slowly down the aisle until she could no longer pretend to ignore him. "May I join you, Ms. Dixit?" he asked gently.

The eyes behind her trifocals appeared confused as she tried to place his voice.

They widened. "Yes, you may, Mr. Ladderback," she replied in a hushed voice.

He paused in front of the chair with the drinks. She immediately snatched them up and put them at the back of the chair on her left. Ladderback removed his gloves, took off his hat, unbuttoned his raincoat, pulled the scarf from his neck and slowly placed himself in the chair.

Her attention was at the front of the courtroom, where people sat in clusters, attended by men and women with briefcases. Ladderback caught a snatch of conversation—"What do you mean you didn't bring the papers? We can't pro*ceed* without them."

The air in the courtroom had that dry, vaguely astringent tang of an old government building. Against this Ladderback caught the faint whiffs of cologne and aftershave that would, no doubt, fade as the morning wore on.

Ladderback shifted in the hard, rickety chair that, like the coldly grand stone courtroom, was a relic of the period when the public face of city government was hard, monumental and unmoveable.

"I am fortunate to have found you, Ms. Dixit," Ladderback said, as he saw a bailiff detach himself from a chair beside a pillar.

He watched her examine him, to make sure that he was truly feeling fortunate. Ladderback blushed and then he heard the command, "All rise." A short, stout, nearly bald man in floppy robe bounded into the judge's box. As Ladderback pushed himself to his feet he saw Neely

Dixit merely lean forward, then back. "The judge gets himself into his chair so fast," she told him, "by the time you stand up, it's time to sit down again."

Judge Alonzo Quihana smacked the gavel. "Be seated."

Ladderback took a breath, and then another. Why was he so short of breath? He had taken a cab from his apartment on Locust Street to the court's handicapped entrance off Seventeenth and Vine, and, aside from two, brief, terrifying moments when he had to be helped into the cab by his apartment house's doorman, and then, from the cab to the handicapped entrance by one of the court guards, he had a rather pleasant, stress-free morning. It had felt too good not to go into that newsroom, where he had never quite learned to ignore the subtle condescension, or outright neglect, he received as the newspaper's oldest staffer.

While he was in the cab, riding with his eyes screwed shut, he imagined himself taking that early retirement option and spending so many good days going to the restaurant through the underground commuter tunnels, opening it up with the key in his pocket, welcoming employees, welcoming guests, welcoming suppliers as they made their deliveries. The restaurant business was far more than just turning locks and saying hello, but he could not shake the feeling that he was appreciated at Jimmy D's and that he could find a new life for himself there.

But he would miss moments like this, when he could savor this place and this person beside him. Neely had been a source for him when he'd done obituaries about courtroom personnel. She had been eager to give him quotes and anecdotes over the telephone and he had been content to remember her how she had been when he had first interviewed her.

He told himself he should not let appearances beguile him. He should not let himself rejoice that the years that disfigured so many young beauties had made her even more marvelous for him. The years had been more than kind.

Ahead of him, the judge on the bench made frantic gestures. A lawyer in a rumpled gray suit apologized that his client had forgotten some papers.

"Being here with you is a luxury for me, Neely," he told her.

"You want luxury, Shepherd, go to the Criminal Justice Center. Serious money went into that building. Very nice seating."

He didn't care what kind of seat he was in with her beside him, but he didn't want to overdo it. He didn't know anything more about this person beside him than that, of the mostly old and anonymous individuals who passed their time as courtroom spectators, none was as beloved as Neely Dixit. The only daughter of a wealthy Bucks County chemical company executive, she inherited a small fortune after her parents died in an automobile accident on the Atlantic City Expressway. She used the money to study dance at Temple University and began frequenting the city's courtrooms when she became the mistress of the notorious Municipal Court Judge Augustus "Playboy" Malamato, a patron of one of the dance groups in which she regularly performed. During the day, Dixit would appear in Malamato's City Hall courtroom, magnificently dressed to accompany the judge to lunch and dinner.

The affair went on for several years until Malamato, who was married, began divorce proceedings against his wife. Malamato was then informed he was the target of a criminal investigation that was expected to charge him with conspiracy and extortion regarding the solicitation of payoffs for favorable verdicts and light sentences. Malamato shot himself in a hotel room days before the indictment was to be announced. His wife was later found to have procured the handgun, brought her husband to the hotel room and poured his favorite bourbon. The jury could not determine if she put the gun in his hand, held the gun against his head and pulled the trigger, or if she had just held her husband's hand as she did so.

Dixit then haunted the back rows of courtrooms throughout the city—every one but Malamato's. She was most often at family court, because it was closest to the small apartment she occupied on Springarden Street. Her parents had left her enough money to live on, though what started out as a small fortune became smaller over the years. Ladderback wrote a profile of her that appeared in the *Philadelphia Press* on the ten-year anniversary of Judge Malamato's death. In that interview, he asked her why she spent so much time in the city's courtrooms, and she replied that she had come to see a courtroom as a sacred space, in the same way that the ancient Greek amphitheaters were invested with religious significance. In court, she said, the extremes of human behavior are enclosed in language, gesture and ritual, and thereby transformed into the most moving, intensely subtle kind of theater. She said she was planning a ballet based around a trial, and that the more she observed courtroom situations, the more material she found for her ballet.

The ballet, as far as Ladderback knew, was never performed. But Neely never left the city's courtrooms. Ladderback called her when he needed a different point of view about a lawyer or someone connected with the Philadelphia municipal courts.

Deadline pressures, as well as his worsening agoraphobia, had limited his contact with Neely Dixit to long telephone conversations at night. Sitting beside her now on an uncomfortable wooden chair in the badly heated courtroom G (the courtroom guards had told him where to find her), he wished he had never been ill.

The judge went through the formality of asking a haggard man in a faded denim jacket if there was any chance for reconciliation. The man did not respond. The judge repeated the question. The man said no.

"The fellow getting that divorce?" Neely said. "He's been up all night celebrating, don't you think?"

Ladderback tried to hear what was being said in the front of the courtroom. Was his hearing going, too? "Have you ever wanted to move any closer than the back row?"

"It's more important to see than to hear. See that man over there, the one with the jacket with vents in the back? His vents aren't open. What's that say to you?"

"He hasn't been to his tailor."

"What if he stole it right off the rack? A man who wears a suit, and doesn't get dirt on his hands, can have larceny in his heart." She gave his hand a squeeze. "Or worse."

Ladderback suddenly felt shy. He told himself he was too old to feel shy.

The silence grew between them and Ladderback, who was normally content to let long silences fill a conversation, felt as awkward as if he were on his first date. He had to do something. He had to say something. He had to distract himself from the fact that it felt so good to be near her.

He asked her if she had ever spent any time in Judge Harlan Whetson's courtroom and, if so, what was Whetson like?

"Judge Whet is your basic ham jurist," Neely told him. "He likes putting on a show. He deals mostly with juveniles and likes to lecture from the bench. He tells them what they're doing wrong, gets them to cry and say they're sorry in front of their parents and their relatives, because what he knows those are the ones that will vote for him when he's up for reelection. He doesn't care why the kid did what he did. He doesn't care if that kid is going to go back to his neighborhood and do the same damned thing again but, maybe, do it a little better so he doesn't get caught. Judge Whet just wants to whip the boy with words. Any lawyer who does juvenile will say, you want Judge Whet—that's what we call him around here—to lightweight—that's a light sentence—or suspend a sentence, you bring in the whole family, or folks who aren't family but look as if they just might—get everybody in their Sunday best and have the kid break down in tears just after Judge Whet works himself up into such a rage that his voice starts to break."

"I once did an obituary about an individual who exhibited similar symptoms." Ladderback nodded. "Have you ever heard of Tourette's Syndrome?"

She wrinkled her nose. "Is that one of those mental things you can have without knowing it?"

"Possibly. I examined some of the campaign literature on his Web page. It said he has a hereditary speech defect and was thought to be mentally deficient in school until he forced himself to speak properly. His sympathy for disabled children springs from this. What is interesting is this rage you mention."

"He expects the offender to abase himself—the good lawyers will teach their clients how and when to cry. The more tears the better with Judge Whet. It's the offenders who just stand there like they're deaf and dumb that he gets mad at. Then he becomes insulting. Mean, even."

"Abusive?"

"Verbally, but he's playing to the parents, he's playing to the people in that kid's neighborhood who see that kid as a threat and won't do a damned thing to rein that kid in. He's being an authority and the kids know he's just some fool in a chair. But the kids don't vote."

Ladderback observed Judge Quihana asking a sulking, smoldering woman in a new bright red dress, if there was any hope for reconciliation. She stared at the man in the denim jacket and said, "No fucking way."

Quihana pulled his microphone to his mouth and recited, in a singsong voice, "Court directs counsel to inform Mrs. Altone that only language as is fitting for a courtroom will be tolerated. Shall I repeat that for you, Mrs. Altone?"

Altone pointed her finger at the judge, once, twice, as if putting a silent curse on him, but said nothing.

Ladderback remembered the reason for his visit. "Did Schuyler Nordvahl ever try any cases before Judge Whetson?"

"Never saw Nord in Judge Whet's courtroom. Nord's got his eccentricities. Speaking Latin like he's the only one that knows. He gets all hot and bothered if opposing counsel acts crude or folksy. You know he actually challenged a lawyer to a duel?"

"He mentioned it to me once. He said he was young and foolish, immersed in his studies of Edward Coke and Francis Bacon. He said the challenge was over the affections of a woman. Forgive me for asking, but, I was always curious if that woman had been you, Neely."

She closed her eyes. "Oh, Shepherd, what a *thing* to ask a woman on Valentine's Day!"

"Have you any imminent commitments, Neely?"

"My time has always been my own, Shepherd."

He glanced at his wristwatch. "Perhaps you can accompany me to lunch. Would Jimmy D's please you?"

She opened her eyes. "Oh, it would. Oh, it would be *splendid*. That's where all the lawyers used to go. And the politicians. And the mobsters. And the stars playing in the theaters. Judge Malamato took me there, you know."

Ladderback knew.

She glanced at her clothing. "Am I dressed for this? It was such a fancy place when he took me there."

"You are dressed perfectly, Neely."

Color flooded her pale skin. "Oh, but not the way I was when I was with Judge Malamato. I could make every head turn my way then, and it was nothing to me. What I wanted was to have the complete attention of an interesting man." She turned to him and raised an eyebrow. "You've always been an interesting man, Shepherd."

"I believe I have been paid a compliment," Ladderback said.

"You have!" Neely said. "But I must tell you, I was not the woman that Nord wanted to duel with McSloan over."

"Was she a lawyer?"

"She was in graduate school to be some kind of a therapist."

"A psychiatrist?"

"Shepherd, you must never ask me who she was, because she was dishonored, and I am old-fashioned enough to believe that some secrets should be kept. Trust me, though, it wasn't the woman he married."

Dixit pointed toward a matter happening in the courtroom. "This is the best part," she whispered. "Judge Qui is doing the equitable distribution. Used to be, the woman would get the house and the man would get the mortgage, but not anymore."

Judge Quihana was reading a list, but he was speaking away from the microphone so Ladderback couldn't quite hear what was being said. He asked Dixit if they should move closer.

"What's being said doesn't matter," she told him. "Just watch."

Ladderback watched the back of the woman in the bright red dress. She slumped forward. The man sat up in his chair and pounded his fist into his palm.

"He got the house," Dixit said. "Another satisfied customer."

As the towers of Center City, Philadelphia rose ahead of the swerving, ten-lane swath of Interstate 95, Rhea told Andy that she was glad she couldn't figure out how to turn off the automatic direction system in her car. "Rawle likes it," she observed.

For most of the trip, Rawle sat quietly in the backseat, studying the small video screen at the center of the dashboard. Whenever the computer's voice spoke, he would tear his eyes away to search for signs and landmarks to correspond with symbols on the screen. He became excited as they passed Philadelphia International Airport, with its curving sprawl of terminals and towers engulfed in the harsh, concrete fortress of parking garages almost the same bleached blue and gray color as the hazy winter sky.

"You having a good time back there?" Andy asked him.

He was so enthralled with the view of the airport that he didn't respond.

"If Schuyler believes he is right, then there is nothing that he can't endure. But if he has one instant of doubt, he will lose his composure. Then he becomes careless, or fixated on things. I once saw him put his arm through a sewer grate because he wasn't sure if he'd lost his keys and he just had to go after them. His arm was wedged so tightly in the grate, it took twenty minutes to work it out. And then he found that the keys were in his pocket."

Andy asked Rhea to drop her and Rawle off at the Kendall School. Rhea asked her if she didn't mind her leaving them in Center City where they could take a subway to the school.

"Just avoid Broad Street," Andy said. "There's a run on the southern part, between City Hall and South Philly, happening around noon. I was supposed to cover it but I didn't know if I'd make it back in time. It's probably going to be crowded because this basketball star, who doesn't talk to the media or give speeches, is going to give a speech."

Rawle turned his head sharply toward Andy.

They went up on a ramp to the bridge that soared over the slumbering vessels in what had been the Philadelphia Navy Yard. "When I was growing up," Andy said, "Steve Carlton, a baseball player with the Phillies, never talked to the media. He finally retired, and by the time he did an interview, nobody was interested. But a lot of people are interested in Ismail Khan."

Including Rawle McSloan, who whooped so loud in the backseat that Rhea almost lost control of the car. He tried to speak but nothing came out of his mouth. He looked around for Andy's computer, then he pulled out his handheld speaking computer, touched the screen with a pointer and held it in front of Andy.

A halting, male voice emerged from the computer: "Is-male can big man to me. Please must see is-male can please please please please."

"Sure," Andy said. "Why not?" To Rhea, she added, "The Law Watch people told me that you have nothing to worry about with Roberta Zetzmeer. They said your ex-husband could get a restraining order if she became too much of a pain."

"I have counseled rape victims who had restraining orders against the men who harmed them," Rhea said. With her left hand on the steering wheel, her right hand punched in the cigarette lighter, removed a cigarette from a pack in her purse and then touched the lighter to the tobacco.

"I will be out of town for a few days," Rhea said after she exhaled.

"Some lawyer yells at you and you run?" Andy said.

"It's not quite that," Rhea explained. "Yesterday, on the way back from our breakfast meeting, our mutual acquaintance, Shepherd Ladderback, said some things to me about Schuyler that have made me want to be away from this."

"Like what?" Andy urged.

"People who make themselves too much of one extreme can, without warning, become the other. Please do this, for the boy: let Schuyler help you with him, because Schuyler dearly believes in using his abilities to help. But if you ever suspect that Schuyler may be withholding information from you, that he may not be all that he seems—"

"He's been that way from the beginning," Andy said. "He gets creepy sometimes."

"And what might creepy mean to you?" Rhea replied in her psychiatrist's voice.

"Creepy means to me, to watch my back," Andy said.

"Then you understand why I am leaving town for a while," Rhea replied.

The only sound for the rest of the ride came from the car's computer, telling them where they were and where they were going.

14 nothing special

Rhea let them off near Jimmy D's. Rawle and Andy walked a block to Broad Street, where they saw men and women in brightly colored warm-up suits stretching, bending, squatting but mostly standing around exchanging business cards.

The southbound side of Broad Street had been closed off from Locust Street down to South Philadelphia. Andy estimated at least a thousand people, some in warm-up suits, some taking pictures, most just milling around between the metal, collapsible reviewing stand mounted on the sidewalk in front of the concert hall and the sleek red, white and yellow Speed Care ambulance, its many emergency lights blinking, flickering and flashing under the gray sky.

Andy saw the TV news trucks lined up, their sharply groomed reporters milling around the throng. She saw one paunchy male lawyer wearing thermal underwear emblazoned with red hearts look into a camera and say, "With all the crises and negativity facing the profession today, it's nice that we can find a way to laugh a little bit, and raise some money for charity."

For a moment, Andy wished she didn't have Rawle with her, because it can be great fun to be a reporter at even silly public events. Most people are willing to talk to you about why they are here, what they hope to do. You get the varying points of view, the veterans versus the first-timers, the people who traveled long distances as opposed to those who live around the block. You talk to the oldest person you can find, and the youngest. She could imagine a kid telling her something like, "I want to hear the siren!"

Then you use your press pass and slip into the VIP section, where the dignitaries, politicians and celebrities are usually not having a good time. The key when you're in the VIP section is to talk to celebrities for a few minutes, see what they look like when they're not in front of a camera.

But the best thing is to stand off the side and say nothing and keep your ears wide open. You hear the person putting on the event who tends to be worried about dozens of things, or really, really mad that someone who promised to arrive has yet to show up. The celebrities who have arrived chafe at where they're supposed to sit on the reviewing stand, or how much time they'll have in front of the cameras, or how they're going to get through the crowd when the event is over.

If you want to have fun, you go to the VIP catering section and talk to the servers and bartenders. They always have great stories to tell about famous people behaving badly, though coaxing those stories out of them can take a while.

And, because you're in the media, you can watch the event in some exalted place, sometimes on the reviewing stand itself. Of course, there's going to be a pecking order for media: TV is always first, followed by out-of-town media, then radio, then print (the *Standard* gets the best seats, followed by *Liberty Bell Magazine,* with the *Philadelphia Press* and the smaller weekly freebies stuck way in the back). Depending on the event, the media will bring friends, relatives, freeloaders and other curious characters whose job it is to be thrilled that they are with somebody who knows somebody.

Because Rawle had been so excited about seeing Ismail Khan, Andy had planned to use her press pass to get into the VIP area so the boy could meet him. She failed to see anyone who resembled a basketball player, so she asked Rawle if he wanted to look at the ambulance. He nodded rapidly.

The ambulance was surrounded by a ring of yellow police barrier sawhorses. Inside that barrier, a wiry white-haired woman in a winter storm coat and new gray coveralls peered into the ambulance's hood.

"Gina!" Andy called.

The woman glanced at Andy and waved.

"That's Gina Dettweiler," Andy told Rawle. "She has a gas station near where I live and she fixes my car."

"Yo, Andy!" Gina said. She pulled off her grease-stained glove and shook Andy's hand. Andy introduced Rawle.

"Up for some fun, eh?" Gina said. She patted Rawle on his head. "You want to see the inside of a big, bad ambulance?"

Rawle became rigid. Then he started swaying from side to side.

"Not right now," Andy told Gina.

"Hey. I got something to show you." She brought up her left hand to show off a huge diamond engagement ring. "Fellow drives into the station, older fellow, asks for a fill-up. Never seen him before. He's a new law professor at Penn. We get to talking. His wife died. Kids are grown. He's always loved cars. I've always loved smart men. Just this morning, he popped the question."

"You set the date?" Andy asked.

"When I do, can you bring Shepherd with you?"

"And Rawle," she squeezed the boy's shoulder, "if he's up for it."

Rawle asked what he was supposed to be up for.

"A wedding," Andy told him.

Gina again asked Rawle if he wanted to see the inside of the ambulance, but Rawle buried his head in Andy's side. "Guess not, then. I got to check a few more things. You might want to visit that fellow in the chef's hat in that truck down aways. I worked on that truck, too. That Plank fellow says he knows you."

Andy smelled a delicious, eggy buttery aroma and looked down Broad Street at a pale white lunch van with a painted sign on the side that said LE TRUCK.

She grinned. "We've met."

A worried Mafouz indicated to Ladderback he had something important to tell him, but Ladderback quietly shook his head as he let Helen Sylvian, the lunch maitre d', show him and Neely to a table where Cary Grant had once dined, carving his initials in the wood as AL: Archibald Leach.

The dining room was about three-quarters full. The sound system featured Ella Fitzgerald singing "You're the Top" from the Cole Porter songbook. Ladderback made a gallant effort to pull Neely's chair out but the effort wearied him.

She sat grandly, like a queen, and showed him the table where she would dine with Judge Malamato. "He liked that one because he said the light coming off that picture would fall upon me just the way he liked it."

The painting showed a square-rigger at sea, and Ladderback couldn't imagine how any light would make Neely more beautiful than she was now.

"If you don't mind, Shepherd, I will indulge myself," she said as she opened the menu. "I will have what I had with the judge. I expect to cry. I expect to become sentimental. I expect to enjoy this food and your company to great excess."

"Excess can lead to wisdom," Ladderback said.

"I'm going straight for the good old stuff. She turned to the waitress. "Shrimp cocktail, cup of snapper soup, Delmonico steak *rare,* sautéed mushrooms—you do them in butter or olive oil?"

"Either," Ladderback said.

"Butter, then, with lots of garlic," she said. "And steamed asparagus with hollandaise, baked potato loaded with sour cream and chives and, for dessert, I don't care what it is, as long as it's chocolate."

"I'll have the same," Ladderback told the waitress. "And to drink?"

Neely asked, "They still make those dumb martinis with a shake of pepper in them?"

"A round of Jimmy D'Tini's." Ladderback smiled. When they arrived, she proposed a toast. *"Vini, vidi, amati."*

It was a pun on Julius Caesar's famous motto, though instead of, "I came, I saw, I conquered," it was "I came, I saw, I loved."

"Et amo omnes vinci," Ladderback added. And love conquered all.

"It always does." Neely sighed. "Though never in the way we anticipate. You didn't just drag me here to pump me for old stale gossip about Schuyler Nordvahl, I hope."

Ladderback frowned.

"That's how we pull ourselves through the days, isn't it, Shepherd? We think we have no life so we live through others." Sadness passed like a shadow across her face. "You can ask me about him, then, though you must promise me that, if we ever do this again, we will speak only of ourselves."

"I promise," Ladderback said.

"I am your witness," she replied.

Andy asked Rawle if he wanted a treat. He pulled her down so he could whisper "Yes" in her ear.

Inside the truck, a small, thin man with a pointed beard in a fire-engine-red chef's jacket and a white chef's toque with a huge red origami heart dangling from the peak ladled a blob of batter onto a broad crepe pan.

"Yo, Matt!" Andy called.

The eyebrows on the face of the city's most famous restauranteur moved together. He glanced up from the crepe pan, about to scold whoever had the audacity to shout during his on-going quest to make the perfect crepe.

Then he saw Andy about four rows back and said, "My muse!"

He turned to a red-garbed assistant inside the truck and commanded her to "complete the order!" He wiped his hands on a red cloth and stepped down from the truck, opened his arms and gave Andy the second best hug she'd had in days.

Andy would have hugged him back if Rawle hadn't shrieked. Everyone around them, including Matthew Plank, jumped back, bewildered, until Andy introduced Rawle as "my special friend."

Rawle peered at Plank distrustfully.

Plank offered his small hand to Rawle, who turned his face into the worn leather of Andy's bomber jacket.

"Matt is a famous chef," Andy told Rawle.

"I am not famous," he boomed. "I am *notorious!*" He gazed up at Andy and told her she looked "good enough to feed. Your usual?"

"I never had a 'usual' with you." Andy beamed at him.

He grinned so buoyantly he might have floated into the air. "The last time you were on this truck, you had the crushed, fire-tossed almond vodka butter crepe, but I was troubled because I neglected to fold in the Hawaiian chocolate that I tried to seduce you with—"

"Matt!" Andy said, gesturing toward Rawle.

Rawle rushed up to Plank and told him, in slow, halting words, that he had better not make Andy angry.

Andy crouched down, held Rawle's face in her hands and looked into his eyes. "Matt makes me happy with very, very good food and he wants to make something for you."

Plank dropped down beside her.

Rawle's eyes darted from Andy to Plank. Finally, he said to Andy, "N-n-n-othhh-in-ggg sp-sp-ec-i-al."

"Nothing special?" Matt asked. "Where did that come from?"

Andy stood, with Plank following her. "It came from his father," Andy said, her voice low enough so that Rawle might not hear. "When I met Mike McSloan, he said Rawle had a special name, but that the boy was nothing special."

Plank crouched down again to face Rawle. He rubbed his chin. "Usually, when people say to me that they want nothing special, that means they want something, but it should be simple to make. Is that what you mean?"

Rawle didn't move. He started to rock from side to side but stopped when Andy dropped down beside Matt.

"When I was your age," Matt said, "The first thing I ever did as a chef was try take my two favorite foods and mix them together. My favorites were peanut butter and chocolate and they can mix together, but it took me about a month before I could do it without making a mess. A crepe is like a pancake—"

Rawle brought up his electronic talker and rapidly touched the screen. The computer voice said, "I know what K-R-A-Y-P is."

"Do you have a favorite food you'd like me to put in it?"

Rawle began to touch the screen of the talker, but Matt said, "I'd like it if you tell me."

"Ba-nannnnn-ah."

Matt smiled. "Perfect! Easy! The most common fruit consumed in this country in its original state. Would you like anything with the banana in the crepe?"

Rawle shook his head.

"Then that is exactly what you will have. Of course, my bananas aren't quite what you might find in a supermarket. Just as there are varieties of wine, there are varieties of bananas, grown with more care, attention and love than the more typical kind and . . ."

"'Scuse me!" a scrawny, beady-eyed woman in a wide hat said, "You got any more peels?"

Plank told her to check the truck's organic garbage pail.

"The can is in your truck?" the woman said urgently. "Never mind." She rushed to the rear of the truck and asked Plank's assistant to "Give me every banana peel you got."

Andy asked him who the woman was.

Plank shrugged. "I never asked." He went into the truck and began to make Rawle's treat.

Neely Dixit said she had never required the services of Schuyler Nordvahl. "I never had a reason to. I did tell him not to feel so bad a couple of days back, on his birthday, when his malpractice suit got nipped in the bud."

"Do you recall who the opposing counsel was?"

"Mike McSloan. Judge Whet was in the grip in that one."

"In the grip," Ladderback repeated.

The shrimp cocktail arrived and Neely demonstrated with her fingers. "You ever get pickles from a barrel? You get this gripper—"

"I believe they're called tongs."

"You fish around in the brine and you pull out a pickle and you say to yourself, is this the one I'm going to eat, or not? I guess it's the same with lobsters, but they're killed before they're eaten. When you're in a grip, it's much more intense. It's kind of like, all this horrendous, emotional, life-changing crap you see happening to the people in a courtroom is suddenly happening to you. A trial lawyer likes to see himself as always being in the grip, because his reputation is on the line with every litigation, even if the only thing a litigator has to be concerned with is the client paying the final installment of his fee if he loses the case. But, when you got a judge in a gripper, that's very interesting. A lot of people find it refreshing to see a judge in a situation where he can be eaten alive."

"Or not," Ladderback said, dunking his shrimp in the cocktail sauce. "I'm surprised this situation was not covered in our newspaper."

"It was what you would call on the dry side. Nord is not an impressive litigator. Oh, he can talk as well as the next, but he doesn't put on a show. Statute of limitations hearings rarely get any attention unless they're about something really nasty. And even then, they're very much an acquired taste. Nord was arguing that the statute of limitations did not apply to a malpractice suit he wanted to file against Mike McSloan."

"Was his client a John Doe?"

"He was. But Nord withdrew the request for a hearing on the same day. He said the parents got to him, said they didn't want it, but, you ask me, it wasn't the parents. It was John Doe himself. This is supposed to be a rather well-known Doe, and a lot of these Does in the woods, they like to stay in the woods, if you know what I mean."

"Did Judge Whetson attend the proceedings?"

"Never saw him."

"But he was, as you say, in the grip?"

She finished her martini. Ladderback refilled her glass from the shaker.

"Way back when the judge had just got himself elected," she said, "he went around getting himself on the boards of all kinds of organizations for kids. I don't think it cost him anything, and it made him look good. He got himself involved in this summer camp located out around Edwinna, up where I was raised. I know about the camp because my parents used to threaten to send me there, but it was all for kids with real mental and physical problems, and I was just a brat. So there was some child, a foster child from the city, and he was hurt rather badly there. The foster parents got Marathon Mike to sue the camp on their behalf. Mike cut a deal so that, in exchange for dropping the suit and sealing all records regarding it, the boy could get a scholarship to some special city school for problem kids."

The turtle soup arrived. Ladderback added a splash of sherry to the dark brown liquid, stirred it once, brought the spoon to his lips and felt himself move just a little bit closer to heaven.

He came back down to earth and asked if McSloan's settlement occurred before or after McSloan married the judge's sister.

"It happened while he was sleeping with her, and a couple of others that Alma still doesn't know about. Everybody knew Mike and Alma were having their fling, but it isn't the smart thing to speak ill of a judge's family."

"How was this deal the subject of Nordvahl's malpractice suit?" Ladderback asked. "There are very few schools for disabled children in the city. A scholarship from any of those schools is a significant benefit."

She ticked off the details on her fingers. "That camp was insured. McSloan could have got a huge settlement out of that insurance company that would have paid for the boy to go to that school. The settlement might have paid for a lot of other things that the boy might also have needed.

"And if the judge didn't hit the boy, I don't know who did. The judge was visiting the camp when the injury occurred. Part of his family-values thing. He was seen at the camp with the boy. The injury occurred while the boy was on the basketball courts. The child was said to have fallen and hit his head. Judge Whetson's name was nowhere in the documents."

"How did it became known that the judge was responsible?"

"He stayed off the bench while McSloan was working his magic."

"Whatever for?"

"Juries love a judge in the grip. They'll convict to put him out of his misery."

15 accidents can happen

Rawle ate the crepe so fast that Matthew Plank obliged him with another. And another after that. He would have made a fourth if a voice on the loudspeakers hadn't introduced Ismail Khan.

Rawle was too heavy for Andy to hoist on her shoulders, but Gina let him stand on one of the sawhorses surrounding the ambulance. He was enthralled with Khan, a towering, pale, hollow-cheeked pillar of a man in a green cap, matching green muffler and a black chesterfield coat. Khan stood solemnly behind the podium, flanked by two other men in similar dark coats.

At the crest of the applause, he turned to the stairway leading down from the podium. Andy was astonished to see Jermaine Haynes mount the stairs in a new chesterfield coat, with a basketball under one arm.

Jermaine went to the podium, found the wireless microphone, put the microphone under his arm and pulled a folded sheet of paper out of his jacket.

"Excuse me," he said faintly as he unfolded the paper. Then he took the microphone from under his arm and began to read.

"Hello everyone. I am Jermaine Haynes, a Philadelphia public school student in the fifth grade who asked a question: what do you do when somebody takes something important from you. My question appeared in a newspaper with my name on it. Mr. Ismail Khan . . ." He looked behind him. Khan nodded. "He thought there was a better answer. So he asked me to be his voice to tell his story."

He glanced up from the paper he held and saw so many people turned his way that he froze. Khan gently put both hands on Jermaine's shoulders.

"Oh. Um. Excuse me. Now comes Khan's part." He paused and resumed, "Before, I, Ismail Khan, was hurt badly by a foolish, angry man. I fell into a great sleep, and when I awoke, my ability to speak, which was never good, was so much worse that you could say my voice was taken from me. This foolish, angry man never said he was sorry. But he let me go to a special school where I learned that just because one thing was taken from me, I have an in . . ." He hesitated. "In fin . . ."

Khan put his lips next to Jermaine's ear. "I have an infinity of gifts. Much later, I discovered that God is the source of all things. To feel bad that I don't have one thing, is to ignore so many others that I have.

"You might think that not feeling bad is easy for me. This is not true. I felt bad recently when a person told a lie about me. This lie was, that I lost my voice because of drugs. I did not lose my voice. It just doesn't work as good as everyone else's. What I lost was not because of drugs. What I lost was taken from me by a man that I used to hate, but I do not hate him now. I am sorry for him, that he feels he has so few gifts that he must take from others."

Irv Kersaw, in a red, hooded warm-up suit with a neck brace under his chin, fidgeted in his chair on the reviewing stand. He finally stood.

"As a member of the NBA," Jermaine continued, reading Khan's speech, "I am a role model, so, when people ask me why I don't speak, I want to tell them not to listen with their ears, but to listen with their heart. Then you will hear me speaking in the way I play. You will hear me speaking in the way I am with others. You will hear me speaking by what I do, and what I don't do."

Kersaw meandered toward Jermaine.

184

"What I don't do is hurt others back," Jermaine read, "even when they say wrong things about me. In sports, wrong things are said all the time. Nobody knows how a game will turn out. Nobody knows what I am thinking when I play. But I know that the reason I can't speak so you can understand me is not because of drugs. It is because someone hurt me a long time ago and I have not wanted to talk about it, until now, because I felt I was alone—"

Kersaw yanked the microphone out of the boy's hand. "That was really terrific," he said. "How about a big hand for Ismail Khan here?"

The crowd was confused and began some feeble applause that ended with Kersaw ripping the paper out of Jermaine's hand and throwing it on the floor. "I'm not so sure I heard what I just heard," Kersaw continued. "We have about five hundred members of the bar assembled here who love to watch you play, Mr. Khan, and we're all happy you showed up here to let us see what you look like and we'll let you model all the roles you want, but, if you don't mind it when you're slandered in public, and you don't want us to teach those lying sons-of-bitches a lesson they won't forget it—do us all a favor: keep it to yourself, okay?"

Jermaine hid behind Khan, who closed his eyes and moved his lips in what might have been prayer. His fury rapidly melted into pity. His entourage tightened around him and they quickly left the reviewing stand and went into the concert hall, presumably to take the elevator to the VIP parking area below.

Then Andy heard the scrawny, beady eyed woman say, "Accidents can happen."

Neely picked the chocolate "nibbler," which included two chocolate macaroons, two heart-shaped Linzer tortes, two chocolate and macadamia-nut butter cookies, two mocha chocolate crisps, two truffles and, in the center, a single thick, nasty chocolate brownie.

Neely almost cried when she saw the brownie. "I remember why they only give you one brownie."

"It was a Valentine's Day tradition here, and still is," Ladderback said.

"You get two of everything, but one brownie because, if lovers are going to fight, they should fight over something sweet." She told him he could have the brownie.

"I'd rather you have it," Ladderback said.

"I'm really not a brownie *person*," she told him. "Take it."

"After you."

"You first."

Ladderback held up his hands. "You win."

"What if I'd like to lose?"

Ladderback reacted with mock terror. "Weight?"

"What if I just want you to have it?"

He took a knife and divided it in half.

She appeared hurt. "What did you do that for?"

"Pleasure shared is pleasure doubled," Ladderback said.

She narrowed her eyes at him. "You said that as if you've said it before."

"I can say it again."

She took her piece. It was still warm. "You look happy."

"You can say that again."

"I won't, just to spite you," she said, gobbling the brownie. "Oh Shepherd. Chocolate is, always will be, to die for. But, you would know all about that."

"Death by chocolate I would list among the natural causes," Ladderback said, letting his teeth sink into the brownie.

"I read all your obituaries and I haven't seen anything about anyone dying from dessert."

"Sometimes," Ladderback smiled, "you have to fudge it."

She made a face. "So how come you haven't done any obituaries about lawyers?"

"I have. I consulted you about at least one a year ago."

"What about Muckler, McSloan, Altmacher and Newarr?" She strung the names together as if they comprised a law firm.

"When it is a news item and mentioned elsewhere in the newspaper, an obituary is not written. The editors consider it redundant."

"What about Kyle Shvitzer?"

"The one who did the commercials?" Ladderback removed from his satchel a printout of the Law Watch's list of "Lawyers We Could Do Without." Bankruptcy lawyer Kyle "Sweat Equity" Shvitzer was near the bottom.

You couldn't watch late-night network television without seeing Shvitzer, in a suit, in front of a bookcase with his spectacles in his hand, promising that "the right bankruptcy attorney can turn your sweat equity into hard dollars." Sweat equity is the value in labor that improved your home or business—and can protect you and your family from collection agencies."

Shvitzer was on the Law Watch list because he was not only inept at rescheduling his clients' debts, he invented additional fees for legal services he did not perform, and then accepted, as payment, personal items from his clients, including the shirts off their backs.

"They found him this morning. They say he must have turned up the heat and fallen asleep last night in the sauna he has in his office bathroom," Neely said. "But don't you believe it. Somebody must've slipped him something before he went in. You put a turkey in an oven, you want it to stay there. Shvitzer was more of a goat than a turkey. With some of his female clients, he'd tell them he had some kind of backache and he'd take something off her fee if she'd give him a little rubdown in that sauna of his."

Ladderback frowned. "His clients would consent to this?"

"Anybody that walks into the office of a bankruptcy lawyer is beyond desperation. They're already a victim."

"Have you heard any theories as to why he would be murdered?"

"I can give you a legal maxim that isn't in the book, but should be."

She held her finger in the air. "Sleep with your client and you lose your fee."

"Mr. Shvitzer lost his life."

"There's a difference?"

A few of the lawyers around Andy were checking e-mail on their hand-held computers as Irv Kersaw prattled on about how much money the race was raising for local charities and worthy causes.

Andy asked Matt Plank if Rawle could stay with him in the truck. Plank agreed. She told Rawle she would be back in a minute.

Andy pulled a notepad out of her shoulder bag, rushed up to the beady-eyed woman, identified herself as a reporter for the *Philadelphia Press,* and asked her what she was doing.

Then Andy got what reporters call a "mouthful"—a torrent of words so swift and complicated that she just had to be still and let it wash over her.

The woman started out by saying that she used to own a parking lot in South Philadelphia and that Kersaw had sued her because someone had slipped on a banana peel and broke a "verdabray" in his spine and she had to sell her lot and the only thing that kept her from "jumping off a cliff" were the novels of Bette Newarr but then she found a SUPER lawyer who sued—

"Do you mean Schuyler Nordvahl?" Andy asked.

She winked. "Coulda been. And he got Kersaw to CEASE AND DE-SIST and we got a LOT of money in the deal and we moved to the shore and my husband got into his investments but when I heard what Irv Kersaw said on his show about Bette Newarr—it was just too HORRIBLE!" the woman shrieked. "They say Bette died because she had that bad ink, but the REAL reason is that he broke her heart! Artists are sensitive people! They should NOT have to put up with an obnoxious, sarcastic, disgusting and pointless jerk!"

Andy asked the woman her name.

The woman was too busy trashing Kersaw to tell her, then she paused and asked if Andy did, in fact, work for the *Philadelphia Press.*

Andy said she did.

The woman made a face. "I can't believe I am standing on the same STREET with you, especially since your newspaper printed that LIE about Bette not even writing her books. Could you write her books? Somebody has to. Now, if you'll excuse me. . . ."

She rushed off.

Andy looked for her in the crowd and then lost her. She went back to the truck and checked on Rawle. Then she turned to the reviewing stand.

"Now, let's get to the main event," Kersaw said. "All participants must sign a release so if you slip and fall, it's not my ass, okay? If you didn't sign a release, your presence in this event will indicate you agree to all conditions and limitations set forth, *et cetera, ipso facto, illegitimus non corundum, ad hoc agricula conc, id est spittle houc!*"

Some of the lawyers applauded.

"According to precedents set a few years back," Kersaw continued, "the official starting gun has been replaced by a loud sucking sound. As soon as you hear that, you are to proceed by any means necessary in a southerly direction down Broad Street behind the ambulance. Everyone following the ambulance must carry a briefcase filled with at least five pounds of unnecessary paperwork. Drop the briefcase, and you're out of here! Because we have Matthew Plank sponsoring us this year—hiya Matt!—the ambulance will stop in front of Matt's newest eatery, Rivincita, where anyone with a briefcase will receive free food and booze. Anyone who doesn't have a briefcase will be billed by the hour or any fraction thereof. Beyond that, I don't care what happens. I don't care if you trip the guy next to you. I don't care if you get in a truck and run over a half-dozen people in front of you. I'm going to be in the front seat of that ambulance laughing at all you suckers. Anything in the way of low blows, prejudicial behavior, grandstanding or witness tampering is okay by me, pending litigation."

He paused to acknowledge some cheers and razzberries, when suddenly his right leg turned out from under him and he went down.

At least three of the lawyers in the crowd hoisted their briefcases and rushed forward.

But Kersaw managed to pull himself up and, red-faced, he held a banana peel in his hand and waved it at the crowd. "Did you see that? I just want to say that what you just saw," he said into the microphone, "does not invalidate my famous Second Vertebra Claim. Accidents *can* happen, and even though damages don't occur doesn't mean they shouldn't occur." He rubbed his forehead. "I apologize if that doesn't make sense but . . . I could've died from that and . . . I didn't!"

He bowed to the applause. "Counselors." He paused, listening to his voice echo off the buildings lining the long, broad street. "Start your depositions!"

Then there was a loud *plock!* as Kersaw dropped the microphone. A crowed gathered around him. Someone screamed.

It would later appear in the *Philadelphia Standard,* the *Philadelphia Press*'s late edition, all local television news programs, a dozen radio stations, five entertainment industry house organs and thirty local and regional blogs, including PR/Hell, that "Slip" Kersaw did indeed suffer from Second Vertebra Syndrome.

Or at least, he did until he turned to go down the stairs to the waiting ambulance, where he slipped on the printed copy of Ismail Khan's speech.

And died shortly thereafter.

divided

Ladderback heard the front door of the restaurant close. The mark of Neely's kiss on his cheek was still warm on his skin.

He had promised her that they would have lunch next week, and they would only talk about themselves.

Until then, he had to go back to the newspaper. He retrieved his hat and coat from the cloakroom and picked up his satchel. He went toward the steps near the dumbwaiter that brought the food up from the downstairs kitchen. He did not see Mafouz, but he didn't ask for him. Ladderback was in that slightly woozy, well-fed daze that can only come from magnificent food, drink and great company.

He hadn't felt this good in a long time, and he didn't want Mafouz's concern to mar that mood. If Mafouz found him before he left, he would talk to him. If he didn't, Ladderback would go down the steps, through the kitchen to the entrance that opened into the underground concourse connecting portions of Chestnut Street to Market Street, go into the *Press* Building's sub-basement and take the elevator up to the newsroom.

Which he did.

He entered a newsroom that crackled with a purposeful, low-level anxiety as reporters struggled to appear as if they were working, or tried mightily to finish their work. In a corner by the copydesk, Bardo Nackels, the newspaper's bulky, slovenly night city editor, who liked to linger into the day shift, wiped his eyes as he tried to come up with a headline long enough to fit into a box on the newspaper's front page. "Slip a dee do dah?" the enormous editor said to himself. "Slip Sliding Away?"

Ladderback was ignored as he went to the coatrack by the lavatories. He removed his hat first, then his scarf, gloves and the raincoat that had never felt a drop of rain. Then he went to the copydesk and saw a photo of Irv Kersaw in the box. He saw the headline Nackels was trying to write. He tried to ask Nackels, in as even at one as possible, if a news item had appeared about Kyle Shvitzer.

"The one they found in the sauna?" Nackels replied. He did a search on his terminal for Shvitzer's name. Nothing came up. Then he pulled up Press Editor Howard Lange's "Off My Chest" column. The date in the header above the article told Ladderback that the column would run tomorrow. The title, called a head, was CONTEMPT OF COURT.

"I think we can just sort of stick him in here," Nackels said. He hit a few keys, and, to the list of names of lawyers who had died in the last few days, he added another. He glanced at Ladderback and told him he "shouldn't get so worked up. It's like Lange says in the column, people die every day."

Ladderback said, "Some of these deaths could be linked."

"Like it's some kind of conspiracy? C'mon Shep. For most of our readers, a handful of dead lawyers isn't going to make a difference."

"It is our obligation to encourage our readers to think about important things," Ladderback said.

"You mean, it's our obligation to make readers think about what's important to *us*. I think Lange says it all here."

Ladderback went to the windowless corner of the newsroom where his desk faced a wall, beside Andy's. The mail on Andy's desk was so high that it spilled over onto the death notices on Ladderback's desk. He saw one of the envelopes had a two-letter return address: IK, and a Gladwyn post-office box.

Gladwyn was only a few miles from the Philadelphia city limits, but it was much further removed, culturally and economically. The tiny hamlet had the highest concentration of Main Line new money inside the Blue Route. It was a rocky, hilly no-man's land of narrow, twisting roads where enormous houses hung from steep, forbidding slopes.

One of those houses belonged to Danny Bleutner.

Beneath the death notices on Ladderback's desk was a copy of today's *Press* and the competing newspaper, the *Philadelphia Standard*.

If he had arrived earlier, he would have spent the morning reading the *Press,* checking to see how his obituaries had appeared. Then he would get a scissors and clip his obituaries, as well as articles that interested him from the newspapers and the numerous magazines to which he subscribed. He would add these to the folders in the vast file cabinet that took up the entire wall beside him. Then, when he felt motivated, he would scan the death notices and select a handful of candidates for obituaries he might write.

He signed on to his terminal and went to the Law Watch list. Shvitzer was on it. Then he called up Howard Lange's column.

> If I were just another a paranoid, connect-the-dots conspiracy theorist instead of an editor of a major metropolitan daily newspaper, I'd come to the inevitable conclusion, after looking back on the events of the last few days, that being a lawyer in this city has suddenly become hazardous to your health.
>
> And I would be no better than what lawyers say of a man who thinks he knows enough of the law to defend himself in court: a fool for a client.
>
> I don't know much about the law, but I know enough about this city to say, without fear of contradiction, that people die, all the time, for all kinds of reasons. Death isn't good news, and, as far as I'm concerned, it doesn't even qualify as news, unless the person who died is well known.

Ladderback stopped reading the column. He found it confusing, meandering, patronizing, insulting. To Ladderback, death was the *only* news. A victim's occupation, wealth, fame or infamy made no difference. Death demanded that we understand every life as unique, important and irreplaceable.

And to take a life was the ultimate arrogance.

He saw a light blinking on his telephone, indicating he had at least one voice-mail message.

He played it back and heard Mafouz's panicky voice. "Mr. Ladderback, I tried to tell you when you were at the restaurant but I understand you do not want to be disturbed. This morning, we received a hand-delivered letter from the city Office of Revenue. It says we owe $2.1 million in back taxes that Mr. Goohan has failed to pay over several years."

Ladderback called the restaurant immediately. "Whitey paid his taxes," Ladderback told Mafouz.

"If I could have spoken with you, I would have told you that I have spent the morning going over what records he has. What is mentioned here, I have not seen before in all my experiences of doing business in this country, but this situation is similar to one encountered by a cousin who was also operating a business in the city. The Office of Revenue was shown to be in error, but by the time the error was ascertained, my cousin's legal expenses were so high that he was forced to sell his business."

"His lawyer could have sued the city to recover fees," Ladderback said.

"Mr. Pescecane, my cousin's lawyer, advised against it."

"Would that be Severio Pescecane?"

"Are there two of them?"

"One is more than sufficient," Ladderback said.

"This amount, Mr. Ladderback, is so high. I'm afraid that, with this additional burden, my family will not be able to purchase the restaurant."

"Did Mr. Bleutner call after this letter arrived?" Ladderback asked.

"Someone from his office did, yes, Mr. Ladderback. He said Mr. Bleutner did not hear from you and expects your call. I know that Mr.

Bleutner is a very powerful lawyer. Do you think that he would help us with this tax matter?"

"Mr. Bleutner has helped us enough, Mr. Mafouz," Ladderback grumbled. He asked Mafouz to fax the documents to him.

He then pulled from his memory the telephone number and left a message for Osiris Murphy, a former forensic accountant now surviving as a professional poker player, to call him as soon as possible.

He brought up the Law Watch list again. He considered how the lawyers had been dispatched. Then he unwrapped a copy of the guest list for Nordvahl's fiftieth birthday celebration.

Ladderback could connect some of the guests on that list—most of them Nordvahl's former clients—to the assaults on the lawyers. He stopped with McSloan. Mike McSloan had been thrown off a computerized exercise machine that had speeded up suddenly. How could that have happened?

Ladderback remembered the man at Nordvahl's birthday party who repaired computers and televisions. He found the telephone number of Raphael O'Connor in an online business directory under electronics repair. Raphael O'Connor answered before the phone could ring. Ladderback identified himself. "I'm calling regarding a mutual acquaintance, a Mr. Schuyler Nordvahl. He told me that you have some facility with computers."

"What I am is the last television repairman standing in Chester County," O'Connor said.

"Standing?"

"I'm sitting down right now, but you know what I mean. I repair most consumer electronics equipment, including computers, but TVs are my first love. I don't know how far back you go, but I used to love the ones that had the tubes in 'em, that had to warm up. Thing is, nobody fixes TVs anymore. By the time I get the parts and put them in, they go out and buy a new set. But I still love them. I got myself quite an assortment, including an RCA TRK-12. I don't expect you would know what that is."

Ladderback asked him to hold. He went to his file cabinet, found a folder marked TELEVISION, COLLECTIBLE. He opened the folder, glanced at the articles saved inside and returned to the telephone.

"It is an early kinescope television system that used a mirror to project an image on a twelve-inch screen," Ladderback said. "RCA's first model for the mass market. It's sale price was six hundred dollars."

"I got a DuMont Teleset, too," O'Connor said. "You know about the DuMont network?"

He removed the file, "TELEVISION, HISTORY." "Named for Allen Dumont, the inventor of the first practical television receiver. He established his own network in an attempt to rival RCA for dominance in the early days of television broadcasting. The first *Honeymooners* sketch by the comedian Jackie Gleason appeared on the Dumont Network."

"Are you a collector?"

"I am not. But I have a question." He glanced over at Andy's desk. "An associate of mine at the newspaper writes a column under the name of Mr. Action, in which we provide advice and information to our readers regarding consumer items, services and problems."

"If it's about TV, I'm the man. You know there were once two different color TV systems? CBS and RCA? Guess who won."

Ladderback glanced at his file. "RCA. The first color set was made by Westinghouse in nineteen fifty-four."

"I got an RCA CT-100, made the same year. Sold for a thousand dollars. The wood's got a little dry rot, but it's the genuine item."

"My question relates more to modern devices," Ladderback said. "As you're aware, many devices come with handheld remote controls. A reader has asked if it is possible to buy a device that would control everything."

"In the same way there were two different color TV systems, there are different remote-control systems. Some are line-of-sight infrared. Others are low-frequency radio transmission. Others are wireless computer networks. The system that gives you the most flexibility is a wireless network. You can get a handheld computer and adapt that to a lot of remote operations."

"Would this system be able to override another?"

"I'm not sure what you mean by 'override.' If you have two identical controls, the computer will respond to the most recent command. You can protect a system with levels of access codes, like the pin number you use when you get your money out of an automatic teller. Now, if someone else gets ahold of your code, or codes, you're as good as cooked, because the controls respond to the codes. In complicated systems, like the kind you have in buildings that control the environmental systems—heating, cooling, lighting, elevators, door locks, security, that kind of thing—you have several codes that can change by the day and the hour."

"Are there computer programs that can crack these codes?"

"You can find them on the Internet but, if it's security your reader is concerned about, the weakest link is always the human one. You get employees that write codes down because they can't remember them, and then leave them right on their desk where anybody can walk by and copy them down. Or they'll talk about them in the bar after work. Sometimes you can have a case of a disgruntled employee—say, they fire a fellow and he wants to get back at the company."

"So if a reader wants some kind of master control system, a handheld computer would be simple enough?"

"The technology is constantly changing, and you do have competing systems, but you already have the capability to run just about everything with a single handheld. That's what I do for a living. I design proprietary remote-operated environmental control systems for commercial, industrial and residential uses."

Ladderback heard a rise in activity on the newsroom's city desk, where information came in about events occurring within local government and the numerous neighborhoods. "And Mr. Nordvahl is your favorite customer?"

"Not really. He likes being up to date on the technology. I help him stay current. He's had some liability cases involving control systems and I've consulted with him on those. If he's got a problem with what he's got at his mill, I'll come out and look at it. He'll call me and ask me how so-and-so can do such-and-such, and I'll tell him."

Ladderback turned and saw Bardo Nackels, the night city editor, arise slowly from his perch on the top of the U-shaped copydesk to see what the fuss was about. "Surely Mr. Nordvahl has not represented you in any legal capacity?"

"Never had him do any legal work for me. No, my relationship with Sky Nordvahl began when he bought the mill. He had that CT-100 stuck up in an attic in that miller's house, and he called me down to take a look at it, and I told him quite honestly that he had one of the most highly prized pieces of double-O tech in the world—"

Ladderback located the word in an article in his TELEVISION, HISTORY file. "Double-O means old or obsolete technology?"

"That's correct. You're quite well informed, I'm happy to say."

Ladderback heard applause from the city desk. "Another one bites the dust!" Nackels exclaimed. He held his fist in the air. "That harpy represented my second wife!" A phone rang and Nackels went for it.

Ladderback accessed the city editor's desktop from his terminal. The *Press*'s police reporter, from her desk beside the dispatcher's den, had sent an e-mail informing them that an ambulance had been dispatched to handle an apparently accidental fatality in a Center City office building. The victim had been tentatively identified as the lawyer Roberta Zetzmeer.

"So I made no bones about what Sky had there," O'Connor continued in Ladderback's ear, "and he let me take it off his hands for nothing. He even helped me carry it out."

"Mr. Nordvahl can be generous," Ladderback said, pulling up the Law Watch list.

"It's more than generosity. Sky Nordvahl has that attitude that we're all in this together, and that what benefits one, benefits all. He refers other people to me that have double-O tech. I won't do appraisals, but, if you or any of the readers have any old technology, and you want to get a handle on what it is, I'll be happy to share with you what I know. Right now, there's a terrific market for the early Apple, Commodore and TRS-80 desktops."

Ladderback thanked him for his time and ended the conversation. He read on the list that Zetzmeer had been called "the Great Divider" for the way she generated unnecessary animosity between parties in a divorce.

"Damn!" Nackels said to the day city editor. "We got this guy works at the building on the tip line. He says it's really messy. Zetzmeer was doing that elevator thing—the same damned thing she did to me, where she stands with one foot in the elevator and the other in the hall, yelling her head off—but this time, the elevator, without any warning and with the doors still open, dropped two floors."

Nackels made a face. "It just about cut her in half."

17 sentimental

Rawle had been silent for the subway surface car ride up to West Philadelphia and Baltimore Avenue. They got out and walked toward the Kendall School.

While they waited in the enormous parlor at the front of the mansion that survived as the "old wing" for Mr. Deheulos (*mister, not doctor,* Rawle had typed on Andy's laptop), Rawle opened his building set and constructed a model of the school. He told Andy, by typing on her laptop, which was the food room, the sleep room, the toy room, the "learn" room. He called the parlor, a peculiar octagonal enclosure that had been stripped of its decorative features and filled with mismatched furniture, odd pillows and cushions scattered across a dark green industrial carpet, the "talk" room.

Andy sat a few feet away from him on a couch, a pad and pen in her hand, and then stood when Sosa Deheulos introduced himself. Prematurely gray, with a drooping gut pushing out a vest that reminded Andy of a baccarat board, Deheulos let himself drop into a gaudy, paisley-patterned upholstered chair that had been pushed back against a paneled wall that was painted a milky brown.

His eyes went to the pad Andy held. "What I say about a student of this school is not for public consumption without the permission from a parent or adult guardian."

"I'm his guardian now, but don't worry about it." She closed the pad. She thought of the column she had written earlier that day. "Tell me how I can help Rawle."

"You can't. Stay calm when you're around him. When you get tired, throw him a ball."

Andy didn't like the sound of that. Rawle wasn't a pet.

Deheulos opened Rawle's file. "Our athletic director reports that he shows excellent spatial awareness and hand-eye coordination. He doesn't appear to understand the nature of team play. Give him a ball, though, and he can occupy himself."

"I want to tell you that being with Rawle has been the most rewarding thing I've ever done," Andy said. "If I knew it would be this good, I would have gone into this."

"I've read what you've written about him,," Deheulos replied. "You're sentimentalizing him. You are trying to fit him into a myth of what you expect from life. This is almost as bad as the ancient Greeks, who killed these children, or exposed them on the side of a mountain for the animals to devour, because they could not care for them."

Andy wanted to strangle the man. "I just want him to be himself."

Deheulos shook his head ever so slightly. "And how are you coping with his dysphonia?"

"I *listen* to him."

He wasn't impressed. "Be aware that there is no cure for his condition," he said, his attention on documents in the file, "though some specialists have talked about injecting Botox into the larynx, which prevents some spasticity so an approximation of normal speech is achieved for a limited amount of time. His father refused to authorize those treatments. His father refused to accept that his son had a permanent speech defect. He believed that his son was speaking badly to annoy him."

"He was wrong," Andy said.

Deheulos turned a page of the file. "Rawle's mother discouraged her son's participation in team sports."

"Why would she do that?"

"Another child with profound developmental difficulties went to this school and became quite adept at sports," Deheulos said. "Mrs. Mc-Sloan did not want her son to become another Ismail Khan."

"Ismail Khan went here?" Andy said.

Rawle looked at her and nodded.

"He wasn't Ismail Khan when he was here. He was James Michael Gravatte and he was recovering from injuries related to massive cranial trauma. Those injuries severely limited his speaking capability. His ability with sports was quite extraordinary. In the brain, the areas related to speech and hand-eye coordination are quite close. If one fails to develop, or is impaired, the other can overdevelop and compensate. Again, I say this to you in confidence. We were asked to comment about Khan's time at our school for the *Liberty Bell* article but we did not because Mr. Khan did not want us to."

"But if you'd said something, the magazine might not have printed that story about him and the drugs," Andy said.

"We don't volunteer information about our students without their permission, or the permission of their parents or guardians."

"So the story about the drug overdose is not true?"

Deheulos turned his attention to the file. "Rawle is variably acutely sensitive to touch. I've seen some of the boys push him on the floor, or against a wall, and he just stays there, stuck to the wall as if he had glue on his clothes. Other times, you raise a hand near him, and he'll scream. He has an intense understanding of spatial relationships. Take him through a room once, and he'll know where everything is, and, when he comes back, if anything was moved around, sometimes a thing as minor as a book in a different position on a shelf or a change in a position of a chair, he will show you and try to change it back. If he can't change it, he'll slip into that trance state, where his attention will go away. Or he'll move from side to side. You've seen that? Good."

Deheulos folded his arms. "How much of this are you writing

about? You know there are invasion-of-privacy laws regarding disabled individuals."

"I'm not writing anything that Rawle wouldn't want to hear about himself," Andy said. "I discuss what I'm writing with him."

"Does he express an opinion?"

"On the ride over I told him about tomorrow's column. He said I left out too many things. I do. I haven't figured out what I should say about his uncle."

"Why should you say anything about Harlan Whetson?" Deheulos said.

Rawle made a shriek so sharp and hideous that it could have cut bone. Andy jumped off the couch and was at his side just as his arms locked around her so fiercely that she could not move. She found herself looking into his big, wide open, empty eyes.

Deheulos became irritated. "What he says regarding his relationships with others cannot be considered to be reliable. You can't be sure of anything he says."

"I *trust* him," Andy said. "He has a right to be listened to. And he has a right to act on what he knows."

Deheulos shook his head. "The rights of the disabled have always been problematic, especially for those who cannot express themselves normally and appear to lack mental capabilities."

Deheulos continued to go through the file. "Rawle has no apparent food or environmental allergies. He has no chronic illnesses. He occasionally fails to react to low temperatures—cold air, cold water, snow on the ground, cold compresses when he's had an injury."

"Just tell me what he needs," Andy said, hugging Rawle even tighter.

Deheulos closed the file. "What he needs is to continue at our school. He has friends here. He has things to do here. In the long term, he needs someone created by God to care for him. I am not that person. His father wasn't. I won't comment about his mother."

Andy shuddered.

Deheulos closed the file and put it on the couch. "As per Mr. Nordvahl's instructions, I've also included copies of treatment logs and incident reports for the last six months. You can read it when you have the opportunity."

Rawle pulled away from Andy. She stayed on the floor beside him.

"Keep in mind, disabled children are *not* defective human beings," Deheulos said. "If anything, we—the so-called functional personalities— are defective because we cannot see that these people are miracles, in every sense of the word." He stood. "May I call you a cab?"

Andy looked at Rawle and didn't see a miracle. Miracles were momentous things and events that you couldn't explain. She saw a boy, a boy playing with a building set.

"I live close to this place," she said. "We're going to walk to my home, then we're going to get dinner and go to my school."

He seemed amused. "You have a school?"

"My best friend teaches a self-defense class," Andy said. "I open the place up for her and lead the warm-up."

Deheulos was skeptical. "And you think that will be good for him?"

"What I learned in that class saved my life," Andy said. She glanced at Rawle, who was still seated but was rocking from side to side. "It just might save his."

On the way out, Rawle led Andy to a section of the old mansion that had been converted into offices. On the right side of the heavy, cherry wood-paneled hall were framed portraits of former directors. On the left were past and current board members.

Rawle stopped in front of a portrait of a jowly, pink-faced man in spectacles with straight blond hair parted in the middle, wearing a dark judicial robe. A small sign on the painting identified the board member as the Honorable Harlan Whetson.

"You're basically fucked," Osiris Jonathan Murphy told Ladderback on the phone. "This is the kind of shit lawyers pull all the time. They make work for themselves. The tax codes applying to businesses in any major municipality are either onerous, or so contradictory as to be incomprehensible. Unless you go in with some kind of political juice, you're taxed so much your business won't make it to the first quarter. The only thing that can save you is to hire a law firm like Bleutner's, who cuts a deal with the city and you pay a lot less, providing you make a nice donation to the political campaign of whoever wins the next election. Then you're okay until they raise your assessment. You either pay the city the assessment, or you pay it to Bleutner, and things go back to normal until the next election."

"Jimmy D's has been a part of the city longer than I've been alive," Ladderback replied, the bustle of the newsroom around him rising to a slow crescendo as the evening deadline approached. "There must be someone to whom I can appeal."

"Shepherd, a lawyer has made trouble for you. You're going to need another lawyer to get out of it. There's this guy I heard about, he once taught an ethics seminar at one of the law schools, Penn, I think it was. He's competent and he doesn't charge a dime and he hates guys like Bleutner. He's got some Dutch-sounding name. I think it's Schuyler—"

"Nordvahl."

"Find him. Talk to him. Get him on your side. If you don't, if you try to fight this yourself, or you get somebody who doesn't know his way around city hall, you're going to wake up with a lien on the property, which will screw up any chance you have of selling it in the immediate future. And then they'll drag you into tax court, where you will not only lose your shirt, but they will charge you for the privilege of taking it from you."

"There must be a better way."

"You know about death, I know about taxes. Get a lawyer, or kiss it good-bye."

Ladderback changed the subject. "I have one other thing to ask you. When you were doing fraud investigations, you had experience with proceedings in which the documents resulting from the investigations were sealed."

"Usually as part of the plea bargain with white-collar crooks."

"What happens to the documents?"

"They are listed and copied. The prosecution gets a full set. The defendant gets a full set, though he usually doesn't take them home. Usually the defendant's lawyer arranges for storage." Sometimes the documents have a convenient way of getting lost, but, in situations where reputations are at stake, it's in everybody's interest to keep those documents right where they can be found. Of course, leaking them to you media guys can get the leaker, as well as the media guy, held in contempt of court and put in jail. You're not going to do that, are you, Shep?"

"I don't expect to," Ladderback said. He said good-bye and felt himself slip into a dour mood. If he were in his apartment, he would listen to music or watch television. In the newsroom, he could only work, or read.

He looked over at Andy's desk. Then he accessed her column, the one that would run tomorrow. Its headline was I KNOW WHAT TO DO.

He read it and it was so good—no, it wasn't good, it was magnificent. He had admired her tenacity as a reporter and her aggressive pursuit of the facts, even if it was just a matter of Mr. Action helping a reader make sense out of an expired repair warranty.

But this was a voice he hadn't heard. Andy had described an ordinary romp in the snow, and then showed how disquietingly mysterious the boy was. Then she asked, very gently, what must be done with people like this boy? How are we to cope with people who don't fit into any category, people who suffer as we do, who experience pleasure as we do, but who are also difficult and terrifying, but deserve every good thing we would want for ourselves?

And she answered it: we trust them. When they stumble or fall, we help them up. When they tell us they know what to do, we believe them, as much as we would believe ourselves.

That something that great could find its way into a tabloid crammed with fatuous editorials and sensational accounts of murder, disaster, overpaid athletes losing sports games, celebrities behaving badly, politicians behaving even worse—as well as his own little page of obituaries—raised his spirits as no music could.

Then his breath grew short. He felt dizzy. He gripped the edge of his desk and told himself that at the age of sixty-three, he shouldn't be feeling this bad.

He called Rhea Nordvahl on the phone. She picked up on the first ring because, she told him, she was still rescheduling appointments, and she would have to postpone his therapy sessions because she was going out of town for a few days.

Ladderback didn't ask her why she was going out of town. He asked her if she would care to have dinner with him that evening at Jimmy D's, and she said yes!

18 a miracle

Rawle said nothing as he followed Andy several blocks to Forty-second Street. He walked clutching his building set tightly across his torso, with his coat open. After a few gusts of chilly, diesel-scented Philadelphia air, Andy tried to button him up. He refused.

He looked at the three-and four-story Victorian mansions along Forty-second Street, their ornamental woodwork and broad porches painted dark brown, gray or green. He began to rock from side to side.

Andy waited. The wind raked across her face and she tried to think of what she could do while he was gone inside his head. She talked.

"We have time for some food. There isn't much in my apartment, but there's a café down the block where we can get sandwiches. After that we're going to take my car to the school we're going to tonight: the teacher is a woman who got hurt a few months ago. Her name is Lucia Cavaletta-Ferko. She's feeling much better now, but there are things she can't do, so she asks me to help her. She's my best friend and—"

He stopped rocking. His face became contorted as he said, without looking at her, "b-es-t f-f-f-fr-ien-d."

"I've known her for almost eight years," Andy said.

He became angry and it took him a full minute to tell her that *he* was her best friend, and that you can't have two best friends.

"I can," Andy said. "You're my best *boy* friend. Lucia's my best *girl* friend."

He frowned at that, as if he didn't quite believe her. Then his face went blank and he began walking.

He followed Andy up a short walkway over a few square yards of dingy green grass to the porch of an Italianate Victorian crowned by a rectangular cupola. She took him through the front door, pulled it closed (the landlady was replacing the spring closing mechanism), removed a clot of junk mail from her box and led Rawle up three flights of stairs, down a sparse, wood-paneled corridor that held a variety of spicy cooking aromas (her landlady was from Calcutta and had offered to teach her how to cook as a ploy to have Andy meet her son Shivkumar who was studying to be a radiologist and wanted to be a novelist like Vikram Seth "but not write big books") to a narrow door that Andy opened with another key.

The door opened into a single windowless room with a tiny kitchen, a tinier closet and a door leading to a bathroom so narrow that it had taken her months to learn how not to bang her hip on the sink while stepping into the shower.

In the center of the room was a flight of steep, open stairs leading up. Rawle shot up those stairs. Andy let him go, trusting that he wouldn't get into trouble. She took off her coat, hung it in the closet that smelled of laundry that really should be done *soon* and moved into the kitchen that smelled of garbage that should have gone out last night.

She put the mail and her shoulder bag down on the tiny dinette table and sat in the chair where—it seemed like a year ago—she had her morning tea and ate whatever was left in the refrigerator for her breakfast.

She took a single breath, inhaling the sweet and sour scents of home— *her* home. She felt the heat from the floor vent rise around her legs.

It felt good to be home.

Then she rose and put a kettle of water on the twin-burner stove. She found her teacup in the small sink and rinsed out yesterday's leaves. Then she opened the cupboard to rows of tea tins. She found her favorite—a dark, brutally strong *keemun* that Matthew Plank had given her for Christmas, and, beside it, the spectacular Vietnamese jasmine tea from Lucia.

She called up to Rawle. Did he want a cup of hot chocolate?

She heard no reply. Did that mean no or yes? She took down the "Official Civilian Police Academy" cup, a present from Lucia's husband, Police Sergeant Vinnie Ferko. The water came to a boil. She filled the cups with powdered cocoa, added sugar and hot water, put them on a small tray, and carried them upstairs.

Her bedroom was inside the cupola, with windows on all four sides. The windows were shielded by wooden blinds and billowy, off-white curtains. From the queen-size futon mattress on her platform bed, she could pretend that she was in a four-poster bed that, on a nice day, was open to the trees and the sky.

She saw Rawle on the small stretch of floor between the bed and a row of bookshelves, building a model of the cupola. She put the tray beside him. He put a plastic brick in place, then moved over and stared down at the steam rising from the cups.

Andy sat on the edge of her bed and watched him. Then she let her mind wander to the barren roof tiles and naked tree branches outside. She checked her cell-phone messages.

She called Logan Marius Brickle. "You're home," Logo said.

"Temporarily." Andy sighed, leaning back on her bed.

"You sound tired."

"I'm relaxing."

"We should celebrate."

"Not tonight."

"At the end of your how-to-beat-up-the-bad-boys class. You'll be all sweaty so you'll feel embarrassed and out of place if I take you someplace hideously expensive."

"I can't, Logo."

"What do you mean—*can't?* We're supposed to be *trying* to sleep together."

"Logo, have you read the paper?"

"Yours? No. I know I should, but Mr. Action's earnest efforts to enlighten the wage-earning rabble haven't been thrilling me lately. It's not your fault, you just work there but . . . how can I say this without really pissing you off?"

"You've already pissed me off," Andy said. "You haven't seen *anything* that's been going on in the paper?"

"We get the *Standard* delivered to the bank's executive offices and, until I move my mother out of the chairman's suite and I remodel her bathroom, I don't really have the privacy to read *two* newspapers. Frankly, Andy, any tabloid that isn't *Barron's* is just not *seen* on the executive floor."

Andy closed *her* eyes and reminded herself that Logo's *thing* was being annoying, that his obnoxiousness hid a deep vulnerability, that he really did care about her and he was probably the closest male friend she would ever have.

But she was in no mood to be teased, insulted or otherwise annoyed.

"You are one cruddy boyfriend," she told him. "I shouldn't have to tell you to read the paper. It should be enough that I write for it, that it's part of my life and you should care about what I do and be interested because I'm doing it!"

"You've been doing *it?*" he said in mock surprise. "With *whom?*"

She cut the connection, sat up in bed and didn't see Rawle. She called for him. She went over to the edge of the bed and peered down the stairs. She clambered out of the bed and went halfway down the stairs.

Her apartment's door was open. She didn't see Rawle in the hall.

She grabbed her coat and ran down the stairs.

Ladderback returned to the restaurant at 5 P.M. and pored over the old tax documents Mafouz had retrieved.

"Perhaps we should consult an accountant," Mafouz said.

"Whitey never used one. He paid his own taxes," Ladderback replied, utterly confused about where to begin.

"I recall Mr. Goohan mentioning that he made other kinds of payments," Mafouz said.

Ladderback's eyes went to the blotter. "Has anyone from Mr. Bleutner's office called about his father's birthday?"

"No one," Mafouz said. "I ordered the olives."

Ladderback went to the telephone. "It's time we made the father aware of the sins of the son."

"Mr. Ladderback, we have no proof that this tax matter has anything to do with Mr. Bleutner."

"We don't need any," Ladderback said, dialing.

The front door was ajar. Andy ran out to the porch. It was dark enough to make the street-lights flicker on.

A car raced up the street. She followed the glare of its headlights, searching for a small boy in a red down jacket who could move really fast when he wanted, who was insensitive to cold, who had never been to this part of the city and would probably get lost. West Philadelphia was dangerous enough for normal people and downright lethal for a person who could not see danger, who would not recognize a threatening glance from another human being, who might just rush into a street and not see a car or a bus coming.

Then she heard a sob.

She turned around and saw him on the porch, his face wet with tears.

She ran to him and he wouldn't look at her. Then he told her, very slowly, that he was not a cruddy boyfriend.

"Rawle, I was talking on a telephone to someone else. I wasn't talking about you."

He began to sway from side to side.

"Oh, Rawle, I'm so sorry. . . ." She tried to hug him and he shrieked and ran to the edge of the porch.

He resumed his swaying and, just for a moment, Andy got mad. Here she was, trying to help him, looking out after him, watching her step

213

everywhere she went, and she has a phone conversation and he goes off and she just felt like leaving the kid, turning her back on him and, if he didn't follow her back to her apartment, he could just stay here on the porch and—

She stopped herself. This was an irrational, angry feeling and she regretted it immediately. Then she was shocked—how *could* she have this feeling about anyone? How could she be like the ancient Greeks who left disabled children to die on the side of a mountain? How could she be that horrible?

She didn't know. She closed her eyes and sank into a fetal position with her back against the wall until she heard someone breathing. She opened her eyes and saw Rawle standing in front of her, his right hand holding some branches he'd pried off a holly bush.

He said they were for her.

She put her hand around his. His skin was very cold.

He struggled to say each word as distinctly as he could but they still came out choppy. "I ammmmm y-y-y-ourrr b-es-tttt b-boyf-f-f-friend."

"Okay," Andy said. "Just don't run off from me. Please, Rawle. It makes me feel . . . bad."

"Y-y-you m-mi-ssss m-m-me?"

She nodded. He followed her back into her apartment. She got her shoulder bag and took him out for a sandwich at the coffee bar down the street. Then she took him to her car, a red Ford Focus hatchback, and drove south, across the Schuylkill River, down Washington Avenue and into the tangled streets of the Westyard neighborhood.

She parked at Panati and fifteenth and put the key in the lock of the street entrance of the Tiburno Academy of Dance at 7:22. Rawle followed her up the stairs to the second floor.

Andy turned on the lights in the studio and led Rawle to a place beneath the ballet bar on the newly sanded and varnished floor. She set up her laptop on the floor. Then she went into the office and turned on the heat and the lights in the changing rooms.

"Now we wait," Andy said.

They didn't wait long. June came in with Edie and Carla. Then Stace, followed by Shaliq and Basha.

Lucia Ferko came up the stairs slowly, her face brightening as she came into the studio. She moved like someone who had been severely injured—which she had been—but wasn't going to let it get her down. She needed a cane when walking and, when new students showed up and wanted to know how a self-defense teacher had gotten so banged up, she would say, "You have to take a few to give it back."

Best girl friend, Rawle typed on the laptop.

Andy nodded.

Best boy friend-me!

Andy smiled and ran her fingers through his hair. She introduced Rawle as "a friend who wanted to watch." Lucia looked at Rawle, then at Andy and mouthed, "Is that him?" The others did not connect Andy, or Rawle, to the events described in the newspaper. She had never mentioned that she wrote for a newspaper and none of the women in the class had ever asked her what she did for a living. The class wasn't social: the women came to the studio, learned what Lucia taught them and then left.

Lucia started the "Valentine's Day Special" class' with one of the many warm-up exercises she still couldn't do. Andy demonstrated: hands on hips and rotate forward—to the right side, to the back, to the left side—three times, then in the opposite directions. Andy spun her arms around.

"Now tighten," Lucia said, leaning on her cane.

Andy made her arms go in smaller circles.

"Now bring the circles in until you're almost waving hello."

In previous classes, Lucia had taught that those simple circular movements could be used to block, parry or strike.

"Now lift each knee, first the right, then the left. Lift it up slowly, pause, then put it down, coming down on the outside of your foot."

As she put her feet down, Andy remembered Lucia telling her not to step directly on the guy's foot, but to try to work the movement close to the guy's ankle.

Finally they practiced the "quick pick-me-ups" in which Andy pretended to be knocked down, only to get up, fast. They did four kinds: the fall to the front, collapse with hands breaking the fall into a crouching push-up, then up; the fall to the back which started with a head-tuck, and then leg-tuck as your butt hit the floor, almost going onto your back until you stopped with your arms, then put your feet flat and spring up; a fall to the right side and then a fall to the left.

"The one thing the attacker doesn't expect after he puts you on the ground is that you can bounce back up," Lucia said. "The bad guys want us to be passive victims. You bounce up fast enough, you show him that whatever he's trying to pull, it's not going to be easy."

Then they lined up on one side of the room for the exercise called "Over There," in which you had to sense when a person was going to attack you without knowing what kind of attack was coming. Lucia designated Edie as the bad guy.

"Remember, the bad guy is over there and you're over here so you have nothing to worry about, until . . . Carla?"

Carla was a short, broad-shouldered union carpenter who lifted weights and had her own contracting business. Andy had heard from Lucia that Carla was getting over a rape and robbery at a job site. She took a position at the far end of the room.

Edie, a puffy, fifty-something grandmother in black winter sweats and an oversized red "Rivincita!" T-shirt, folded her short arms and tried to look mean.

Carla looked strong enough to toss Edie on the ground, but even the phony anger that Edie projected unnerved her.

"Nothing to worry about, Carla," Lucia said. "You know something's coming. This is all about seeing it coming."

Suddenly, Edie charged and Carla stopped dead in her tracks—the one thing you're not supposed to do. But just as Edie was about to grab her, she stepped away and Edie ran past her.

"Excellent!" Lucia said, tapping the floor with her cane. "Okay, Carla, you're the bad guy. Andy?"

Carla went to Edie's position.

Andy told herself she would not think of anything, she would act normally, she would take her typical, loping, long-legged strides as if she were crossing Rittenhouse Park to see Logan at the Hampton Bank building. She saw Rawle observing her, his face emotionless. She winked at him.

Just then Carla pounced, rushing toward Andy with her arms extended, as if she wanted to choke Andy. Instead of doing the simplest thing—swerving out of Carla's way—Andy wanted to show off for Rawle. She let one of Carla's hands come close to her throat, then she brought her right hand across her chest, trapped the arm and stepped back.

Carla was supposed to fall forward onto the floor but Andy's arms became tangled in Carla's. Andy tried to twist away and they both fell down in a heap, with Carla on top of Andy.

Carla didn't stay on top of Andy for long, because Rawle shrieked so loudly that the sound made them jump apart.

Andy sprang up and went to Rawle. Rawle ducked and ran from her so quickly that she almost fell against the wall.

She turned and saw him dart among the women like a pinball ricocheting through a field of bumpers. Then he was out the door, his steps hammering down the stairs to the street.

Andy ran after him and prayed, prayed that he wouldn't run off here, not in Westyard, where the streets didn't form a grid and went off in all kinds of directions.

She caught the aroma of the Italian bread bakery in the night air. She looked in shadows. She called his name and heard cars moving on the streets and a loud clunk from the relay box controlling the traffic light at Fifteenth Street, and the rustling sound of a jacket moving back and forth.

She found him in front of her car, rocking from side to side. He stopped moving as she came closer. His face was streaked with tears and he clamped his arms around her so tightly that she could not breathe. She felt his breath on her ear: "No-t hu-rrt, Andy."

"I'm glad you're not hurt, Rawle. I'm not hurt either. I'm just . . . happy I found you."

She let him hold her and tell her, slowly and awkwardly, that he did not want the other girl to hurt her, and that he ran away so Andy would follow him and be safe.

She started to tell him again that this was a school and they were learning to help each other, not hurt each other, when Rawle told her he was hurt at his school.

Andy demanded to know who hurt him.

He shuddered.

"Did they hurt you like your uncle?"

He said no, not like his uncle. At school, they didn't want him to be hurt. They wanted him to be happy.

It took him almost a minute to say, *But . . . when you can't do . . . what you want . . . everything hurts. . . .*

Andy held him tightly. What else could she do?

As Ladderback waited for Rhea at Jimmy D's bar, Mafouz told him that Danny Bleutner had called again, and that this time, he insisted that he speak with him.

Ladderback tried to catch his breath but he couldn't. He was halfway through his first Deet of the evening, and he should not have been feeling as if he had just spent some time underwater and was now coming up for air.

"You told him I am not taking calls?" he said to Mafouz.

"He says he does not believe me, that he knows you're here, that he is contemplating some kind of legal action against you, possibly for harassment, and that you were wrong to tell his father that he was destroying his father's favorite restaurant when it is the city that is pursuing the tax matter."

"At no time did I tell Mr. Bleutner's father about our taxes," Ladderback said. "I merely informed him that his son had canceled an affair here. That the father knows about the son's manipulation of the city hall tax office as a threat to the restaurant indicates that others may also know of this."

"But why would Mr. Bleutner do such a thing?" Mafouz asked. "He was such a good customer."

"Hang up the phone," Ladderback said.

"That is undignified and discourteous. All customers must be treated with respect."

"This is a man who has set into motion a series of thoroughly unnecessary events that may drive us out of business," Ladderback told him.

"I would invite him to dinner, listen to him. If possible, I would ask him to pray with me, so that he understands we worship the same God, and that it is God's will that we resolve our differences."

"Failing that?"

"There is no failure, Mr. Ladderback. If God wishes that my family not own this restaurant, then it is a success that we discover this and find another restaurant to acquire."

Was this piety or fatalism, Ladderback asked himself. While he was alive, Whitey Goohan could probably have solved it all with a phone call to one of his numerous city hall cronies. Bleutner had these cronies, but Ladderback did not. He had written obituaries of a few current and several former city hall functionaries, and he could call a few current city hall officials who had contributed to those obituaries.

But not one of those officials would cancel a $2.1 million delinquent tax bill for him, even if Ladderback could establish that the bill was in error.

He sipped his drink. "Then you should do what you think is best. Invite him to dinner, Mr. Mafouz."

Mafouz went to the telephone behind the bar. After a second, he told Ladderback that Bleutner had hung up.

"We'll hear from him again," Ladderback told him.

"You're sure of that? I hope so. I'm sure he will be a very useful friend," He glanced at the dining room. "You will excuse me," he said, and went back to the handful of customers in a room that used to be crowded with dinner guests.

Ladderback finished his drink. While the second was being mixed, he heard the front door open. Rhea came in, apologizing for being late.

He asked her what she was drinking. "I will be driving a while tonight, so I will have nothing."

Ladderback led her to the table. When she was seated he said, "Tonight, I need some information that I hope you can tell me."

"You are working on an obituary?"

Ladderback nodded.

"Whose?"

"Your ex-husband's."

She paused. Her color changed. Ladderback signaled Mafouz, who arrived in time to hear her say, "I'll have what Mr. Ladderback is drinking."

After a while, Andy told Rawle to stay in her car. She went back up and got her laptop and his building set.

Rawle sat obediently in the front seat, eyes straight ahead, his body not moving as Andy started the car, moved into the street, stopped at a traffic light and navigated through Westyard's counterintuitive maze. She found Washington Avenue, turned left toward the Schuylkill River and went over the bridge of West Philadelphia.

At Forty-second and Biltmore she began to hunt for a parking space. She didn't find one close to her apartment house, so she expanded her search until she found one four blocks away, across from a public school's asphalt-covered basketball courts.

Rawle turned his head toward the courts.

Andy had been looking forward to the loose, sweaty, self-empowering workout that Lucia's self-defense classes provided. Her only other exercise consisted of the occasional long walk through the city which required too much careful attention now that winter left the sidewalks covered with ice and shooting layups which was a very personal relationship with a basketball and a basket that did NOT include another person.

Definitely not.

She kept at least one basketball in the car, filled to the right pressure, so that no matter where she might be, no matter what she was wearing, if she saw a court and nobody was watching, she could shoot a few, no matter what the weather was, just as long as the court was free of ice. She usually put the ball in under the lid beneath the hatchback, though she sometimes put it in the backseat.

Then she saw it in Rawle's hands.

He was out of the car before she could tell him that it was dark, that there might be ice on the court and that she carried the basketball because it was part of her life and not part of anyone else's—

He was inside the court, skipping lightly over the asphalt, dribbling the ball awkwardly, arhythmically. Then he got the beat down: ka-chuck, ka-chuck, ka-chuck as he stood still, dribbling as he turned, first, to the far edge of the court, then to the backboard and the basket, then to four corners of the court.

Somehow, it reminded Andy of the "quick pick-me-ups" she did in self-defense class.

He moved to the foul line, took a shot. It missed the backboard entirely. He watched the ball fall short of the net, waited until it stopped moving. He made a small squeak, went to the ball, picked it up, dribbled it back to the foul line then did his four corners ritual again.

Andy came onto the court as he took a second shot. It hit the backboard but missed.

"Rawle . . . ," she began.

He picked up the ball and the rhythm changed. The ka-*chuck*s were firm, assured. There was no awkwardness as he walked the ball back to the foul line.

He shot and the ball kissed the backboard and went right in. He made no sound as he ran to pick it up.

Andy let him take position for another foul shot. Just as he made the shot, she trotted across the court and positioned herself near the basket so she could grab the ball when it came down and tell Rawle that they had to go, though she didn't quite know where, but somewhere that was warm, maybe with a roof over their heads, where they could wait for Nordvahl—

She was holding air. The ball had come down from the basket and

Rawle—who was maybe five feet tall—had snatched it away so fast she didn't even see it happen.

She put her hands on her hips as she went back to the foul line. Then she hunkered down, hands on her knees, eyes on the ball.

He sent it high, in a soaring arc with just enough backspin so it went up and just hung in space before falling perfectly through the rim. She had her left hand on it as it came down and sent it down hard so it would rise back into her right hand as she took it downcourt.

But it didn't come into her right hand. She felt a rush of wind and saw Rawle zooming away, the ball *ka-chucking* tightly as Rawle returned to the foul line.

"Rawle!"

The ball was in the air again and she jumped up and pulled it out of the air, coming down into a wide-legged crouch. She looked around for Rawle and didn't see him.

She felt the ball leave her hands and turned around and saw Rawle zooming back to the foul line.

He was playing one-on-one and she hated one-on-one because it was a guy thing, a who's-better thing, an urban-cool thing, a *competitive* thing and she hated competing over a ball because . . . she *hated* losing. Here was this adorable kid who couldn't say a single word without mangling it, who may or may not have seen his father die and was getting pulled this way and that by a bunch of selfish grown-ups *who should know better* . . . and she hated letting him take the ball away from her.

He stood at the foul line and didn't even see it when, just as he was about to take his shot, she flew into space, her impossibly long beanpole legs in black denims snapping her into the air, her wiry but much too thin arms in a bulky, beat-up leather bomber jacket spread wide, her hands reaching for the ball and pulling it in as she spun around, spied the backboard and, just as her feet made contact with the ground, sent the ball flying.

Only to see him come up *even higher,* his shorter arms and smaller hands waving the ball down, coming back to the foul line and sending it up again so fast that Andy couldn't block it.

The arc was just . . . perfect. The ball didn't even touch the rim. The ball came down and bounced once, twice. He rushed past her and got it and came up to her, rocking from side to side.

She crouched down and he stopped moving. Then he put his hands on her ear and whispered, "My-y-y s-scho-oo-l."

She eyed him skeptically. "You're teaching *me* how to play basketball?"

"Y-yo-u n-n-ot h-h-h-urrrrr-t?"

"Nothing I can't take," Andy said.

He became confused. "T-t-ake?"

She took the ball out of his hands, dribbled to the far end of the court, turned back and threw it high enough so he'd have to jump.

He jumped like one of the huge killer whales zooming up out of their pool to catch a fish. His jump had no grace, no calculation, no arrogance—none of the physical sass and power-playing that she despised in professional basketball, where the athletes weren't playing a game as much as they were vying for attention in an improvised performance that required them to do so many tricks.

Rawle moved with a determined, innocent joy. He reached the apex of that jump and put his hands on the ball like a dog grabbing a Frisbee out of the air. He came down and took a very long shot that skimmed the backboard, snagged the inner side of the rim and fell through.

He came back, went to a different part of the court and almost handed it into the air where an invisible force accepted the ball and sped it in another perfect arc that peaked with a faint twang of ball against metal hoop that ended with a resounding smack on the blacktop.

For the next several minutes she watched him dart all over the court, and just about every shot he took got into the basket. He missed one in ten. No, one in twenty. Then he stopped missing altogether.

Andy could have understood it in terms of his autism. Autistic individuals typically showed prodigal skills with memory, numbers, calculation. Rawle had already demonstrated an uncanny spatial awareness when modeling buildings, furniture, objects near and far. Transfer that spacial awareness to a basketball court and, yes, you could *explain* his talent with the ball as a highly focused sensitivity to distance and scale.

But you can know where things are and still fail to have the ball hit the backboard. To put a ball where you wanted it, or, in Rawle's case, *where the ball had to go,* you needed an unconscious awareness of your body, as well as the ability to process characteristics of the ball, the air temperature, the nature of the court and the backboard itself.

And to be able to snatch the ball away from someone of Andy's height and skill, you had to have been practicing for a *long* time.

He was eleven years old. Andy had been doing layups, off and on, for at least a decade. She never considered what she did with a basketball to be a sport—it was something she did for herself, to get her mind off her anxieties, to let her forget about everything but herself and the ball.

And then, after she had become so winded that she noticed hours had passed, when she was so weary she almost couldn't move, she would feel a powerful, oxygenated energy crackling through her body. She'd know, deep in her bones, that she'd done something good for herself.

What Rawle was doing would not just happen to an eleven-year-old. This kid wasn't just good at basketball. He was . . . a miracle.

She gave up. She gave in. She ran to him and grabbed the ball, tossed it up, and the shot missed but he caught it, took it across the court, and snapped it back to her. She brought up a hand and touched the ball so gently, just nudged it slightly and yes, it went up, slipped against the backboard, rolled around the rim and went in!

She tossed off her coat. He shed his down jacket. She didn't know how long they kept at it, in the cold, their faces glossy with sweat.

And then her cell phone rang. She stopped in midair, came down to earth.

It was Nordvahl. It was bad enough that she hadn't told him she was going to the city. Why didn't she at least check in with him? Where were they? What were they doing?

"Playing," Andy said. "Basketball."

"You sound out of breath. Are you in a gym?"

She told him the location.

"Do you have any idea of how dangerous it is in that part of the city, being outdoors, at this time of night?"

"No," Andy said, panting. "No idea at all."

"I'm coming to pick you up. We're going to Mike McSloan's place."

"You got it unsealed?"

"Am I a superhero or what?"

home

"You can smoke," Ladderback said.

"I have decided to quit," Rhea announced as they sat down in a corner table for two beneath a dim painting of a storm-drenched New England seascape.

"Bette Davis carved her initials into this table when she passed through town," Ladderback said. "I always thought, of all the actresses who used them, she could do more with a cigarette than most men."

"Then I will do the very least," she replied.

A waitress brought the drinks and the menu. Ladderback heard Tony Bennett sing, "You Must Believe in Spring."

She selected the grilled eggplant with fava beans on minted couscous. "Since when has Jimmy D's gone vegetarian?"

"It's a Lebanese dish that Mafouz added," Ladderback said. He picked the prime rib, broccoli rabe and baked potato. "We've also added a clear soup called *pho*. I've learned it's a Vietnamese variation on the French *pot-au-feu*. A bowl can cure whatever ails you."

She folded her arms. "Nothing ails me, Shepherd. I do not know why you need to write my husband's obituary with him still alive."

"It is a way to save time."

"You say that as if you expect him to die soon."

"I expect that his actions will generate consequences that will prove unfavorable for him."

"You are referring to his actions with the boy?"

"His actions with the others," Ladderback said.

She told him how she had warned her husband about Roberta Zetzmeer.

"You should have warned Ms. Zetzmeer," Ladderback said.

"I still can't believe that Schuyler would be doing such terrible things."

Ladderback frowned and then glanced around the dining room. "We can discuss our beliefs later. I just want to appreciate this with you for a while."

"You sound as if this is all going to go away."

"It might," Ladderback said. "In a better world, I would want your ex-husband—"

"Husband," Rhea said. "We never divorced. I wanted to. He did not. He said we could say we were divorced and if I ever found another man I wanted to marry we would do it then."

"Was Whitey that man?"

She shook her head. "Whitey helped me make the decision. You helped me keep to it."

Ladderback didn't move.

"Go ahead and drink," she told him. "What I learned about you when you were in therapy confirmed my hope: that if Schuyler was not to be the man I would spend the end of my life with, there would be another." She put her hand on his. "Who you are, what you are, has always appealed to me."

"But you know too much about me."

"Not nearly enough, Shepherd. But what I do know I admire."

Ladderback suddenly thought of Neely Dixit, with whom he had shared an absolutely wonderful lunch. He glanced around the dining room. It was nearly full with mostly older couples who were warming to the music, the food, the alcohol on a cold winter night devoted to sentiment and love.

Was he too old to have two women vying for his attention?

No, he decided. He was just old enough.

Rawle began to whimper when Nordvahl steered his car into the condo building's parking garage. Andy, who had let herself slip into a daze after so much exertion on the basketball court, sat up suddenly. This was the same garage that she and Rawle had been driven into twenty-four hours ago, though the driver had been Mike McSloan.

Nordvahl gave the keys to the valet, stepped into the vestibule and dialed his cell phone. A few minutes later, they were met by a dark-haired, freckle-faced uniformed maintenance man whom Andy recognized from Nordvahl's birthday party. Rawle said hello to him.

He said, "Hello, Rawle."

Nordvahl introduced him to Andy as Harry Arthur.

Arthur seemed to know Nordvahl rather well. Andy asked Nordvahl if Arthur was a client. "Not precisely," Nordvahl said, looking away.

"It's been wild since yesterday," Arthur said. "You want me to let you in anyplace else, you let me know, Mr. Nordvahl."

"What places has he let you into?" Andy asked suddenly.

"Anyplace Mr. Nordvahl wants," Arthur said.

As they went into the elevator, Arthur told Andy that Nordvahl had been "a godsend to my brother. Couple of years ago, my brother got hurt working construction. Couldn't work again. His lawyer found some way to pocket all the money my brother was supposed to get. Mr. Nordvahl got that money back."

"Mr. Arthur runs the show here," Nordvahl said.

Arthur waved a handheld computer and winked.

The elevator opened onto a small landing. Against a wall were two red leather chairs, a table with a reading lamp and a telephone. One of the chairs was occupied by a crisply efficient policewoman Andy had met in Howard Lange's office.

Directly behind her was one of three numbered doors, entrances to apartments. A piece of yellow tape had been stretched across the frame of the door marked 103.

Rawle shot past them and stood expectantly in front of that door. He did not seem to notice the tape.

Sergeant Hess stood as they approached. She handed forms to Nord-vahl and Andy. "You're here to get the boy's clothes and personal effects, right? You're going to sign these forms, and then you're going to show me some I.D. You, too," she said to Arthur, "unless you're not going in."

Arthur said he was just opening the door and that he would be happy to stand outside until it was time to lock it.

"If you can pack up the boy's things," Nordvahl said to Andy, "I can stay outside, also. I'm sure you can find some kind of bag to put them in."

"When we go in," Sergeant Hess continued, "no one is to go into Mc-Sloan's office or his bedroom. Anything you take out, I write down on a list. If I say so, it stays. Got that?"

Andy said she did. She signed her name and showed her driver's license. Sergeant Hess removed the tape, took the seal off the door lock and stood aside.

"Used to be, I carried around a mess of keys," Arthur said to Andy. He produced a hand-held computer. "Now, everything's wireless. Anywhere I go in the building, I can control the elevators, the lights, hot, cold air and water delivery systems, the sprinkler systems, security zones, the fountains, and open any electronic lock, with this thing right here."

Before he could finish his explanation, Rawle slipped by him, touched the keypad over the knob and had the door open in seconds.

Andy watched him rush inside. She saw lights come on. She went through a vestibule and down a short hallway to a seating area with huge, orange leather sofas and end tables made of hammered metal. A clear glass wall revealed a view of the city almost identical to that from the Skyline Spa on the roof.

Rawle showed her the kitchen. He showed her his favorite cereal. He showed her the milk in the refrigerator. He opened and shut every cabinet and kitchen drawer.

He took her down the corridor to a guest room "f-orrr sl-eep ov-er-s." He showed her his bathroom, with its oversized tub crowded with toy boats.

Then he led her to his room. Brightly colored jet planes hung from the ceiling, model trains and cars crowded shelves and, in the center of the room, taking up most of the floor space between the unmade bed and the small desk, was a sprawling, highly detailed cluster of building-set skyscrapers that, Andy saw immediately, duplicated the cityscape as seen from the window at the far wall.

Rawle let go of her hand, pulled out a plastic basin filled with building bricks and began to assemble them with a focused joy that was even more intense than what she had seen on the basketball court.

She moved around the model city. "Rawle, is it okay if I take some things for you from your closet?"

He ignored her. She opened the closet door and confronted an enormous poster of a sweating Ismail Khan, his long fingers clamped around a basketball.

So Rawle had a role model. Why, then, did the boy's mother not want him to play basketball at his school?

She lifted down a suitcase from the highest shelf in the closet and began filling it with pants, shirts, underwear. She saw a sand bucket and shovel in a corner and took that, too.

"Ann-dee!"

She turned around and saw that he had built a model of the subdivided mansion that contained her apartment. He inserted it into a corner of the city on the floor and then pointed to a boxy cupola on the top. "R-r-r-oo-fff."

"That is really great," Andy said, squatting down beside him. She saw he had found colored bricks corresponding to the dark brown trim on the porch, the pale green stucco and the position of the windows. He had even gotten the number of steps right going up to the front door.

He began to assemble the basketball court.

"So," Rhea Nordvahl began. "Do you do this often?"

"Ask a woman to dinner?" Ladderback said.

"That I would never ask you about. I would expect that other women have shared your company." She put down her drink. "What I asked was, do you often write obituaries about a person who has gone out of his way to avoid publicity?"

"How can I stop him?" Ladderback asked her.

"You can't." She sipped her martini and shivered. "I forgot how cold these things are." She took another sip.

"Pretend he's dead," Ladderback said. "Pretend I'm calling you and asking you to comment about him, as a person who knew him, who consulted with him on some of his cases."

She rubbed her fingers as she thought. "I would say that he wanted to be a good man, and that he wanted to use the law for the betterment of others."

Ladderback nodded. "And how did he practice?"

"Obsessively. He would seize upon a situation and give it his complete attention."

"To the exclusion of his personal life?"

She nodded slowly.

Now it was Ladderback's turn to be silent. Finally, he asked her why she had no children.

He saw her cheek tremble. "Because . . . how important is this?"

"It may have no importance. I don't mean to awaken uncomfortable feelings."

"Then I won't answer that question," she said. "I can tell you one thing he said to me, when we were married, about how he knew of another lawyer whose worst fear came true."

Ladderback listened.

"You must know that there must be a level of impersonality between any professional and his client. In your case, if you are writing about someone, and you become emotionally involved . . . it can make it difficult for you to work effectively."

"In journalism we talk about the importance of maintaining our objectivity," Ladderback said. "But I have since grown to believe that there is no such thing as a purely detached emotional state. I find that the effort to be unemotional constitutes a refusal to feel."

"Are you emotional now, Shepherd? I want to be. I want to let go of my professionalism. Can you do that too? Can we forget about him?"

Ladderback felt his heart pounding under his blue suit. "No," he said.

She leaned back in her chair. "Schuyler was a very emotional man— I mean, he *is* emotional—he is still with us, though I am pretending he is not. He would see every client's situation as somehow relating to himself."

"Was that what Freud called narcissism?"

"A while ago you told me about Jung, now you tell me about Freud. We must be careful not to fit individuals into categories as much as we must attune ourselves to their current situation."

"I'm not a therapist," Ladderback said.

"But you told me, when you were in therapy, that you saw your work as a healing process. When you said that, I began to wish you weren't my patient, and that I had found you in some other way."

Ladderback became silent.

She let him cope with his silence for a while. Then she said, "Schuyler believed it was important not to form emotional attachments. He told me of another lawyer—he never said who this lawyer was, and I never asked him. The lawyer had a son born out of wedlock. The son was given up for adoption and, many years later, the foster parents contacted this very same lawyer to represent them in a case regarding the boy."

"It just happened that the parents selected him?"

"It didn't just happen. This lawyer felt a deep sense of guilt about his child. When he heard about the boy's problem, he manipulated the legal system so the case would come his way."

"I find that a rather honorable act of conscience," Ladderback said.

"Schuyler did not. He felt this was the worst thing that could happen, a perversion of professional practices, especially regarding the way it was settled."

"How was it settled?"

"I never asked and he never told me. But I know Schuyler made several offers to the foster parents for several years to reopen the case as a malpractice matter."

"Did they ever take him up on his offer?"

"I can't tell you. Part of the difficulty of being married to him was that he would only talk about his work, or the history of the law, and I reached the point where I needed someone else with whom I could be emotional."

She looked around and became startled. "I just thought I saw him." She put her napkin over her mouth. "Whitey. Standing right over there." She glanced toward the maitre d' station where Mafouz, in a black tuxedo, was checking the list of reservations.

"He would have wanted you to be here," Ladderback said.

That unsettled her further. Ladderback thought he would offer a bit of levity, and asked her if she believed in ghosts.

"I believe I'm going to have a cigarette," she said, opening her purse.

Rhea had been correct, Andy decided. Rawle needed to be where he felt comfortable and secure.

Andy told him that she would be back in a few minutes. He didn't seem to hear her.

She went to the sitting room and found Sergeant Hess at the window, a clipboard in one hand, a cell phone in the other. "I'd like to let him stay here for a while," Andy told her.

"She's here," Hess said to the cell phone. She took a step toward Andy and handed her the phone. "He wants a word with you."

Andy put the phone to her ear.

"Andy, it's Jeff Everson. Is Nordvahl with you? Can you see him anywhere? Is he close enough to observe you?"

Andy glanced down the entryway. "He's in the hall outside the apartment talking to the maintenance guy."

"That would be Mr. Arthur. I just want to ask you this, off the record, unofficially, and you don't have to answer it if you don't want to, but . . . when I told you to tell Nordvahl that he might be next, how did he react?"

"He laughed."

"He found it funny?"

"Not quite. I don't remember it clearly. Why?"

"We've looked at some in-store video surveillance from a bookstore where we had a poisoning earlier today. The poison was put into an open inkwell. She ingested the poison when she sucked on the nib. The cameras didn't get a clear look at all the customers who came close enough to the inkwell to do it, but we narrowed it down to a few customers who also charged their purchases, so we could get their names, and the name of one customer was represented by Nordvahl at one time. These, and other things I'd rather not go into right now, indicate that Nordvahl might know something about whoever it is who has this thing for these lawyers."

"I think I saw a truck today that looked like the one that passed me when Muckler was killed," Andy told him. "Want the plate number?"

He paused. "Just because a truck looks familiar to you doesn't mean it—"

"The owner makes sculptures out of sand he pumps in, and he's one of Nordvahl's clients."

"I might be interested in that number."

"I might give it to you, then, but in the morning. Rawle and I are going to spend the night here. I want Rawle to stay in his own place from now on."

"No way. That apartment is still sealed. I haven't had time to go over Mike McSloan's personal effects."

Sergeant Hess caught Andy's eye and mouthed the words, "Go for it."

"I'll be in the guest room. If Rawle is okay in the morning, I want him to go back to his school."

"You're forcing me to ask a question I was hoping not to ask, until later: do you have any reason to believe the boy saw someone who might have been involved in the death of his father? If the answer might be yes, then I have to consider assigning someone to protect you. Did Nordvahl tell you what happened to Roberta Zetzmeer?"

Andy asked what happened to her. Everson told her. Andy gasped.

"It could be an accident in the same way what happened to Mike Mc-Sloan was an accident. Nordvahl was on the building's floor when it happened. He didn't say much to us, but he suggested that it might not be accidental. Now, if Nordvahl happens to say more to you about it—"

"You'll have to get it from him," Andy said. "About staying here: I think we're safer here than any other place I can think of. The door has a dead bolt that locks from the inside. I also have an idea who might stay with him tomorrow when I'm not around."

"Someone with law-enforcement experience?"

"More than enough."

"I still can't let you stay there," he said.

"You said you wanted the truck's license plate number. . . ."

She thought she could hear him thinking. "You're asking me to take some risks."

"I'm asking you to do what's best for Rawle."

Another pause. Then Everson said, "Let me speak to my sergeant."

She handed over the phone to Hess. She listened, then gave Andy the thumbs-up sign.

"You know Schuyler will be upset with us when he finds out we've done this," Rhea said as she finished the baklava—another of Mafouz's additions.

"One more thing," Ladderback said. "He told the police that he thought McSloan was murdered. He told me his concept was a kind of coercive terrorism against bad lawyers. But could he also have the serial criminal's need to play with the police? Does he want to be caught?"

"He has a collection of old comic books," Rhea told him. "He would hate that some of his superheroes had flaws."

"But comic-book heroes are only interesting in light of their flaws," Ladderback said.

"If I were to turn my husband into my patient, I would say that here you have the major distinction between you and him. You are too comfortable with your agoraphobia. You believe that flaws make the man, so to speak. Schuyler does not. He is constantly striving—burning, really—with a desire for perfection. If he is, in fact, doing what you say he is, then it is possible he is searching for a way to put that fire out."

"You mentioned that, when you were married to him, there were times when he became too caught up in his work. What did you do then to make him come to his senses?"

"If I could answer that question, I would still be married to him, though I don't know if I would be comfortable in the marriage. If we had children, their needs would have made everything different. Schuyler's clients function like substitute children for him. He feels fulfilled when he can satisfy their needs. He enjoys being appreciated and he expects them to do what he says."

"What happens when they don't value what he does, or when they disobey him?"

"He refers a client to another lawyer, or merely announces that the relationship is over."

"What if he can't get rid of his client so easily?"

"Then I will be very sorry for the both of them. Children who do not redeem their parents can destroy them." She pushed back her chair. "Where shall we take this, Shepherd? It is still Valentine's Day and I can't think of anyone else I would like to spend the night with."

"I have been short of breath lately," Ladderback said. "I am not sure if I have the strength."

"I'm not asking you to be strong, Shepherd."

He closed his eyes and felt the terror overwhelm and surround him. Then he opened his eyes and said, "I'll make the attempt."

Nordvahl didn't want to let Andy and Rawle alone. "You saw how easy it was to unlock this door," Nordvahl said, his tone of voice just a little too urgent. "Who knows who could come in here while you're sleeping."

"I'll deal with that," Andy said, arms folded, blocking the doorway.

"And what happens tomorrow?"

"He goes back to his school. I find someone to take care of him until you settle this thing with his mother. I go back to work. And then, if he's up to it, we go to Atlantic City."

Nordvahl's pale skin lost even more color. "How—"

"Any way we want. We can take a bus, a train. I can drive."

"You're taking a dysfunctional child to a dangerous place just so he can make sand castles?" Nordvahl was indignant.

"He's not dysfunctional," Andy said. "You should see him play basketball."

"You're being unreasonable," Nordvahl replied.

"I'm being perfectly reasonable. I have an assignment down there. We'll go early. We'll have some fun. Then I'll have some fun."

"But he's unpredictable. He could get into trouble."

"Then I'll get him out of trouble. Or I'll call you."

He nodded. "Yes. If there is the slightest problem, do that. May I ask you the nature of your assignment?"

He sounded almost like Ladderback. "I'm covering the opening and dedication of the Atlantic City Aquarium's shark habitat. It's named for a Philadelphia laywer."

Nordvahl's expression changed. "Severio Pescecane."

"You know him?"

He narrowed his eyes. "We've met."

Nordvahl left reluctantly. Andy closed the door and locked it, throwing the dead bolts. She checked on Rawle, who did not say a word to her as he took a bath, brushed his teeth, changed into his pajamas and went to his bed. He fell rapidly to sleep.

Andy went to the guest room and opened her laptop on the small, blond wood desk. She accessed the Internet and, instead of checking e-mails, she signed on to the *Press*'s Web page to catch the cover of to-morrow's edition.

Her column was mentioned on the front page with her byline!

She saw she had two staff memos. One was from Howard Lange, the *Press*'s editor.

You've been syndicated! Five newspapers have
picked up KNOW-WHAT-TO-DO. You won't get any
money, but it looks good. Congrats.

The second was from Chilly Bains.

CHECK YOUR E-MAIL! I've found out that Ismail
Khan wants to meet you. Yes, he's THAT Ismail
Khan. The SAME Ismail Khan who doesn't talk to
the media. The same Ismail Khan that won't
even talk to me! Find out what he's sending
you and copy it to me. This is WILD!

So she checked her e-mails. She saw one from Ismail Khan. She
opened it.

Jermaine Hayes spoke for me. Did you hear his
voice?

She wrote him back.

Rawle and I saw you at the Broad Street Run.
Kersaw should have let Jermaine finish speaking
for you. You and Rawle seem to have a lot in
common. Rawle plays GREAT one-on-one. He also
has a picture of you in his room. I'll have a
column about this soon. Do you want to meet
him?

She glanced at the rest of the e-mails, deleted some spam and signed
on to the newspaper's Web page. She looked through some of the questions to Mr. Action. Few questions seemed promising.

Then she went back to tomorrow's column.

She never got used to seeing her work in print. She either found flaws in the editing—lines that should have run but didn't, or, worse, lines that slipped that should have been cut—or she saw parts that she could have described differently, written better.

This time she had a definite feeling that she had done something good. She wasn't sure exactly what that good might be, but she couldn't deny the feeling.

She pulled up her word processor and started writing about Rawle and basketball. She wrote a paragraph beginning with what Deheulos had said about miracles.

Would she need Rawle's permission to quote Deheulos? The boy would certainly give it to her. She wrote about what happened on that basketball court, and how wonderful it was, not to play with someone who has dysfunctions, but to find common ground in playing: to play, to catch, throw, leap and dodge and let fate take them where it would.

She read back what she wrote and it sounded precious. She imagined Bardo Nackels or some other copydesk editor grumbling that miracles *happen all the time.* They are not *news.*

And yet, they become news when the miracle feels right, when it touches you deep inside. She sent that to the newspaper and dialed the second phone number in her speed-dial cue under the name Ferko.

Lucia's husband, Philadelphia Police Sergeant Vincent Ferko, answered. "Hey."

"You still on disability leave?"

"For the next eight months, at least."

"You want something to do?"

"With you? Andy, I got a wedding band on my finger. I'm still so banged up, there's not much I could do with anyone."

"Can you get around, at least?"

"At least. My physical therapist says I should do chores around the house, and you'd be surprised how hard it can be to move a sponge in a circle. The place is spotless. It's getting so I clean what I already cleaned. Lucia and me, we have his and hers canes, though mine's more like a crutch. It takes me so long to go up stairs. I was never big on watching TV. I'm getting a little tired of clean, you know?"

"There's somebody I want you to meet. He's a boy, eleven years old."

"The one you've been writing about?"

"You read the paper?"

"I always was your biggest fan, Andy."

How is it that she can find out she's getting syndicated—a big deal to a journalist—and it doesn't move her, but this adorable brown-eyed Italian cop who just *happened* to marry her best friend could tell her he was her fan, and that would *thrill* her?

"Tell Lucia I'm going to borrow you for a while. I want to go back to work and he needs somebody to look after him until I can find somebody permanent."

"How long is that going to be?"

"I don't know. He's going back to school tomorrow. I'll be in the newsroom. I want to leave your number with the school so that they can call you if he has any difficulties. If they call you, call me. If I can run out to get to him, I will. If I'm tied up, take a cab and sit with him until I get there."

"I don't know, Andy. He sounds like he has problems."

"He does. You had problems, too. And you beat them."

He sounded unsure. "Some of them."

"*All* of them. I'll get my car and pick you up with him tomorrow. You can get acquainted while I take him to school. Then I'll drop you off at his apartment—it's really nice. Then you take a cab to pick him up, or, if I can get off early, I'll get him. We're supposed to go to the shore later in the day. I promised him he could make sand castles."

"Thanks, Andy, but . . . I don't think so."

"Vinnie! This boy is a gift!"

"I'm sure he is, but not for me."

She would have slammed the phone down, but she didn't want to wake the boy. The quiet of the apartment slowly calmed her down. She yawned again. Though it was late, she felt like a cup of tea. She went into Rawle's room and saw him curled up on his bed.

She closed the door, turned on the hall light and went past the sitting room into a stone and black metal kitchen with no handles on the cabinet doors. She saw a black mug in the sink with the residue of coffee at the bottom. Had McSloan drank from that?

She found a cabinet with black coffee mugs with the name of McSloan's law firm printed on them in gold. Another cabinet revealed a box of supermarket orange pekoe tea bags that smelled stale. She put a bag in a cup, ran hot water from the sink, filled the cup and then stuck it in the microwave oven for a minute.

She had a little time as the tea steeped. She went out of the kitchen and saw that incredible view from the sitting room. She turned and was about to return to the kitchen when she saw the open door leading to McSloan's home office.

She poked her head in, groped for a light switch. She saw a broad antique desk with a slim laptop computer on it beside a stack of files. She went a little closer and saw a letter atop those files, from Schuyler Nordvahl and Associates. Something about a John Doe.

Was that the case Nordvahl had mentioned that had put him in such low spirits?

Her tea was probably ready now, and she had told Lieutenant Everson that she would stay out of this office, but . . .

Her eyes were drawn to a red label on the very bottom file. The label was printed *Sealed By Order Of . . .*

Andy didn't pay attention to who had ordered that file sealed. She only saw a name: James Michael Gravatte, Ismail Khan's previous name.

Andy forgot about her tea. She forgot about the possibility that this room and everything in it might be fingerprinted.

She pulled out that file and started to read.

# 20 glory

He had loved her little Rittenhouse Square apartment, even if he could not endure the view. And he had loved her, slowly and gently and easily, knowing with each easy movement, each simple pleasure, that this just might heal him in ways that nothing else would.

When he woke the sunlight was streaming onto the ceiling over the bedroom. He looked at that ceiling for at least a minute.

Then he had to catch his breath, and close his eyes.

The doorman of her building walked him to a cab, and the doorman of his building helped him out of the cab.

By the time he reached his apartment, he saw that he would be late for work.

He didn't care. He showered, rubbed his electric razor across his face, dressed, grabbed his satchel and, just before going, picked up his phone and ordered a dozen red roses sent to her apartment.

Then he took the elevator down to the sub-basement that opened into the subway concourse leading to the underground tunnels below South Broad Street. He couldn't walk fast enough and he had to stop occasionally to catch his breath. In a bakery in one of the food courts below Market Street he bought himself a double espresso and a lemon-poppyseed muffin that he ate much too quickly as commuters rushed past him.

The brightly groomed, aftershave-and-cologne-scented rush-hour throng hurried to their jobs, while he sat at a laminated café table and waited for the coffee and the sugar in the muffin to give him the energy to continue the final quarter mile to the *Press* Building's basement entrance, up the elevator to the newsroom on the eleventh floor.

When he finally rose from the table, he found himself moving even more slowly. He felt his heart beating beneath his raincoat. Each step was an effort, but he persevered. He came into the newsroom, too tired to see anyone, or even say hello, though no one said hello to him. Most of them had started their day an hour previously. They were busy, or trying hard to appear so.

He saw Andy's column featured again on the front page. He read it again and felt the words lift his spirit.

Then he saw the light blinking on his phone that said he had at least one message in his voice-mail box.

The first was from Mafouz. "Mr. Ladderback, I am very pleased to tell you that I called Mr. Bleutner this morning and he explained everything to me. He said that he heard we were having a tax difficulty from his father and that he is confident he can help us with it. He told me that he loves the restaurant so much that he wants to become a partner because he feels there is no way we can survive without additional resources. He said he is sending Matthew Plank to help us with the details. I did not say yes or no to his offer. After all, I do not own the restaurant yet. I am just an employee. But I am very excited that Mr. Plank will visit us, and that Mr. Bleutner wants to help. We pray to the same God, after all."

Ladderback put the phone down and wished he knew the telephone number for the main switchboard in hell, or heaven—wherever Whitey Goohan's soul might be. If he had the number, he'd make the call and ask Goohan if the manner in which Bleutner and Plank had "moved into" Jimmy D's was not slightly similar to the way Goohan had moved into businesses when he was in the mob. You cause a problem that makes

244

everyone suffer, then you take the problem away, in exchange for getting a little piece of the business. Then you take more, and more, and more.

Ladderback reminded himself that he was still the executor of Goohan's estate. He had to agree to the eventual sale. It might be difficult to keep Bleutner and Plank out, but, if that was what it took to preserve the restaurant as Goohan wanted it, Ladderback would find a way.

And yet, all of Plank's restaurants were successes in ways that restaurants in Philadelphia had never been. If Plank was merely giving advice, it would be worthwhile to listen. Maybe Ladderback would invite Andy to come along—they had become acquaintances. Andy and Plank had met when a critic died at one of Plank's restaurants. He sent her flowers on her birthday, gifts at Christmas.

He glanced at the desk next to his. In less than a year the young woman hired to do the consumer column and be his assistant had surpassed his expectations.

The second message was from Nordvahl. "Wasn't it just marvelous what happened to Kersaw yesterday? Don't you love it when things . . . fall into place? I have learned that the Blue Boy is screwing with your taxes. *Volenti non fit injuria.*"

If one consents, one is not injured.

"I do not consent to have you, or anyone, unjustly injured," Nordvahl continued, "especially by the Blue Boy. I'm putting my staff at the Law Watch on it. I'm sure the documents that were filed regarding the tax matter have errors. If we find enough, the city's filing is rendered invalid, which means it has to be filed again, which means it won't be filed because the tax office knows it was one of Bleutner's shakedowns and now they know *we* know it. If we don't find enough errors, then we challenge and prove that the initial assessment has been paid, which will prove that the assessment was invalid. Admit it, Shepherd, I should not be stopped because what I'm doing is right. I have that certainty, and so should you. Bleutner will again be on the Law Watch list for next month, with a new assortment of embarrassments to the profession. I suggest you judge the current matters ignoramus and leave my ex-wife alone."

By mentioning the word ignoramus, Nordvahl was not insulting him. The term was originally used in early English law, when a group of peers did not have enough evidence to convict, or it was found that the original charges were invalid. The writ was then marked "ignoramus," which means, in Latin, "we know nothing."

The term became a synonym for stupidity during the reign of James I, when students at Cambridge University presented a play called *Ignoramus* featuring a boob of a law professor that the king believed was a parody of Sir Edward Coke. Coke's anti-authoritarian stance in Parliament was annoying the king, who attended a command performance of the play before he became so angry with Coke that he locked him in the Tower of London.

Coke was one of the greatest legal minds England ever produced. The common law that Coke admired took moral, civic and social responsibility away from gods and kings. It gave ordinary people the opportunity to have faith in themselves.

Ladderback had hoped, when he had told Andy to ask Nordvahl about Sir Edward Coke's imprisonment, that Nordvahl would understand this, and, perhaps, redeem himself.

But Ladderback and Nordvahl did not pray to the same god.

Ladderback decided it was time to tell Andy about Nordvahl. He removed from his satchel printouts from Web pages he had viewed over the last few days. Then he signed on to his terminal, did a series of searches of the databases of the *Press* and *Standard,* and came up with an old gossip item by Chilly Bains's predecessor, Lincoln Fretts that mentioned Nordvahl's duel with Michael McSloan. Fretts had identified the "mystery lady" as a graduate student in training to be a therapist.

Ladderback hadn't yet identified that therapist. He wasn't sure why he needed to know this woman's name. He wasn't even sure if he was doing anything more than wasting his time.

He arranged the printouts on his desk and saw that one of them, a campaign biography of Judge Harlan Whetson, mentioned that his sister, Alma Whetson McSloan, had a background in speech pathology.

The word-spinners who write campaign biographies use language like cheap plaster. To have a background can mean that one doesn't have a degree or professional accreditation.

He was about to do a broader search for Alma Whetson when he heard Bud Pielsberg, the newsroom's receptionist, say, "Nice piece, Andy."

He turned in his swivel chair. Andy paused by the desk and reporters, editors, copy aides—people who had things to do, or were pretending that they did—stopped what they were doing.

They saw Andy in her standard, cold weather, I'm-not-going-to-meet-anybody-important ensemble of black pants, winter boots, a knitted cap pulled down low over her ears and her shoulder bag hanging off the sleeve of a well-worn leather bomber jacket.

One of the sportswriters, a woman who covered golf and tennis, sauntered by and told her that the "piece about the boy was just fine. We need more of that in this rag."

A new hire who was supposed to be the newspaper's blogwatcher looked all the way up at her and said, "Your name is in more blogs than the mayor's right now."

She permitted the ends of her mouth to turn up, just slightly, and she grew even taller as she crossed the clusters of desks to her own. She stopped when she saw the piles of mail.

Ladderback muttered something.

"Was that Latin?" she asked him. "I'm really getting to *hate* it when people quote Latin at me."

Ladderback lifted his hands slowly from his keyboard and said, "*Mea culpa.*"

"Just tell me what it means, okay?"

"*Mea culpa* means it is my fault."

"Before that."

Ladderback gazed up at her. "In Roman times, when a hero accomplished great things for the empire, usually in terms of conquest, he would be welcomed back to the city in a rather elaborate parade."

"It was called a triumph," Andy said. "I took history."

"As the man of the hour passed though the city, usually on a stupendously decorated chariot, the multitude was ordered to hail the conquering hero. And yet, a tradition arose for an anonymous slave to ride in the chariot with the conqueror, and to repeat just loud enough for him to hear . . . what I said."

"In English!" Andy said.

"All glory is fleeting."

"I knew it!" she exclaimed as she dropped into her chair. "I knew that, no matter how good I felt about what I've been doing, the moment I came back into the newsroom somebody was going to give me shit."

"That was not my intention."

She slid her chair close to his. "I just did the one thing you told me I shouldn't do as a journalist."

He thought about that. "I remember telling you several things not to do. I also remember telling you that the reason I have the authority to tell you not to do those things is that I have done them."

"You told me that a reporter reports the story. She's not supposed to influence the events or take over. I took over. Rawle's back home, permanently, as far as I'm concerned, and he's back in school. I tried to get a friend to look after him but he was too scared. So I thought it was all going to be over and then I found someone who wants to take care of him. It was like a miracle. Everything fell into place."

Ladderback winced.

"Now what I have to do is square it with his mother, which I plan to do while Nordvahl is busy handling all these new and former clients who are afraid that the police think they know who killed these lawyers."

Ladderback turned to the neat pile of printouts beside his terminal. "I can give you information that may shed light on a prior relationship between Michael McSloan and Mr. Nordvahl."

"I could do that, too," Andy said. "But I won't."

Ladderback was quiet for a while. "There is also the matter concerning Mrs. McSloan and her brother, the judge."

"That's solved, too. Rawle isn't going near him ever again without supervision."

Ladderback's eyes moved behind his thick glasses. "It would appear that you have taken the law into your own hands."

"Not quite. I'm tired of seeing Rawle suffer."

Ladderback took a breath. "I must tell you about some other things that Mr. Nordvahl is handling."

"Later," Andy said, digging through the pile of mail until she found the envelope with "IK" in the return address. "I've been up all night. I just want to have a normal, quiet morning, catching up on things, getting back to doing what I used to do."

"That may not be possible," Ladderback said.

"Let's make it possible, okay?" She opened the envelope, pulled out the single sheet of paper and said, "I knew it!"

Ladderback was about to tell her that the reason she might not be able to return to her previous duties with an anonymous consumer column was that the work she had been doing about Rawle had been so superb that it would bring unanticipated consequences—

But then Howard Lange put his hands on Andy's shoulders, leaned forward and said, "Got a minute?"

Andy dropped the letter, planted her left foot on the blue carpeted floor, rose up and shot her right leg out until the edge of her boot was an inch from Lange's jaw.

"Don't you *ever* put your hands on me again," she said.

He backed off. "Hey, hey, no reason to get excited—"

She pulled her foot back and set it down. "I'm *not* excited."

"Well, you should be. I got something for you that's going to put you on the map."

"You said the column has been syndicated to five newspapers," Andy said. "I'm already on the map."

"It's twenty-seven newspapers now. You're hitting a nerve, what can I say? But that's nothing compared to what I've got for you now."

He tilted his head toward his office. Andy followed him warily.

Ladderback examined the day's death notices and the police reports and selected two possible obituary candidates: a retired saleswoman for a candy firm, and a homeless street-corner saxophone player who had died of heart failure outside the shelter the night before.

He heard Lange's office door close. He waited for a few minutes. He recalled that Andy was taking self-defense courses. He thought about the exaggerated series of movements she had made. The movement was more an attempt to push the letter away than it was to defend herself against the newspaper's editor.

Ladderback took a breath. He saw the letter on the floor. It had no address for a letter-head, no e-mail, no phone number. Just a name: Ismail Khan.

The letter held a single sentence. What had Mafouz said about God leaving the manna close to the tents of the righteous?

Ladderback did a Web search for dysphonia and was on his fourth Web page when the door of Lange's office flew open with a bang and Andy rushed out and nearly fell into her chair. She put her elbows on her desk, covered her face in her hands and began to cry.

The newsroom was quiet for an instant, and then it became very, very busy.

Ladderback sat quietly for a minute.

"*Don't*," she said.

"I wasn't going to say anything."

"You were, too!" She sobbed quietly. "And it was going to be in Latin."

"No."

"Did you read the letter?"

Ladderback said nothing.

"You're so nosy!"

"It is the journalist's trait," Ladderback said. "If you did not want me to see it, you would have taken it with you, or put it somewhere else."

"I didn't want *Lange* to see it," Andy said. "Lange knows Ismail Khan has been trying to contact me. Lange wants me to interview Ismail Khan about the *Liberty Bell Magazine* story that says he can't talk because of a drug overdose. There's a rumor going around that *Liberty Bell* paid a source for that information, and that the source fabricated the story, and Lange wants me to get Khan to trash *Liberty Bell*."

"Our union permits you to refuse an assignment if you can show cause."

"To hell with the union. I quit." Andy sobbed.

Ladderback waited. Then he said, "You've become emotionally involved in your subject."

"You're going to tell me I screwed up?"

"No," Ladderback said. "I'm going to tell you that you've done a good thing."

"By quitting?"

"By being willing to let your emotions lead you to a greater truth that, at this point, you feel you cannot express."

Andy took her hands away from her face. She wiped her eyes on the sleeves of her gray sweatshirt.

"Though there is great rivalry among the news media in this city, I doubt if Mr. Lange asked you for a story merely to embarrass *Liberty Bell*," Ladderback continued. "He wants to use you to get an interview with a public figure who rarely makes public comments. Such an interview would sell newspapers and make a reputation for you. It is also possible that Mr. Khan may want to speak through you, and not just about his speech difficulties."

She stared at him. "You read the letter."

Ladderback shook his head.

"You were about to."

"Judge Whetson suffered from dysphonia as a child. It was mild enough that he was able to suppress the symptoms. Rawle inherited it, complicated by what may not be autism, but a form of Tourette's Syndrome, which the judge also may have. Tourette's manifests itself in fits of sudden, inappropriate rage, regular spasmodic movements or speech, and contrasting demonstrations of physical strength, stamina and agility. Some athletes have it, though they tend not to want to admit it, because its treatment requires a drug regimen that can affect their performance.

"Alma had enough awareness of her family's hereditary problems to study speech pathologies at Temple University. But she never graduated with a degree. Why? We can speculate, given a public disagreement between Michael McSloan and Schuyler Nordvahl over the honor of an unnamed woman. The date of the disagreement is close enough to the published birth date of Ismail Khan, a child who, according to the *Liberty Bell* article, as well as his team biographies; was given up for adoption. Whatever problems Ismail Khan had speaking were no doubt made worse when he was injured at a camp for disadvantaged children—"

"He was in a coma," Andy said. "He almost died."

"You found Mr. McSloan's copy of the sealed documents?"

"They were just . . . there," Andy said. "I read them last night. Then I e-mailed Khan about what I found out. He e-mailed me back this morning that I didn't have to read anything, that he had sent me a letter telling me everything I needed to know."

She picked up the letter and handed it to Ladderback.

He didn't look at it.

"It may be worth your while to speak with Mr. Khan," Ladderback said.

"I intend to," Andy replied. "I intend to speak with his people, and with Rawle and Alma McSloan, and maybe even that awful judge. I want to do what my father used to do: get people to sit down for a meal and work out their differences, without lawyers, and without the media looking on."

"Your father did his best negotiations at Jimmy D's," Ladderback said. "At the appropriate time, I will have his table reserved for you. Until then, I suggest you say nothing further to Mr. Lange until you have met with Mr. Khan."

"Lange told me that when I leave this newsroom, I can't come back unless I have a story."

"Did he specify what kind of story?"

She shook her head. "I mean, it's the Khan interview that he wants but, with Kahn's schedule and Rawle in school, the soonest I can set that up will probably be tomorrow night."

"Let me know the time and the table is yours. Until then, you need a big story to make Mr. Lange happy."

"I want Lange to go fuck himself," Andy said.

Ladderback thought for a moment. "I recall, when I met you and Rawle for breakfast, you were planning to take him to Atlantic City."

"Tonight. I actually got an assignment. I'm taking Rawle to the beach. And then Chilly Bains is letting me cover the opening of some new wing at the Atlantic City Aquarium."

Ladderback turned to his word processor, accessed the *Press*'s list of special events. "That would be the Pescecane Shark Habitat. Is Mr. Nordvahl going with you?"

"Why should he?"

"Ask him. He probably was not invited, but he may want to go."

"If he doesn't, I can manage without him. My friend, the cop on disability, can come along with us."

"If Mr. Nordvahl comes with you, watch him closely." He showed her the paperwork he had gathered. "Shall I leave this where you might read it?"

Andy frowned. "Why?"

"You may have a big story."

"Not as big as this." She showed him the letter. The single line said, *I want to be my brother's keeper.*

21 two birds, one stone

"I always have a variety of concepts," Matthew Plank began. "They circle my mind like jets waiting to land at an airport."

Ladderback sat across from him at a dark table in a dark corner of Jimmy D's. He said nothing.

"I'm not used to discussing my ideas with owners," Plank said. He leaned back in his chair like a bored model in an advertisement for the lustrous, irridescent black sport jacket and retro seventies gray mock turtleneck knit shirt. "When I come in, I'm given complete freedom."

"I am not an owner," Ladderback said, wishing he had worn his better suit rather than his typical rumpled uniform and nondescript dark necktie. "And I don't believe you have been asked to come in."

"Danny Bleutner asked me," Plank said. "The reason he's my lawyer is he likes getting involved. If things had been different, I'd be making cheese steaks in a South Philly luncheonette and he would be one of those street-corner mayors hanging around at the counter, talking to this one, talking to that one, setting up all kinds of deals. As an artist, I don't need him. But I appreciate him and I respect him. There is no way this restaurant is going to survive without hugely significant changes, and I will not make those changes until I am placed in complete control. That's what he's going to do. That's what he knows *how* to do. Why can't you just let it happen?"

Ladderback was silent.

Plank smacked his hand on the table. "I feel like I'm auditioning. I've never done that, as a chef. I've never had to prove myself. Everything I've ever done has been a smash."

"I am not asking you to prove yourself," Ladderback said.

Plank grinned. "The new name for this place is going to be 'Gangsters at Noon,' " he said. He waited for Ladderback to react. Ladderback didn't.

"I originally wanted to call it Lansky's, after the mob accountant, but some people in my generation don't like restaurants named after dead people."

"My generation came to Jimmy D's more after Gianni Delano died."

"Time to wipe the slate clean," Plank said. "The concept I have is about the big, greasy, highly spiced messes that aging New York mahoffs and goombahs ate when they went to Miami Beach to show how powerful and humble they could be, as if they were just guys from the neighborhood. There will be a third, secret, emergent cuisine, the muted Puerto Rican *tropicalismo* of chorizo, plantains-and-beans and pickled and burnt fish, and a mirrors-and-blue-red velvet bar called Rum-Ba with at least one hundred different Caribbean rums and every kind of teaky-tacky parasol cocktail known to man."

"Who would want to eat there?" Ladderback asked.

"Not you, obviously. But we're dealing with white-collar aspiration. There is a deep, desperate need among workplace drones to act out their anxiety in tediously personalized consumerism. Also, Kennedy-era Miami Beach has a misty nostalgia now. In the same way that disco was all about pre-AIDS sex, the transplanted European pig-out cuisines represent what was served in hotel coffee shops in an innocence of mere gluttony, the calm before cardiology. The boomers who fear a Reuben sandwich more than unprotected sex are going to stay away, so that overpaid office drones of my generation will fall over themselves to get their table and order their thing, and lay down severe amounts of cash for some stupid parasol drink."

"I have no difficulties with cholesterol," Ladderback told him. "Would you care to have dinner?"

Plank looked at him slyly. "Are you going to have your chef poison my food?"

Ladderback permitted himself a grin. "Would I tell you if I was?"

"It's almost time to go," Andy called out, pulling her scarf around her as a cold, briny breeze rolled in off the Atlantic Ocean. She sat on a small rise in the sand, her arms and legs drawn in tightly to conserve warmth.

Rawle held up a finger. He was on his knees in the sand about ten feet from her. He was without a hat, without gloves. His winter coat was speckled with sand, and Andy, though she worried about him catching a cold, had never seen him happier, not even when they were doing layups together.

A row of precisely modeled casino and residential towers lay before him. He'd even included the boardwalk and two of the piers.

Maybe he'll be an architect when he grows up, Andy thought. She watched him take a fragment of a clamshell and carve out a curved fin on the roof of his model of the building directly in front of them: the Atlantic City Aquarium's Pescecane Shark Habitat.

The aquarium itself was inside the King Neptune Casino Resort. According to the press releases e-mailed to Andy by the casino's owner, Brilliant-Savarin Corp., the Shark Habitat was an added "architectural statement" to the casino's $864 million expansion of its existing boardwalk "entertainment" facility. That statement included a nautical-themed retail shopping arcade called the Flotilla, two lounges, three new restaurants, an "exclusive" high-roller slot pit, an enlarged poker room and an off-track-betting parlor featuring plush seats with built-in mechanical back massagers. The press release went on to describe the "full service" law firm of Severio Pescecane, LLP, with its offices in Atlantic City and Philadelphia, as a "longtime pioneer in gaming related law."

Rawle stepped back, admired his handiwork, then leaped over the row of buildings, rushed toward Andy, clamped his arms around her and almost knocked her down on the sand.

She looked up in the hazy, cloudless night sky and heard him say in her ear, "Th-tha-nk y-y-ooou s-s-so mu-ch, And-d-d-ee."

"You're welcome, Rawle. Now we're going to go to a place where I'll have to talk to a lot of people. They'll have food you can eat. There's supposed to be a band. And we get to see a real shark have dinner. You can stay with me, or with Schuyler. He's supposed to meet us here."

He let go of her and sat up. His face became serious as she swept the sand off their clothes with her gloves. He raced past her, through the sand dunes, to the stairs going up to the boardwalk.

She found him waiting obediently at the King Neptune Casino's clamshell-shaped boardwalk entrance. Andy led him into a buzzing, beeping, jangling expanse of slot machines. The noise bewildered her until she saw a casino lounge against a far wall. Inside the lounge, perched on a bar stool, was Schuyler Nordvahl in a dark suit with a glass of orange juice in his hand.

As they drew closer to the lounge, Andy saw that Nordvahl had his handheld computer out. He was using his touch pen to copy a series of numbers from a piece of paper into the computer.

"Right on time," he said, looking up from the computer. He saw the way Rawle was staring at him. "Something wrong?"

Andy crouched down beside the boy. "Schuyler isn't here to take you back to his house, Rawle," she explained. "He's here because he knows the man who paid for the shark habitat."

"Pescecane actually sent an invitation to the Law Watch," Nordvahl added, "so I'm not here as your guest."

Andy saw that Rawle's attention was on Nordvahl's computer. Rawle put his mouth next to her ear and then took it away.

"What is it, Rawle?" Andy asked her.

He whispered a halting question: was Nordvahl her friend?

"He's just a man who has helped us with some things," Andy said.

He cupped his hand around her ear and said, "Mon-st-er."

The word almost knocked her over. Andy put her hand on the lounge's carpeted floor to steady herself. She rose slowly.

Nordvahl looked at the boy, then at her. He picked up the piece of paper from the bar, crumpled it and put it in his pants pocket. Then he put the handheld in his jacket pocket. "Let me show you something," he said.

"We're going to the opening," Andy said, not facing him.

"This is on the way."

"Stay away from us," she said.

But he did not. They were together as they left the lounge and skirted the casino toward another sheet of falling water, that, as they drew near, parted to reveal a three-story, theatrically lit blue and green undersea grotto ringed by boutique shops and restaurants bulging out of the fake volcanic stone. A glowing shark's fin pointed past a fountain toward the entrance to the Atlantic City Aquarium.

"Stop here for a minute," Nordvahl said. He had his hands on a sculpted stone wall.

Andy didn't want to stop, but Rawle paused beside her.

"Beyond this wall are a series of concrete pillars," Nordvahl said. "They support what used to be a parking garage that was eventually closed when stress fractures appeared in the concrete. The original plans for this expansion required the replacement of the pillars. They were not replaced and, a year ago, you may recall that two of the pillars collapsed, killing one construction worker and injuring another. The worker who died was a mother of two children. One of those injured workers was Lonnie Arthur, brother of Harry, the maintenance supervisor who opened the door to Rawle's apartment building. Lonnie Arthur lost both his legs. Severio Pescecane, whose firm does some legal work for this casino, negotiated a settlement with the construction union's lawyer, who then joined Pescecane's firm."

"I don't want to hear about this," Andy said.

"You *must*," Nordvahl said. "Pescecane's firm was supposed to administer the benefits paid to Lonnie Arthur. Pescecane's firm charged itself an administration fee that was so high that it kept more than half the money that was supposed to go to Arthur. Arthur couldn't find a lawyer who was willing to take Pescecane on. His family had to get a second mortgage to pay for medical expenses not covered by his insurance, which were considerable, as well as rehabilitation and changes to the house so a man without legs could take care of himself when his kids were in school and his wife was at work. Arthur then came down with secondary illnesses that he believed were related to his injuries. The union insurer did not agree and Arthur's family was about to sell their house before I learned of his situation and represented him. I got back the money Arthur should have received, plus compensatory damages. I further made sure that the union's insurance company would cover secondary illnesses."

"So?" Andy said cautiously, trying to stare him down. "So why don't you just leave us alone?"

"Because I must serve the interests of my client," Nordvahl said.

"You haven't done enough?"

"Not yet," he said. "On the way down to meet you, and my client, I stopped off at Lonnie Arthur's house to say hello. Lonnie has many friends in this city, some of whom are employed here, at this casino, doing what his brother does in Philadelphia. Lonnie Arthur considers me a hero for what I have done on his behalf, and for others. And I'm here because I want to see Severio Pescecane, who still practices what might best be described as predatory law, in his moment of triumph."

Andy finally looked him in the eye. "I don't want you to be Rawle's lawyer anymore."

"I don't think you can take me off this case, Andy. You've looked after him, but if you examine the documents that I have filed on his behalf, you will see that *I* am his legally appointed guardian."

"Unappoint yourself," Andy said.

"I expect to, but not until his father's estate has been settled and a system is in place to provide for his needs, I have set up a foundation for the administration of his father's estate. I assure you, I won't charge any fees for that service. I do not practice predatory law. My motivation, now, and always, is *quid igitur agendum est.* I ask what must be done, and I do it."

"But it's wrong," Andy said. "It's all wrong."

"How can it be wrong if you, Rawle and others like Lonnie Arthur have benefited?"

She felt Rawle's hand in hers. "Rawle hasn't benefited," Andy said.

"Who got him away from his mother? Who is protecting him from his uncle? Who made sure he was fed, housed and clothed? Who is making sure that he will have resources on which to live for the rest of his life?"

"Who killed his father?" Andy said.

Nordvahl looked her right back in the eye. "Who can say? Do you have any additional facts? If so, share them with me. Do you have any witnesses who will be believed? Let's hear them out. I am on the side of what is good. I told you, you must trust me."

Rawle was rigid. "Trrrrrr-u-s-s-s-t m-eeeee?"

"I trust you, Rawle," Nordvahl said. "What do *you* want to do?"

"K-k-k-illll m-m-on-st-er," Rawle said to him.

"Myself, also," Nordvahl said. "Now let's not keep Mr. Pescecane waiting, shall we?"

Rawle pulled Andy into the aquarium entrance.

Plank had a bowl of snapper soup before him. "I could criticize this for you," he told Ladderback. "There are restaurateurs who would pay me per hour, just to tell them what's wrong with their place."

"Taste it," Ladderback said.

Plank put a spoon in the dark brown liquid and stirred it. He took the spoon out, observed how the soup adhered to the spoon. He raised the spoon and inhaled. "Smells okay."

Ladderback waited.

He put the spoon in his mouth. "I'd use a grated white pepper instead of powdered black. And a little paprika, to bring up the flavor and round out the finish. As a soup it's okay."

"Does it please you?" Ladderback asked.

"It's fine, but . . . understand me, this is the past. You can't just please people with food anymore. You have to create an entire experience, and a bowl of soup is not enough."

"Your steak is coming," Ladderback said. He had his bowl of Vietnamese *pho* just under his nose. He raised a spoon to his lips and let the warm, clear broth warm him all the way down to his toes.

Andy and Rawle put their coats in a cloakroom and rushed to an elevator fast enough so that the doors closed with Nordvahl on the other side.

The elevator took them up to the Feeding Chamber. A man and a woman sat at a control desk in front of the jaw-shaped entrance. Andy told them she was with the *Philadelphia Press*.

The woman at the desk introduced herself and offered to show them around. Andy took out her pen and pad.

The woman led them to a room redolent with the briny odor of seawater. "You want to eat, there's a sushi bar by the band, and a wet bar and a pretty good spread of eats. I'm supposed to tell you that the feeding area isn't finished. We're a little behind on the construction, so there's only a temporary barrier at the edge of the tank, which makes it much easier to get photos of the sharks feeding, if you want them. Not that you or anyone wants to swim with the sharks, get it?"

She led Andy into a rounded room that contained about two hundred people, some in tuxedos and gowns, others in sweaters and blue jeans. Animated projections of fish swimming swirled on the pale walls. Just below the skylight, a catwalk thrust out above the churning, circular pool, ending in a bulbous contraption that reminded Andy of the bucket on an earthmover.

Andy told Rawle they had to stay back from the sawhorses ringing the pool.

"There is only one shark in the tank right now, a three-hundred-fifty-pound, twelve-foot tiger shark, species *galeocerdo cuvieri*," the woman continued. "He was caught about a hundred miles due east of here and is very, very hungry."

Rawle whispered in Andy's ear. "He wants to know if the shark has a name," Andy said.

"Not officially," the woman replied. "The Habitat wants to sell the naming rights."

262

"Who would want his name on a shark?" Andy asked.

The woman pressed her finger to her lips. "That's the big secret, okay? Mr. Pescecane is supposed to make some kind of presentation in a few minutes. He's going to do the first official feeding. After that there will be twice-daily shark feedings for tourists, who can either watch here, or in the glass viewing stations on the floor below. Anything else you need?"

Andy took out her pen and her pad. "Not really."

"Great. Oh, and if you see Nordvahl, tell him I've been trying to get in touch with him."

"He came in right behind us," Andy said. "He's in the black suit."

"He *is?*" The woman scanned the room until she saw Nordvahl standing by himself, tapping things into his handheld computer. "See ya!"

Andy looked at Rawle, whose face had gone blank. She held her pad in her hand. The lights began to dim, the five-piece band in a corner did a fanfare and a spotlight appeared at the door in the wall leading to the catwalk.

All eyes turned to the man in the spotlight. Big, wide Severio Pescecane almost sparkled in his blue-gray sharkskin suit. He stepped out onto the catwalk and held a microphone under his lips like a nightclub singer.

"Ladies and gentlemen," he began. "Lend me your ears. I was born in the great city of Philadelphia but it was in the summers, on the beach in Ventnor and Margate, that I really came of age. I'd sit on the beach, and I was just a little runt of a kid from Eighth and Passyunk, and I'd watch the big guys go into the water, and, you know, a big guy, it didn't matter what he did for a living, he always had to make a splash going into the water, because the public expects it and you don't want to disappoint the public. So, long before I began to practice law, and put on the few pounds you see before you, I wanted to make a splash in everything I ever did. I'm proud to say, the law firm of Severio Pescecane, LLP has done that in just about everything we've ever done. That's why, when we heard that, in their infinite wisdom, the Atlantic City Reinvestment Authority was going to build its very own shark habitat, with daily feeds and all kinds of other educational opportunities for the community, in Atlantic City, of all places, we had to make sure that this, the Pescecane Shark Habitat, would make the biggest splash of all."

The drummer hit a rim shot and, if Andy had been capable of listening to music, she would have recognized the familiar bass vamp leading into Bertold Brecht's and Kurt Weill's most famous ditty, one that, like so many other signature songs in musical theater and film—"Over the Rainbow" in *The Wizard of Oz,* "On the Street Where You Live," in *My Fair Lady,* "A Comedy Tonight!" in *A Funny Thing Happened on the Way to the Forum,* and "My Object All Sublime" in Gilbert and Sullivan's *Mikado*—was tossed into the production as an afterthought.

Andy could hear lyrics, and what she heard was Severio Pescecane singing with a voice that was more fury than sound, singing about a shark that has many teeth, dear. . . .

Pescecane finished to light applause. "Okay, okay," he said. "Only reason I did that was, all my life, I wanted to sing that song in front of people who wouldn't run away, okay?"

Andy glanced around the room and saw Nordvahl, alone now.

Pescecane took a remote control from his pocket. "And now," he said into the microphone, "the big feeding. The way this is supposed to work, is, all automatic. Food gets loaded up in back of that door I came through, comes down on a belt, goes into that bucket thing at the end. The bucket opens at its dinnertime. There's normally not supposed to be anybody up here because it's too easy to fall in, ha, ha. But I just wanted to be up here, you know? Why else are you going to bust your ass through law school, build a practice and get a reputation, if you're not going to get up in front of people every once in a while?"

He stepped onto the catwalk until he was over the water. "You ready?" he said to the shark racing through the churning waters. "You ready for some professional courtesy?"

He aimed the remote control at the bulbous contraption. The jaws of the bucket opened a crack and then jammed.

"What is this?" Pescecane growled. "I spend all this money and it screws up?" He stepped forward until he was on top of the feeding bucket. He got down on his hands and knees and began to bang the bucket with the remote control.

Then Andy felt Rawle go rigid at her side. She saw him looking at Nordvahl, who had just come in. Nordvhal had his handheld out and aimed at the catwalk.

Rawle took off. He rushed up to Nordvahl, snatched away the handheld and threw it at Andy, but Andy was just a little too slow to react. Nordvahl's handheld bounced off her leg, skidded over the tiles, slipped under the sawhorses and went in.

Nordvahl tried to lunge for it. Rawle jumped up, arms wide, and tried to block him as he had blocked Andy when she tried to set up a shot. Nordvahl struck the boy in the face and Rawle let out a shriek.

The shriek did different things to different people. Most were startled. They tensed, froze, winced and eventually put their hands over their ears.

For Pescecane, the sound was just enough to make him lose his grip on the catwalk, which made a low, metallic vibration as his big body swung out and down over the water. He held on, though, with his hands.

But not for long.

Before she saw Pescecane go in, Andy had taken off toward Nordvahl. As far as she was concerned, nobody was going to get away with hitting Rawle. Nobody!

He didn't see her—he was too intent on locating his handheld, which was riding the churning water like a piece of flotsam that couldn't wait to sink—so Andy had time to bring her left leg up and around in a roundhouse kick that put the top of her foot below his ribs, just about where his right kidney was. As he crumpled, she let the kick's momentum take her foot around and down. With her left foot firmly planted, she spun again with her leg, this time catching him behind his neck with the edge of her right foot.

Nordvahl went down, still reaching for the handheld, when a loud splash made him, and everyone else, turn toward the water.

———

"Listen to me." Plank set the scene with his hands. "You walk into this bright, bold, severely air-conditioned retro futurism of Portman-era Miami Beach—steel and plexiglass staircases, curved lines, ludicrous water fountains, with indirect lighting, deco-echo curves and swirls."

Plank waited. "Aren't you going to ask me about the menu? It's going to be *huge*. Pages and pages. The first-timers and tourists will read it—tourists read everything. But the regulars will show how cool they are by not reading it. They'll order what they want, as a way of showing off, like it's their place and they have their own special thing, and we'll train the staff to nudge them up toward the specials. Every day we'll have a special deli meat, special fish, special cheese, special sauce, special sandwich, special dessert, and then we'll have the 'nothing special,' which we'll be a very ordinary thing, like, say, a tuna fish salad sandwich, that we will max out."

"Max," Ladderback said tonelessly.

"We'll make it tableside. Start with fresh tuna fillet, grill it on a portable gas grill, or flambé it in a hundred-fifty-proof rum. Then we'll dice it, and, while it cools, we'll do the mayonnaise with eggs and oil and a fork—do you know most human beings have never even seen mayonnaise made and have absolutely no idea what it consists of? So we show them. Then we toss it with the diced tuna, add maybe a little Madras curry or ground habanero pepper, serve it warm on a bread of choice, or maybe a flame-toasted sourdough kaiser, with bibb lettuce and a screaming red Jersey tomato sliced so thin you can see through it. And that's just tuna fish.

"We'll have thirty-seven different varieties of smoked or pickled fish—five herrings, at *least* ten salmons; eighteen different pâtés—including three chopped livers, six vegetarian terrines. With fifty different kinds of deli meats, and close to a hundred cheeses—you have to be careful about cheeses because your most exquisite Emmenthaler will spoil while you run out of American Swiss—we're going to make hoagies so astonishing that people in New York and D.C. and maybe even Boston will come here just to eat sandwiches that will numb their minds. Fifteen mustards, six horseradishes, five slaws. Rye, white, wheat, Italian breads and bagels baked on the premises, still warm from the oven. But that's just the deli."

Ladderback took a long breath. He could barely keep his eyes open. Why was he so tired, at the moment when he needed to be strong enough to show that this wasn't just a restaurant, it was part of the historical fabric of the city? If you wipe the slate clean, you lose more than you could ever recover.

He glanced down at his rare Delmonico steak, steamed asparagus in hollandaise sauce, and roasted new potatoes.

"Shep, you're looking at that like it's your last meal," Plank said. "I don't let everyone call me Matt, but you can. Can I call you Shep?"

"No," Ladderback said.

"We contrast deli," Plank continued, "with the scorched breath, red sauce, pasta palace Southern Italian main courses: four different lasagnas, manicottis and raviolis with twenty different fillings stuffed to order, with ten different red sauces, with a sauce *del giorno*, but we'll give them silly names, the way they did in the Miami hotel coffee shops, starting with . . . 'No-Lead,' for the puree of uncooked vegetables, to 'Regular' for marinara, made daily of course; 'SAE30' for the olive oil with chopped olives—"

"Kalamata?" Ladderback asked, struggling to concentrate.

Plank made a face. "You get the same olive from Italy and I can taste the difference in the soil and the sunlight but . . . all right, kalamatas it is for the SAE30. I'd love to do a dry red wine sauce with Palermo pistachio clam sausage with a dash of lemon and basil—the 'Hi-Testarossa.' The 'Jet Fuel' would have to include something alcoholic so it can arrive in flames. We can set on fire . . ."

He paused. Ladderback did not seem thrilled.

"You don't like it?"

"It's not . . . ," he frowned, "this."

Plank stared at him. "It's better," he said finally.

Ladderback folded his hands. "This is sufficient."

"Sufficient, maybe. But spectacular, sensational, the kind of place that will be a destination on par with the finest restaurants in the city, and then, after we get the kinks out, above and beyond anything else anywhere? No."

"You don't understand," Ladderback said. "People eat here."

"And you have your favorites and they have their favorites and you think that just by having things the way you like them, that everything will take care of itself?"

Ladderback said nothing.

"You're afraid that if I come in and make this as incredible as it's going to be, it will completely obliterate what's gone before."

"I respect what's gone before," Ladderback said. "Interesting people have eaten here. Some have carved their initials in the tables. Al Capone, for example."

"The tables look terrible, by the way. And Al Capone is dead."

"W.C. Fields."

"Also dead."

"The Reverend Leon Sullivan."

Plank shrugged. Ladderback dropped other names: Arturo Toscanini, Richie Ashburn, Jacqueline Susanne."

"All dead," Plank said.

"Mario Lanza."

"Who's that?"

"One of the greatest singers. He was born in Philadelphia and . . ." Ladderback began but let his words fade. It seemed too great an effort. He felt himself losing his strength. "And . . ."

Plank sat up. "Andy?"

Ladderback blinked. "Andrea Cosicki has eaten here, yes."

Plank turned red. "Are we talking about the same person?"

"My assistant at the *Press*," Ladderback said, struggling to concentrate.

"Your *assistant!* With all that attitude, I wouldn't think she'd assist anybody." Plank looked around. "Which is her table when she's in here?"

Ladderback had to force himself to focus on the dining room. "The longer one in the center was her father's. He had invited her to a luncheon on the day he died. She also uses this one."

"This is *her* table? I didn't think she was the Jimmy D's type.'"

"She is her own type. She is unique. She is extremely capable. She is an excellent reporter. She is irreplaceable."

"And she's famous now," Plank said, slouching back in his chair. "I mean, she's not a brand, like I am, but that series she did about that kid with the problems is really getting around. What she's been for me, is like, a muse. She came into Loup Garou and she asked me for a cheese steak and I maxed one out for her. Totally. She only had one bite but you should have seen her light up. I saw her with that boy Rawle, yesterday. I maxed him on a banana crepe. He was the one who gave me the idea for the nothing-specials, but Andy was there. She's always there when the big ideas happen."

Plank patted the tabletop. "I'll keep this table, just for her. But the rest goes. Then we'll gut the place. People that eat at my places have expectations."

"But you don't always grant them," Ladderback said, finding himself short of breath.

Plank bristled. "I am an artist. I please myself by exceeding ordinary expectations."

"Could you . . . ," Ladderback stopped. He felt weak. "Could you please yourself by merely making this restaurant better?"

"I can," Plank said. "I could make this the most incredible old-style Philadelphia surf-and-turf joint in the world. Surf-and-turf is so easy. Too easy. I could max this up until it was completely astonishing in every way. But that would be too easy. I wouldn't have to reach for that."

"Sometimes, all that we truly need is within our grasp," Ladderback said, suddenly dizzy. "What is surprising is how long it takes us to . . ."

Plank looked around. He turned back to Ladderback.

". . . learn this," Ladderback breathed before he collapsed.

———

Nordvahl almost got his hand on his computer, then Pescecane grabbed his arm and, in attempting to pull himself out, pulled Nordvahl in. Pescecane pushed him down in the water, frantically crawling over Nordvahl until several people, one with a long fishhook, helped pull him out.

Nordvahl turned back, saw people gathering with long poles and hooks. He swam awkwardly for the edge of the tank.

Then Rawle went to the edge, looked right at Nordvahl and screamed, "MON-STER!"

Andy wasn't the only person who could have seen Rawle's face. Those standing close who were still frozen in the terror of what had occurred could see in Rawle's eyes an intensity, a sense of purpose and triumph.

But only Andy had seen Rawle play in a shopping-mall food court with a toy building set, in which he put together a precise model of the open balcony of the Skyline Spa, with four toy figures, one representing her, one representing him, one representing his father on the treadmill and a fourth that he had called a monster.

A bystander might think that what Rawle called a monster was the tiger shark in the water.

But Andy knew that Rawle had said it to Nordvahl, who was about to pull himself out when a single word from a boy stopped him.

It stopped Andy, too.

Perhaps Nordvahl realized that, too, because he turned away from Rawle, as if he had been hit, and then the shark found him.

And then Andy's maternal instincts took over. She put her arms around Rawle, turned his head to her, and pulled him back and away, because the world can be a hideous place, and some things a child should not have to know.

He held her tightly, as if to agree.

22 pro bono

Though the curtains had been closed, the daylight leaking in unnerved him. Then there was the tube in his hand, and wires connecting the monitors, and the anticipation that these hours might be his last.

It took him a while to be sure that the telephone was ringing. The ring was different from his apartment telephone, far different from the newsroom telephone. And there was that damned television. The person in the bed beside his kept the set on all the time.

He groped awkwardly for the phone, and almost said, *Philadelphia Press,* N. S. Ladderback.

But he didn't have the strength so he just said, "Hello."

"Shep, it's Andy. I'm calling you from your restaurant."

She sounded pleased with herself.

"Jimmy D's was never my restaurant," he grumbled. "I'm not sure whose it is now."

"You really blew Matt away when you told him it was my favorite place. I really don't have a favorite place, but he's into it now. He changes his image with every restaurant he develops. Now he's going jazz-bop: baggy suits, a beret, horn-rimmed glasses. He says he wants the mood to be like an old speakeasy."

"Jimmy D's was a speakeasy," Ladderback said, hoarse from the breathing tube that had been inserted down his throat. "Fats Waller and Jelly Roll Morton played the piano in the back room. What will he be doing to the food?"

"It'll still be there when you get out, though I think you'll have to change your eating habits."

He said nothing.

"Anyway, I called because I just did the meeting with Rawle, Alma McSloan and Ismail Khan. Everything's set. They're all moving into Khan's place in Gladwyn. Rawle will be taken to his school every day by one of Khan's drivers. The judge will not be visiting, or in the same room with Rawle, without one of Khan's bodyguards present. Oh, and one more thing. Khan just *loved* the baklava."

"Mr. Mafouz will be pleased."

"He's more than pleased. Khan wants to buy into the restaurant. We had some of that champagne at the end of the meeting, so, if I'm a little woozy, it's because . . . I'm a little woozy."

Ladderback almost smiled. "I haven't seen the newspaper, but the person beside my bed keeps the television on all the time. I heard what happened to Schuyler. He died a hero's death."

"He wasn't a hero. He wasn't trying to save Pescecane. But, it's like you told me, there are always details that never quite make it into the story."

Ladderback wanted to ask what those details might be, but he let her continue.

"You were right: I got my big story and Lange has backed off. It's possible that Khan will do an interview with me later. I'm writing my final column about him and Rawle now."

"A book is a great challenge to write."

"You sound like you've written one."

He said nothing.

"I wanted to tell you that, before I left for Atlantic City, I read what you left on your desk."

"I'm happy that you did. You could pursue those leads. Your story could become bigger."

"And what would I get for it? I would destroy a man that a lot of people need to be a hero."

"But you might reveal something more important, and that is the nature of a man who wants to be a hero, and the compensation he sought to fulfill that need."

"And I'd hurt a lot of people."

Ladderback had to force the words out. "It is our obligation as journalists to report the story. We cannot assume responsibility for our subject's feelings."

"But didn't you tell me that when you do your obituaries, you put in the things that will help the living deal with the loss?"

"I would expect you to despise the man who killed Rawle's father."

"I did. I still do. But what matters to me—me personally—is that a family is back together, and Rawle's in a better place than he's ever been. After what I've been through, that's enough. I don't want to ask any more questions. I don't want to probe. I don't want to find out how much I don't know. I just want them to stay happy."

"You will have to discuss that with the police."

"I'll tell Jeff Everson anything he wants to know—when he asks me. Right now, he's trying to get to some of Nordvahl's former clients and he's having a tough time with their new lawyers."

"The Law Watch is handling them?"

"With Danny Bleutner consulting pro bono."

Bleutner! "I'm not sure if his presence is for the good," Ladderback said.

"Mafouz told me Bleutner fixed up some tax problem for your restaurant and brought in Matt. What's so bad about that?"

Ladderback changed the subject. "Now that your situation with the boy has ended, what do you expect to do?"

"Go back to writing Mr. Action. I have a question already picked out. Dear Mr. Action: How am I going to take this grumpy, lonely agoraphobic old guy to the wedding of Gina Detweitey, his former flame?"

Ladderback took a deep breath. "I've been told that, though this procedure is relatively routine, a stent is to be inserted in a blocked blood vessel. The procedure can dislodge pieces of plaque inside the vessel and those pieces can cause strokes during the recovery period. There is a small chance I may not survive. You would not need to answer your question."

"Shep, you're going to that wedding with me. What's the worst thing that could happen?"

"I'd rather not think about it," Ladderback said. "And I would rather you did not tell anyone that I have agreed to resume therapeutic counseling regarding my illness, presuming I survive my physical difficulties. I want to scatter Whitey Goohan's ashes in the right place."

"Shep, that's wonderful! There's so much in the city you should see."

"S.J. Perelman called Philadelphia the city of bleak afternoons."

"You can call it whatever you want. The doctors are *not* going to screw up! You have to stop being afraid of things."

He sighed again. "That is not as easy as it sounds. With the years I have been given, I will have failed more than I have succeeded, and what success I have had has been undistinguished. Perhaps if I had your temperament I would have done more that mattered."

"Shep, everything you do is a matter of life and death."

Ladderback eyed Neely Dixit and Rhea Nordvahl, each sitting at opposite ends of his bedside, struggling to pretend the other did not exist.

His spirits began to lift. "You might be correct."

"I just might," Andy said.